*Ryan's mood was buoyant—until his son shouted, "Look! There's Tess!*

"She has a flat!" Mike bubbled. He looked at his father, first eager, then crestfallen. "Aren't you gonna stop?"

Ryan opened his mouth to tell him that these days liberated women changed their own tires, but before he could, the woman who had become the bane of his existence straightened up from the open trunk and turned around with the jack in her hands.

"What the—?" Ryan's eyes bulged, and his jaw dropped. Then he cut loose with a string of colorful curses that had Mike gaping, and he stomped on the brakes.

As the car screeched to a halt, he stabbed his son with an irate glare. "Why the hell didn't you *tell* me she was pregnant!"

Dear Reader,

Welcome to Silhouette **Special Edition** . . . welcome to romance. Each month, Silhouette **Special Edition** publishes six novels with you in mind—stories of love and life, tales that you can identify with . . . as well as dream about.

We're starting off the New Year right in 1993. We're pleased to announce our new series, THAT SPECIAL WOMAN! Each month, we'll be presenting a book that pays tribute to women—to us. The heroine is a friend, a wife, a mother—a striver, a nurturer, a pursuer of goals—she's the best in every woman. And it takes a very special man to win that special woman! Launching this series is *Building Dreams* by Ginna Gray. Ryan McCall doesn't know what he's up against when he meets Tess Benson in this compelling tale. She's a woman after the cynical builder's heart—and she won't stop until she's got her man!

On the horizon this month, too, is MAVERICKS, a new series by Lisa Jackson. *He's a Bad Boy* introduces three men who just won't be tamed!

Rounding out the month are more stories from other favorite authors—Tracy Sinclair, Christine Flynn, Kayla Daniels and Judith Bowen (with her first Silhouette **Special Edition** title!).

I hope that you enjoy this book and all the stories to come. Happy 1993!

Sincerely,

Tara Gavin
Senior Editor
Silhouette Books

# GINNA GRAY

## BUILDING DREAMS

Published by Silhouette Books New York

**America's Publisher of Contemporary Romance**

SILHOUETTE BOOKS
300 East 42nd St., New York, N.Y. 10017

BUILDING DREAMS

ISBN: 0-373-09792-1

First Silhouette Books printing January 1993

Printed in the U.S.A.

## GINNA GRAY

A native Houstonian, Ginna Gray admits that since childhood, she has been a compulsive reader as well as a head-in-the-clouds dreamer. Long accustomed to expressing her creativity in tangible ways—Ginna also enjoys painting and needlework—she finally decided to try putting her fantasies and wild imaginings down on paper. The result? The mother of two now spends eight hours a day as a full-time writer.

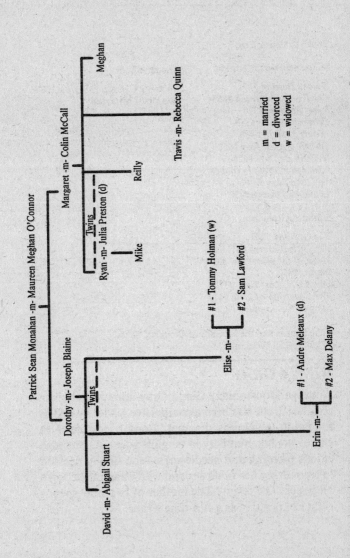

Patrick Sean Monahan -m- Maureen Meghan O'Connor

Margaret -m- Colin McCall

Meghan

Twins
Ryan -m- Julia Preston (d)

Reilly

Mike

Travis -m- Rebecca Quinn

Dorothy -m- Joseph Blaine

David -m- Abigail Stuart

Twins

Elise -m-

#1 - Tommy Holman (w)

#2 - Sam Lawford

Erin -m-

#1 - Andre Meleaux (d)

#2 - Max Delany

m = married
d = divorced
w = widowed

# Chapter One

It was too quiet.

The thought struck Ryan McCall halfway up the stairs, and he paused, his expression puzzled. Normally by that point he could hear rock music rattling the walls of his apartment. Or, at the very least, the television blaring. His son rarely did anything in moderation.

Ryan trotted up the remaining steps, curious but not particularly alarmed.

The first vestige of the latter feeling came a moment later when he unlocked his door and opened it to a dark apartment. Stepping inside, Ryan flipped on the living room lights and checked his watch. It was only nine—too early for Mike to be in bed. Maybe he had fallen asleep watching television in his room.

"Mike! You here?"

There was no answer. Frowning, Ryan tossed the mail onto the coffee table and strode across the room, heading for the door that led into the bedroom hallway. "Hey, Mike! Where are you?"

His son's room was empty. The bed, on which the boy wallowed periodically throughout the day, was made up in Mike's usual haphazard manner but it showed no sign of having been touched.

The room was crammed with a thirteen-year-old boy's clutter. A catcher's mitt and a bat and ball lay on the desk, along with dozens of baseball cards, two crushed soft drink cans, a deflated football, a pair of dirty socks, a pocket electronic game, and an assortment of candy wrappers, rocks and scraps of paper. A squadron of model airplanes hung from the ceiling and another half-finished aircraft sat on a sheet of newspaper in the middle of the floor. In a pile in the corner, where Mike had tossed them, were a torn kite, a Frisbee and a skateboard. A ratty sneaker with a hole in the toe lay on its side beside the bed. Yet, for all its messiness, the room had an undisturbed air.

Real alarm began to spiral up inside Ryan. Where was Mike?

The front door slammed. "Hey, Dad. I'm home!"

Ryan whirled, his relief so great his knees nearly buckled. The debilitating emotion lasted only an instant, just long enough for parental ire to override it. Dammit, where the devil had that boy been? No matter what, he was damned well supposed to be home by dark with the doors locked.

Ryan stalked toward the living room. Mike was heading for his room, and father and son nearly crashed into one another when Ryan stormed through the door.

"Oh, hi, Dad. Wait'll you hear—"

"You've got some explaining to do, young man."

"Huh?"

"Where the devil have you been? You know you're not to leave without permission."

"I didn't leave! Well...not really. I was next door."

"Next door?"

"Yeah. I've been helping our new neighbor move in."

Ryan stared at his son, taken aback. Mike was a good kid. He was responsible and cooperative, but like most teenage boys, when it came to things like household chores or anything that involved physical labor, he groused long and loud.

"Well, hey, that's great, Mike. I'm proud of you." Ryan hesitated. "Uh...you *did* volunteer to help, didn't you? I mean...they're not paying you, are they?"

"Heck no! I wouldn't take money from someone like Mrs. Benson," Mike declared, affronted. The next instant he brightened, his young face lighting up with enthusiasm. "Wait'll you meet her, Dad. She's really great. She's a high school teacher—or she was until school let out last week for the summer. She says she's not going back next fall. She's going to take a real long sabba...sabbat..."

"Sabbatical?"

"Yeah, that. Man, I bet it'd be cool, having a teacher like Mrs. Benson. She young. Well...sorta...for a teacher, anyway. And she's real friendly and all, and she laughs a lot. And guess what else, Dad? Amanda Sutherland...you know, that lady who does the news on television? Well she'n Mrs. Benson are best friends. Ms. Sutherland is helping her move."

One corner of Ryan's mouth kicked up in a faintly scornful twist. "Is that right?" he replied without a trace of interest. Women were far from his favorite topic of conversation.

He retrieved the mail from the coffee table and started riffling through it. "So how about Mr. Benson? What's he like?"

"Oh, there's not a Mr. Benson. At least, not anymore there isn't. Ms. Sutherland told me he died about seven months ago."

Ryan's head snapped around, his eyes narrowing. "You mean our new neighbor is a widow?"

"Yeah. And she's—"

"Oh great. That's just great," Ryan snapped. "Just what I need—an unattached female right next door. That's the perfect piece of news to cap off what's been a really rotten day."

Ryan and Mike had lived where they were for almost eight years. Until his death the previous month, a doddering old bachelor had occupied the apartment next door. Ryan had hoped that the next tenant would be someone equally innocuous.

"Ah, c'mon, Dad. Don't be that way. Mrs. Benson is different. She's nice and ... well ... special. You'll like her. Really."

"Yeah. Right." His jaw tight, Ryan returned his attention to the day's mail.

Mike headed for the kitchen. "Tonight Mrs. Benson just brought over some small stuff. The movers are bringing her furniture tomorrow, and she's moving everything else herself in a rented trailer. So anyway, I told her I'd be back to help some more after my softball game tomorrow," he said with his head inside the refrigerator. "That's okay, isn't it, Dad?"

"I guess," Ryan replied through gritted teeth. "But first you have to do your Saturday chores."

"Ah, *Daaad*. Do I have to? Just this one time, couldn't—"

"You know the rules, Mike."

Actually, Ryan half hoped that the additional work would make Mike change his mind. On the one hand, he was proud of his son for generously helping out a neighbor, but he hated the idea of a single woman living next door, and he certainly did not want Mike to spend a lot of time with her. In Ryan's experience, unattached females were usually on the lookout for a man.

He tore open an envelope with more force than necessary, his teeth clamped together so hard they ached. At the first opportunity he intended to make his feelings about women crystal clear to this new neighbor.

The opportunity arose the very next morning.

As usual whenever Mike had a softball game, Ryan's identical twin, Reilly, came along. Depending on the previous evening and the woman with whom he had spent it, Reilly sometimes appeared on their doorstep on Saturday mornings looking a bit frayed around the edges—but he came. He was nothing if not a devoted uncle. So far, he hadn't missed a single game.

That particular Saturday morning Reilly arrived early bearing a box of warm donuts for their breakfast and whistling off-key. Ryan took one look at the devilish twinkle in his brother's eyes and raised a sardonic brow.

"You're bright-eyed and bushy-tailed this morning. Don't tell me you actually got a decent night's sleep for a change. What's the matter? Get stood up?"

Reilly grinned. "Hardly. If you want to know, I spent last evening with a dynamite gal. You ought to try it sometime, Hoss. Does wonders for your outlook. As a matter of fact, I know a fantastic lady I could fix you up with."

"Forget it. When I want a woman I know where to find one. Besides, there's nothing wrong with my outlook."

"Wanna bet," Reilly muttered, trailing his brother into the kitchen.

Between the three of them, the McCall men quickly devoured the whole box of donuts. A short time later they clattered down the stairs and headed for the parking lot amid laughter and good-natured jibes.

Just as they reached Ryan's Jeep Cherokee, an older economy car towing a rental trailer pulled into the parking lot and sputtered to a stop a few feet away. Mike's face lit up.

"Hey, look! It's Mrs. Benson!"

Ryan groaned and tried to stop him but he was too late. His son rushed over to the car and leaned down beside the driver's window before the woman could kill the engine.

"Hi, Mrs. Benson. Ms. Sutherland," Mike added, sparing the woman in the passenger seat a quick glance. "I didn't expect to see you again so soon." Grinning, he glanced over his shoulder and motioned eagerly to his father and uncle. "C'mere'n meet Mrs. Benson, Dad. You too, Uncle Reilly."

Ryan gritted his teeth, but he had no choice. Reilly, who needed no second urging where women were concerned, was already sauntering toward the car. Ryan followed him reluctantly.

Beaming, Mike made the introductions.

"I'm delighted to meet you," the woman behind the wheel said, smiling up at Ryan. "And please, do call me Tess. We're neighbors now, after all."

Ignoring her outstretched hand, Ryan responded with a curt nod, then deliberately looked away, his expression stony.

Whatever his greeting lacked in courtesy, his brother's more than made up for in charm. With a hand braced on the car door Reilly leaned down and flashed his most devastating smile. "Morning, ladies." His gaze slid back and forth between the two women, and he sighed dramatically. "I swear, it just isn't fair. This brother of mine has always had the devil's own luck. Imagine having two beauties like you move in right next door. Nothing like that ever happens to me."

"Oh, brother." Rolling her eyes, Amanda gave a disgusted snort and scooted down in her seat. Arms crossed tightly beneath her breasts, she stared straight ahead.

Tess's uncertain gaze flickered from Ryan's rigid face to his brother's smiling one. "Uh . . . I'm afraid you're mistaken, Mr. McCall—"

"Reilly," he insisted with an affable grin.

"Uh . . . Reilly. You see, I'm the only one who'll be living here. Amanda is merely giving me a hand."

"Really. Hey, in that case, perhaps I can talk your friend into moving into my building?"

"Don't hold your breath," Amanda muttered, but she didn't deign to look at him.

Reilly grinned. His eyes twinkled as they roved over Amanda's stiff profile. "Say aren't you . . . Of course! Amanda Sutherland. I thought you looked familiar. You're a roving reporter for Channel Five, aren't you?"

"That's right."

"I'm a big fan. Maybe we can get together sometime so I can tell you how much I admire your work. Say . . . over dinner tonight?"

Amanda cut her eyes around, giving him a look that would have shriveled most men. Reilly McCall's grin widened.

"I'm busy."

"How about tomorrow night?"

"No."

"The night after that?"

Amanda shook her head.

Ryan shifted impatiently and made a point of checking his watch. "The woman's not interested, Reilly, so count yourself lucky and come on. We have to get to the park." He gave Tess another curt nod and turned and walked back to his own car without another word.

"It was nice meeting you," Tess called after him, but his only response was to yell to his son to shake a leg.

Crestfallen, Mike gazed after his father. He sent Tess an apologetic look. "Gee, I'm sorry, Mrs. Benson. Dad doesn't really mean to be rude. He's got a lot on his mind, is all."

"That's all right, Mike. I understand."

His father hollered again, and Mike darted away toward the Cherokee. "Don't forget," he called back over his shoulder. "I'll be over as soon as the game ends."

He had barely tumbled into the back seat when his father reversed out of the parking space and sent the utility vehicle shooting out of the lot.

Ryan's expression did not encourage conversation, but Mike was too upset to care.

"Shoot, Dad. Why'd you have to go and act that way to Tess?" he demanded glumly.

"Yeah, Hoss." Reilly's eyes twinkled with devilment. "I'd like to know that, too. You were a real jerk back there. If a looker like Tess Benson moved into my building I sure wouldn't bite her head off. I'd woo her with soft words and flowers." He waggled his eyebrows. "You'd be surprised how far a little sweet talk can get you."

"Ah, knock it off, Uncle Reilly," Mike snapped, surprising both men. "Tess isn't that kind of woman."

"Hey, Mike...buddy. What gives? I didn't mean any—"

"Oh, just forget it." Flouncing back in the seat, Mike stared out the window, his young face sulky.

The two brothers exchanged a baffled look and fell silent.

Mike didn't say a word all the way to the ball park, but he was never able to stay angry for long. When they arrived and he spotted his teammates he let out a whoop and rushed off to greet them, his pique forgotten.

"Now, what do you suppose that was all about?" Reilly mused.

Ryan stared after his son, a worried frown drawing his thick eyebrows together. "Beats me."

For several seconds the two women sat in Tess's car, staring after the McCalls' departing vehicle.

"Well," Amanda huffed. "He certainly won't win the good neighbor award. That man's about as warm and friendly as a coiled rattlesnake. Who would've guessed that a sweet boy like Mike would have a father like that."

"He was rather abrupt."

"*Abrupt!* The man was downright rude."

"Yes...well...maybe we shouldn't be too quick to judge him. It could be that he's just having a bad day or something."

Amanda groaned and rolled her eyes. "I swear, Tess Benson, you are the most tolerant, good-natured, incurably optimistic person I've ever known. It's disgusting. The man is mannerless and abrasive. He's got the personality of coarse-grit sandpaper, for heaven's sake."

Tess laughed. "Maybe. Or maybe he's simply got problems right now. Or maybe he's just in a bad mood. We all have days when we're mad at the world and would just as soon people stayed away. Since I'm going to be living next door to the man I'd prefer to give him the benefit of the doubt."

"You would," Amanda muttered.

The rumble of a diesel engine and the squeal and hiss of air brakes announced the arrival of the moving van. The long tractor-trailer rig lumbered into the parking lot and rolled to a stop beside the car.

Tess looked up at the apartment building, and drew a deep breath. "I guess it's time to get started. This stuff won't get unloaded by itself." With a determined sigh, she reached for the door handle and slowly, awkwardly, hauled her very pregnant body out of the car.

Four hours later, Tess stood in the kitchen of her new apartment, knee-deep in boxes, wadded newspaper and bubble pack, wearily rubbing her aching back.

"Where ya want me to put this one, Mrs. Benson?"

She looked around in time to see Mike come through the front door, staggering under the weight of the carton he carried. The thirteen-year-old was sweating profusely, and the tendons in his neck and underdeveloped arms were corded and straining.

"Mike! You shouldn't carry something that heavy up the stairs all by yourself! Here, let me help."

From the look of horror on his young face you would have thought Tess had suggested she bench-press five hundred pounds. He clutched the carton tighter and held it out of her reach when she came around the end of the bar. "No! You can't do that!"

"The kid's right." Amanda sauntered in through the open doorway carrying a half dozen clothes-filled hangers hooked over each shoulder. "In your condition, you haven't any business trying to manage something that heavy."

"But—"

"I can handle it, Mrs. Benson. Honest. Just tell me where you want it."

"C'mon, sweetie, follow me. I'll show you." With a don't-you-dare-say-a-word look for Tess, Amanda maneuvered through the maze of boxes and jumbled furniture with her unhurried, hip-swaying walk and led the boy out of the room.

Tess watched them go, feeling properly chastised and more than a little useless.

"How about it, Mike? Whaddaya say we take a lemonade break," Amanda suggested a minute later, when she and Mike returned.

"No thanks, Ms. Sutherland. But you go ahead. There're just a few more boxes left in the trailer. I'll get 'em while you rest. They're too heavy for you to carry anyway."

"Now there goes one heck of a nice kid," Amanda drawled, hitching herself up onto a stool beside the bar.

"Yes, he is. But I'm afraid we're taking advantage of him."

"Are you kidding! He's having a ball. Look, Tess, trust me on this. If there is one thing I know, it's the male animal. The early teens are tough on a boy. Their hormones are just beginning to bubble and they're filled with all kinds of doubt and anxiety about their budding masculinity. Believe

me, lending a hand to two women makes Mike feel manly
and strong.''

"Still...I could have helped. I'm not an invalid you
know.''

"No. But you're too far along to be doing any lifting and
toting. And remember, when I let you talk me into this, our
agreement was that you would leave all that to me. With
Mike helping there is even less reason for you to concern
yourself. We can take care of the heavy stuff. You just un-
pack boxes.''

Tess made a face, but she didn't argue—not when
Amanda used that tone.

As her friend drank her lemonade, Tess studied her, bemused. Amanda wore a pink tank top and skimpy white
shorts that showed off her spectacular leggy figure. Her li-
oness mane of streaked blond hair was piled atop her head
and twisted into a loose knot. Her appearance today was not
quite that of the sharp sophisticate seen daily on television
reporting local news events, but despite the heat and humidity and hours spent in sweaty, back-breaking work,
Amanda still managed to look elegant. She made Tess feel
like a beached whale. An exhausted, washed-out beached
whale.

They had been best friends since grade school. Even then
Amanda had been a beauty, exuding an innate female mag-
netism that not even obnoxious six-year-old boys had been
able to resist. With the passage of time her allure had merely
grown stronger. The combination of keen intelligence,
stunning looks and an aura of sultry sensuality continued to
draw males like flies to honey.

For the same reasons, most females felt threatened by
Amanda. For Tess, however, her friend's looks and appeal
had never been a problem. Tess had been the only child of
adoring parents who had showered her with love and attention and made her feel special and confident of her own
worth.

Not that she wasn't aware of her shortcomings. Tess knew full well that she was at best attractive, in a girl-next-door sort of way. Her shoulder-length hair was carroty, that aggravating shade between red and blond that was both, yet neither. Unfortunately, she had the fair skin that went with it, the kind that never tanned but turned lobster red when exposed to the sun for even a modest period of time.

Even now, at twenty-nine, Tess had a splattering of freckles across the bridge of her short, slightly turned-up nose. Her mouth was just a little too wide, her chin just a bit too firm for her heart-shaped face. Her only claim to real beauty was her eyes. Big and wide set, they were the color of mellow whiskey and surrounded by long, dark brown lashes, which Tess considered a minor miracle, considering her fair coloring.

Though far from being a drop-dead gorgeous femme fatale, Tess had long ago discovered that there were plenty of men around who preferred the wholesome type. Certainly, she had never lacked for male attention, not even when out with Amanda.

Amanda fished an ice cube out of her glass and popped it into her mouth, crunching it with her teeth. "I still don't like the idea of you living here alone, you know," she muttered around the icy chunks. "I don't see why you don't just come and live with me."

"Amanda, we've been all through this. I appreciate the offer. Truly I do. But surely you can see it would never work. You're not accustomed to children. I don't think you have any idea of how completely a baby takes over your life. And anyway, you know you like living alone, not having to accommodate anyone else. As much as I love you, you have to admit, we have completely different life-styles. Believe me, for the sake of our friendship, it's much better this way."

Besides, not in her wildest dreams could Tess imagine raising a baby in Amanda's chic mauve and gray condo among all that modern chrome-and-glass furniture. Her own tastes tended toward old-fashioned patchwork quilts, needlepoint pillows and homey antiques.

"Maybe you're right," Amanda conceded grudgingly. Pulverizing another ice cube, she sniffed the air. "What smells so good?"

"A casserole. I knew by the time we finished unloading we'd be too tired to cook or go out to eat so I prepared it last night. There's a salad and a jug of iced tea in the fridge to go with it."

Amanda rolled her eyes. "Gawd, but you're domestic. If ever a woman was meant to be a wife and mother it's you."

Pain stabbed at Tess.

Seeing her stricken expression, Amanda grimaced. "Oh, Lord, Tess, I'm sorry. I'm so sorry. That was a stupid, thoughtless thing to say. Me and my big mouth. When will I ever learn to think before I speak? I should have—"

"It's all right, Amanda. Really. I don't expect you to tiptoe around me forever. I have to accept that Tom is gone. Anyway..." She patted the rounded mound beneath her oversize shirt. "I may not be a wife anymore but at least I am going to be a mommy soon." With a determined smile, she opened another box and began unwrapping a set of hand-blown tumblers.

Mike came and went several more times, hauling in the last of the items from the trailer. When finished, he returned to the living room and looked at Tess over the bar, shifting from one foot to another. "I'm all done, Mrs. Benson. The trailer is empty. What do you want me to do now?"

"Oh, Mike, you've done more than enough already. You've been a tremendous help. I don't know how we would have managed without you. But I certainly don't expect you to do more."

The boy flushed to the tips of his ears but looked enormously pleased. "That's okay. I want to. Honest."

"But won't your parents be expecting you home for dinner soon?"

"Naw. Anyway, my folks are divorced, so it's just me'n my dad. He decided since I was going to lend you a hand he'd catch up on some stuff at the job site tonight. When he works late, I usually just zap a frozen pizza in the microwave."

"In that case, why don't you join Ms. Sutherland and me for dinner? There's plenty, and it's the least I can do after all your hard work."

Mike's face lit up. "Hey, that'd be great!"

A short while later when they sat down to eat he nearly tripped over his own feet in his rush to hold out Tess's chair for her.

She bit back a smile. It had been the same all day. Mike treated her as though she were made of fine china. Since introducing himself the evening before and volunteering to help, he had insisted on doing all the heavy work and had fetched and carried and hovered over her like a mother hen. Tess found his awkward attempts at gallantry sweet and endearing.

She wondered, though, if he had ever been around a pregnant woman before. He seemed fascinated by her condition. Several times she had caught him watching her, the look in his eyes a mixture of awe, curiosity and terror.

Mike devoured his food, eating with more gusto and appreciation than the simple meal merited. "Man, this is super," he exclaimed, digging into a third plateful. "You're a terrific cook, Mrs. Benson. I haven't eaten anything this good since the last time I visited my Grandma McCall in Crockett."

"Why, thank you, Mike."

"Me'n Dad usually eat stuff like pizzas or burgers, or TV dinners. Once in a while he'll grill steaks and nuke a couple of spuds in the microwave, but mostly we eat take-out. Dad's no great shakes in the kitchen."

Mike forked up another mouthful of food, but in mid-chew he looked suddenly worried and hastily swallowed it down. "Course, he's real busy an' all," he tacked on anxiously, as though afraid he'd been disloyal. "He works real hard and puts in long hours. He doesn't have time for stuff like cooking. But he's a really great dad."

"I'm sure he is." Tess's smile offered gentle reassurance, and Mike relaxed visibly. She passed him the plate of crackers and he scooped up a handful. "What sort of work does your father do, Mike?"

"He'n Uncle Reilly build houses."

"Oh, you mean they're carpenters?" Amanda commented.

"Naw...well...yeah, sorta, I guess. Dad'n Uncle Reilly can do just about anything it takes to build a house if they have to," he said, flashing a proud grin. "Clear the land, pour concrete, wiring, plumbing, lay carpet—all that stuff. But mostly they've got other guys to do those things 'cause they're always busy with suppliers and inspectors or down at city hall getting permits and junk.

"See, Dad and Uncle Reilly own this company called R and R Construction an' Dad says that dealing with bureaucrats is a real pain in the bu—" Flushing, Mike ducked his head. "Uh...that is...being a builder is a real headache," he mumbled into his chest.

Tess fought back the urge to laugh. "I'm sure it is," she agreed with a straight face, then tactfully changed the subject. Within minutes she had Mike chattering away once more, telling them all about his baseball team and their chances of making the play-offs.

By the time they had eaten, it was getting late. There was still a lot left to do, but their number one priority was to set up Tess's bed. They had just completed that task when heavy footsteps sounded on the stairs outside, followed by a door closing.

"That's Dad," Mike announced. "I hate to leave you with so much left to do, but I'd better go. I'll be back tomorrow, though, to help you get things straightened up."

Tess thanked him profusely, making him blush again, but he looked pleased. When he had gone, Amanda gave Tess a sly look.

"Well, well, well."

"Well, what?"

"I think that boy has a crush on you, that's what. At the risk of sounding immodest, I'm somewhat of a local celebrity. Usually people get all flustered and excited around me, especially males, but Mike barely paid me any notice all day...except, of course, to ask questions about you."

"Don't be ridiculous, Amanda."

"C'mon. You've got to admit, he's been practically tripping over his feet all day, fetching and carrying for you."

"That doesn't mean he has a crush on me, for heaven's sake. I think he's just looking for a mother substitute."

"Mmm. You may be right. If so, his instincts are good. They don't come any more maternal and nurturing than you."

The two friends sat in silence, slouched on the sofa, their napes resting against the top edge of the back, feet outstretched. After a while Amanda chuckled. "Right now Mike's all knees and elbows and big feet, but give him a few years, put a few pounds on those bones, and he's going to be drop-dead gorgeous. Exactly like his father."

"His father? I thought you didn't like Ryan McCall."

"I didn't say that, exactly. Anyway, so what? I may find his personality grating, but I'm not blind. I mean, just look at the man—tall and broad-shouldered, black hair, blue eyes, chiseled features. He probably has to fight the women off with a stick."

"If you think he's so handsome then why were you so short with his brother? They look just alike."

Amanda snorted and shot her friend a sidelong look that reeked disgust. "That lightweight? Forget it. Reilly McCall is nothing but a glib-talking skirt-chaser who coasts through life on looks and charm. I've seen his type before and take my word for it, he'll never amount to a thing. I don't waste my time with men like that.

"Now his brother, on the other hand, is serious and dependable. Those qualities, combined with good looks are much more appealing. I bet even his abrasive attitude probably draws more women than it repels. Personally, the brooding angry man type doesn't do a thing for me, but a lot of women can't resist a challenge—the more standoffish a man is, the more they want him.

"Of the two, Mike's father is by far the better prospect." Amanda rolled her head on the sofa back and smiled at Tess. "And just think, you've got the inside track, living right next door, you lucky devil."

"*Me?* Amanda, for heaven's sake! I'm hardly in the market for a man. I've been a widow for barely seven months. Besides, I'm expecting a child, remember? A handsome hunk isn't going to look twice at a woman who resembles a pumpkin with legs."

"Maybe," Amanda conceded in her laconic way. "But grief eventually fades and life goes on." She rolled her head on the sofa back again and sent Tess a slow, wicked smile. "And you, my friend, won't always be pregnant."

## Chapter Two

"Well? What do you think? Do we stand a chance?" Reilly shot his brother a hopeful look. The two men strode side by side through the lobby of Texas Fidelity Bank, heading for the exit.

"Maybe. Houston's economy has picked up some, but things are still tight," Ryan replied. "It could go either way."

"So all we can do is wait, huh?" Reilly grinned and winked at a pretty blond teller. Despite the serious nature of their conversation, he was aware of the feminine sighs and dreamy stares that followed their progress.

So was Ryan, but, as always, he ignored them.

The women's interest was understandable; the McCall brothers were an impressive sight. Except for subtle, almost undetectable differences, the two men were identical. Tall and broad-shouldered, they had the same ruggedly handsome features and both had the fit, muscular build of a man whose job involved physical labor. Each man's thick hair had the glossy blue-black sheen of a raven's wing, and long hours spent out-of-doors had tanned their skin to a deep bronze, creating a startling contrast to vivid blue eyes.

For the meeting with the bank's loan officer both brothers had worn dark blue suits. There, however, the similarities ended. Ryan's white shirt and diagonally striped navy and wine tie were conservative and sober, but Reilly sported a shirt the exact color of his eyes and a tie in multihued splotches of red, yellow and blue that looked as though it had been created by a berserk artist.

"That's about all we can do," Ryan acknowledged. "Wait and see if our loan application is approved."

"I'm not worried. We'll get the money. We've dealt with Larry Awkland before. He knows we have a reputation as first-class developers."

"He also knows we damned near went under when the bottom fell out of the economy."

"But we didn't. That's my point. While other construction firms were going belly up, we hung on."

"Yeah. By our fingernails." Ryan pushed open the plate glass doors and they stepped outside. The humidity and blistering June heat hit them like a suffocating wet blanket. "Awkland knows that, too. Anyway, it takes more than reputation to swing a loan these days."

"So? That's a prime piece of property we're offering as collateral. If we get that interim loan we'll develop it into a first-class preplanned neighborhood with all the amenities."

Ryan's Jeep Cherokee was parked around the corner from the bank. As he stepped around to the driver's side to unlock it he looked over the hood at his brother.

"That's true. But whether or not the bank feels there's a need in Houston right now for another community of upper priced homes is something else again."

"Aw, you worry too much, Hoss," Reilly chided with a grin, climbing into the vehicle. "We'll be breaking ground on this project within two weeks. You just watch."

Ryan grunted, and his brother gave him a playful sock on the arm. "Loosen up, man. It doesn't do any good to worry. I want this project to go as much as you do. But hey! If it doesn't happen, it doesn't happen. One way or another, we'll get by. We always do."

"Maybe you're right," Ryan conceded, and pulled out into the traffic.

Though at times his twin could be exasperating, Ryan envied his easygoing nature. Reilly took life as it came and rolled with the punches, always bouncing back with a grin. Nothing bothered him for long, nothing worried him, nothing—or at least very little—roused him to anger. Reilly, like their younger brother Travis, was blessed with a sunny disposition and an eternally optimistic outlook. It was Ryan and their baby sister Meghan who were the serious ones.

Ryan wished he could be as casual and unconcerned as Reilly, but he couldn't. For one thing, it wasn't his nature. For another, he didn't want to just "get by." Dammit, they had been just barely getting by for the last eight or nine years, ever since Houston's housing market went bust.

He and Reilly had started their company right out of college. They had hustled their butts off and worked like dogs those first few years, but they had succeeded in building R & R Construction into a thriving business. In the process they had built a reputation as first-class builders and developers. It had been a bitterly frustrating experience to stand by, helpless to prevent it, and watch it all crumble because of circumstances beyond their control.

Memories of that time were painful even now, and Ryan's jaw clenched. He remembered how desperate he had felt, how hard he and Reilly had struggled to hang on. They had been forced to unload almost all of the property they had acquired for future development, taking a loss just to get out from under the debt. All they had managed to retain title to was the wooded tract in northwest Houston, and that only because it was theirs, free and clear. Ryan had even been forced to sell his home—the enormous, extravagant home that he had built for Julia—just to keep the company afloat.

Ryan's fingers clenched around the steering wheel. Julia had never forgiven him for that. To his wife, that luxurious house, their upscale life-style, all the trappings that went with it, were essential. More essential, it turned out, than their marriage, or him . . . or even their son. Julia had been unable, or unwilling, to face a life without money and status.

It had been tough, these past eight years, raising a boy alone and at the same time scrabbling to hold on to his business. For a while it had been touch and go, but he'd gotten through it. Mike was one hell of a kid; a father couldn't ask for better. And despite several shaky years, the company was still operating.

It galled Ryan when R & R, a firm that had once built prestigious homes, had been reduced to bidding on remodeling jobs or any other piddling project that came along. However, it had been those small jobs that had paid the bills and allowed them to scrape by . . . barely.

Their most recent job was an apartment complex renovation that was nearing completion. They were scheduled to meet with the owner in less than an hour for a walk-through inspection. Rather than waste time going home to change, Ryan drove straight to the project. Both he and Reilly kept a set of spare work clothes in the trailer that served as their on-site office.

They had almost reached the site when the car phone emitted a chirping ring.

Ryan snatched it up at once. The instrument was an expense he normally would not have bothered with, but after Julia left, he had gotten it so that his son would be able to contact him wherever he was.

"R & R Construction. Ryan McCall speaking."

"Hi, Dad. It's me. I'm over at Tess's."

"Again? I thought you got her place straightened up yesterday."

"We did, but today I'm helping her hang curtains. I just wanted to let you know that we have to make a quick trip to the hardware store for some bolts. Just in case you called looking for me."

Ryan sighed impatiently. "All right. But look, son, be home early, okay? The Astros are playing in the Dome tonight. I thought we'd take in the game. How about it?"

"Aw-*right!* You gotta deal, Dad! See you about six."

"Damn." Ryan slammed the receiver down. At the same time he brought the Cherokee to a sliding halt in front of the office.

"Something wrong?" Reilly asked, but his brother was already out of the vehicle and striding for the trailer. When Reilly followed him inside he found Ryan sprawled in his desk chair, his face like a thundercloud.

"An Astros game? Since when? You said earlier we were going to stay late and work up a bid on the McElhaney project?"

"I changed my mind, okay. I think it's more important that I spend some time with Mike."

Reilly leaned back against his own desk and crossed his arms over his chest. "All right. What's bugging you?"

The question earned him a sour look. "What's bugging me? I'll tell you what's bugging me. Mike is spending practically every waking moment at the widow Benson's apartment. He's been over there everyday for four straight days, ever since Saturday when she started moving in. In the mornings he gobbles down his breakfast and bolts out of the apartment like he's going to a fire. All I hear out of him is 'Tess this' and 'Tess that,'" he mimicked in a nasty singsong. The mere mention of the woman's name made Ryan want to grind his teeth.

"It'll pass. Anyway, where's the harm? She seems like a nice person."

Ryan snorted. "People are seldom what they seem. Especially women. Regardless, I don't want Mike to get attached to her."

"Why not? The boy could use some feminine influence in his life."

"He has Mom and his aunts for that," Ryan argued. "And there's Erin and Elise and David's wife, Abby. He has plenty of women in his life."

"C'mon, Ryan. They all live in other towns. Erin and Elise live in another state, for Pete's sake. Mike sees them on holidays and at family gatherings. Look, the kid's been motherless for the last eight years. It's only natural that he'd try to find a substitute. Face it, brother. Mike needs a mother."

"The hell he does! Mike and I are doing just fine on our own." Glaring at his brother, Ryan thumbed his chest angrily. "Whatever my son needs, I'll give him."

"Hey. Don't get defensive on me. You've done a great job with Mike. Nobody's saying you haven't. But face it, there are just some things that only a mother can provide."

"And you expect me to believe that's why Mike is hanging around the Benson woman? Because he's looking for a mother substitute?" He gave a bark of scornful laughter. "Yeah, right. That's why he picked a delectable redhead with sexy eyes."

A grin spread over Reilly's face. "So you noticed, huh?"

"I'm not blind," Ryan snapped. "Just because I don't care for women or trust them doesn't mean I can't appreciate the way they look."

"Good. I'm glad to hear it," his brother said with a wink. "Maybe there's hope for you yet where women are concerned." With a smug smile on his face, Reilly walked over to a metal locker, removed a pair of jeans and a chambray work shirt, sent his brother a taunting wink and disappeared into the bathroom.

Ryan's icy stare followed him and bore into the bathroom door. His eyes narrowed into two slits. *Don't count on it, brother.*

Balancing on Tess's kitchen step stool, Mike hooked the curtain rod over the bracket and snapped it into place. "There. That does it. That's the last one," he said, and jumped down in one agile leap.

Tess moved in and attached the tiebacks to the dotted Swiss curtains. When she had fluffed the folds and adjusted the drape just so, they both stepped back to admire their handiwork.

"Oh, Mike. They look lovely. In fact, the whole place looks lovely."

Turning in a slow circle, she surveyed with pleasure what she could see of the apartment, which at present was the nursery, where she and Mike were, and a bit of her bedroom across the hall. All of her furniture was arranged where she wanted it, curtains or draperies framed every window, her pictures and paintings hung on the walls and all of her familiar keepsakes and decorative items were in place. Every box and carton had been unpacked and their contents put away. There wasn't so much as a scrap of bubble wrap or packing material in sight.

"I can't believe we got it all done so quickly. I really don't know how to thank you, Mike. You've been such a tremendous help. With Amanda out of town on assignment these past few days, I would have been on my own if it hadn't been for you. I never would have managed without you."

She turned to Mike, but her grateful smile collapsed when she saw his face. He looked as though he had just lost his best friend. "Why, Mike. What's wrong?"

"Nothing." He shrugged and looked at the floor, his mouth sulky. "We're all done, huh?"

"Yes. There's not a single thing left to do."

"I guess that means I won't be seeing much of you any-more. I mean . . ." He shrugged again and dug the toe of his sneaker into the carpet. "Now that we're all done, there's no reason for me to come over."

Abruptly, the reason for his distress became clear. Tess gazed tenderly at his woebegone face, her heart melting. "Oh, Mike." She grabbed his hand and squeezed it be-tween both of hers and looked deep into his eyes. "Of course there's a reason for you to come over. We're friends. That's all the reason you need. You're welcome to visit me anytime you like."

Mike looked up, a glimmer of hope in his blue eyes. "Really? You mean it?" His voice broke, sliding from a manly baritone into a squeak, but for once he didn't look discomfited.

"Yes, of course I mean it. The truth is, I'll be hurt if you don't come over often. I'm new here, remember. You're the only one in the whole complex I know. If you don't visit me I'm going to be terribly lonely."

"Oh, don't worry," he said, perking up dramatically. "I'll be here. I promise."

"Good." She gave his hand a brisk pat. "Now that we have that settled, you'd better hurry if you're going to that game with your father."

"Jeez! I almost forgot. I've gotta get cleaned up before he gets home." He took off at a lope. Smiling, Tess fol-lowed more slowly. She waddled into the living room just in time to see Mike streak out the front door. "Bye, Tess! See ya tomorrow!"

Chuckling, she shook her head and eased down onto the sofa.

Tess was getting so large, her body was becoming more cumbersome by the day. Almost all movement was awk-ward for her, but sitting down was particularly difficult. Getting up was even worse.

Leaning forward, Tess stuffed a pillow behind her back and lifted her feet onto the hassock. With a sigh, she leaned back and splayed her hands on top of her swollen tummy.

"Well, baby. Here we are. This is home now. No matter what anyone else thinks, I know I'm doing the right thing. When you get here, you're going to have my time. All my time."

Beneath her palms, the baby kicked as though he or she understood, and Tess smiled. "And you know what else? We're going to make each other happy, too, you and I. We'd better," she added with a wry chuckle. "We're all we've got. It's just the two of us, sweetheart."

Tess had read that a newborn infant recognized its mother's voice from hearing it while in the womb, and that the baby drew comfort from the sound. It worried her that, living alone as she did, she seldom had anyone with whom to talk. To compensate, she had started carrying on one-sided conversations with her unborn child so that the baby would grow accustomed to her voice. Also, it made Tess feel less alone.

Rubbing her distended abdomen, Tess wrinkled her nose. "Well...actually...that's not absolutely true. There is your daddy's family. But the Bensons live way up north. And anyway, they and your daddy were estranged. That means they didn't get along," she added in a confiding whisper.

"Not that the Bensons are bad people, mind you. In fact, they're considered pillars of Boston society. The problem is they're...well...managing." Actually, Tom had called them manipulative and domineering, but she hesitated to use such harsh words when talking to the baby. They were also distant and snooty, but Tess kept that thought to herself. "That's why Daddy stayed away from them. And somehow I don't think he would like for us to go to them for help, either."

The baby kicked again, and Tess moved her hands over her tummy in a slow, hypnotic rhythm. Resting her head against the edge of the sofa back, she gazed at the ceiling through half-closed eyes. During her six-year marriage to Tom she had met his parents only once—briefly—when they had come to town to attend some sort of charity gala. She and Tom had met them for dinner at a posh restaurant, where they had endured three interminable hours of stiff, at times interrogating, conversation. She had gotten the impression that the elder Bensons had not been all that taken with her.

Tess shook her head at the memory, a bemused half-smile tugging at her lips. It still boggled her mind that her warm, loving, unpretentious husband had been the offspring of two such stuffed shirts as Harold and Enid Benson.

Tess knew Tom's older brother Charles only slightly better. He had visited them three or four times when he'd been in town on family business. Though not as stiff as his parents, he was ultra sophisticated and polished, but at least he had made a halfhearted effort to be friendly.

As yet, the Bensons did not know about the baby. The last contact she'd had with any of them—Charles included—had been at Tom's funeral, and she hadn't known then that she was pregnant. She had written to them twice but received no reply. She could only conclude that to Tom's family, his death had severed whatever tenuous tie had existed between them.

Should she write and tell them about the baby? Tess groaned. She had been asking herself that question for months. On the one hand, it seemed wrong not to. But on the other hand, she was uneasy about how they would react to the news. Tom had always maintained that the only way to remain independent from his family was to have as little to do with them as possible. She certainly did not want them interfering or trying to take control of her child, as they had tried to control Tom.

Tess didn't know what to do, so she kept putting the decision off. There was plenty of time.

From the McCalls' apartment on the other side of her living room wall, came the faint sound of a shower running and Mike singing at the top of his lungs in his cracked voice. Tess grinned and closed her eyes. A minute later she heard Ryan McCall climb the stairs and enter the apartment.

Suddenly an idea occurred to her. Tess opened her eyes and sat up, mulling it over. Of course. Why hadn't she thought of it sooner. She had been trying to come up with a way to thank Mike properly for all his help, and this was perfect. She would do it right now.

Getting up off the sofa proved difficult but after three tries she finally heaved herself to her feet and headed for the telephone.

Mike's father answered on the second ring.

"Mr. McCall, this is Tess Benson. I—"

"Mike can't come to the phone right now," he said shortly. "He's in the shower. You'll have to call back later."

"Oh, but I'm not calling for Mike," Tess said in a rush, sensing he was about to hang up. "I called to talk to you."

The statement met dead silence at the other end of the line.

Suddenly, Tess felt uneasy and she wasn't sure why. "I uh...I called to invite you and Mike over for dinner Friday night. After all he's done to hel—"

"No."

"I beg your pardon?"

"I said no. I'm turning down your invitation."

"I..." Tess was so flustered she could barely think. She had never met anyone quite as abrupt as Ryan McCall. "Oh. I see. Well, look, if Friday isn't convenient we can make it—"

"The answer would still be no. It isn't a matter of inconvenience. I'm simply not interested in having dinner with you."

Tess was shocked to the core of her being. She could not utter a sound, and for several seconds the line hummed with a stunned silence. Never in her life had anyone spoken to her with such brutal frankness. Hadn't the man ever heard of tact or social grace?

Finally Tess cleared her throat. "I see. Mr. McCall, have I offended you in some way? If so, I assure you it was unintentional."

"Very good, Mrs. Benson. That really sounded sincere. But you're wasting your time."

"I— Pardon me? I don't understand."

"You can cut out the innocent act. I know what you're up to."

"Up to?"

"Having Mike over constantly. Flattering him, making him like you. Inviting the two of us over for dinner."

"Mr. McCall, I have no idea what you're talking about. I merely thought that you and your son would enjoy a home-cooked meal. It was just my way of thanking Mike for his help and you for allowing him to give it."

"Yeah, right," he sneered. "You know, at first I thought you were one of those licentious women who get their kicks by seducing young boys."

"*What!*"

"But now I realize that you were just using Mike to get to me," Ryan continued without missing a beat.

"Using— Me—? You—? You mean you thought I would seduce—? Oh! *Ohhh!* Why, you . . . you . . ."

Tess sputtered and fumed, too shocked and enraged to think of anything vile enough to call him.

"Save your outraged act for someone else," Ryan snapped. "It doesn't work on me. As I said, you're wasting your time, Mrs. Benson. I'm just not interested."

Tess gulped a deep breath and fought for control. "Mr. McCall, you are not only a colossal egotist, you're sick and disgusting! I am hardly at the peak of my sexual attractiveness at the moment, but even if I were, let me assure you that I would not be interested in you!"

She had started off speaking slowly and distinctly through her clenched teeth but with each word her voice rose in pitch and volume, until by the time she reached the end she was shrieking.

"Good. Then we understand each other," he said matter-of-factly, and hung up.

Tess gasped and jerked the receiver away from her ear. She stared at it. "Oh! Of all the—!" She slammed the phone down so hard it jumped out of its cradle and she had to do it again, which made her all the more furious.

Unable to move, she stood there, shaking all over, her heart pounding, breathing hard. Several seconds passed before she noticed. Oh, Lord. It couldn't be good for the baby to get so upset, she thought. Calm down. Just calm down.

Leaning back against the wall, she closed her eyes, splayed one hand against her heaving chest, the other across her belly and drew several deep breaths.

"I'm sorry, baby. I'm sorry," she soothed in a caressing voice. "I shouldn't have yelled like that. But Mommy's okay now. Everything's fine."

Gathering her scattered composure, Tess pushed away from the wall and returned to the sofa, lowering herself gingerly onto the cushion. She still felt shaky. No one had ever made her that angry before. She hadn't known she could *get* that angry.

But then, who wouldn't if they had to deal with an obnoxious man like Ryan McCall?

When she had met him, she had given him the benefit of the doubt and put his abruptness down to a bad mood, but not this time. The man was a rude, evil-minded, ill-tempered brute. Imagine! Accusing her, in her condition, of coming on to him! And worse, of trying to seduce his thirteen-year-old son. It was a mystery how that hateful man ever produced a boy like Mike.

Mike. Tess sighed, sadness washing over her. As bad as she hated to, she would have to break all ties with the boy. His father obviously did not approve of their friendship. Anyway, the way things stood, she doubted that she could hide her feelings. Certainly she wouldn't be able to hold her tongue whenever Mike mentioned his father, which was sure to be often. Mike and his dad were close, and the boy clearly adored him. Whatever else he was, Ryan McCall was apparently a good parent.

Tess discovered that she did not have the heart to tell Mike that they could no longer be friends. When faced with those guileless blue eyes and that eager face, she simply could not utter the words. So she tried to discourage him by withdrawing.

Over the next few days she avoided him whenever she could. When he knocked, she didn't answer her door. She monitored her telephone calls through the answering machine, never picking up when the caller was Mike. When she left her apartment or returned, she did so quietly, tiptoeing in and out like a thief, and feeling as guilty as though she were one. On the few occasions when she did run into him, she pretended to be either in a hurry to get somewhere or terribly busy.

Mike, however, was not one to be put off by evasions. On the evening of the third day after the disastrous telephone conversation, he waylaid Tess in the hallway outside their apartments.

It was late when she climbed the stairs and found him sitting on the floor outside her door. He looked as though he had every intention of staying there all night if he had to.

Tess jerked to a halt at the top of the stairs so suddenly that Amanda nearly barrelled into her.

"Hey! Watch out," her friend yelped, but Tess didn't hear her.

"Mike! What are you doing here? It's late."

Mike looked up, his expression sullen. "Waiting to see you."

"Oh." Tess licked her lips and glanced uneasily at her friend. "We've...uh...we've been to a Lamaze class. Amanda's my coach."

"Hi there, sweetie. How ya doing?" Amanda said, but he merely shrugged and mumbled, "Okay" before returning his attention to Tess.

He climbed to his feet and brushed off the seat of his pants. His gaze never left her.

"I thought you said we were friends."

"Why...we are, Mike."

"Then how come you didn't answer your door this morning when I knocked?" Both his look and his tone accused.

"I...guess I wasn't here."

"Your car was in the parking lot. I checked."

"I see. Well, then..." Tess gestured vaguely. "I must have been in the mail room."

"Uh-uh. I checked there, too."

Amanda remained silent. Her shrewd gaze switched back and forth between them.

"I see. Well...I, uh...I suppose we just missed each other somehow," Tess said lamely.

Mike stared at her in silence. Tess could feel the guilt written all over her face, but there was nothing to do but brazen it out.

"Can I come in?" he asked finally.

"Oh. Well...I'm pretty tired, and it's getting late. Maybe some other time."

Hurt flashed in Mike's eyes. Then pride took over and his young face grew remote. "Yeah. Sure." He nodded and stuck his hands into his back pockets. "See ya."

Tess watched him walk away with a lump in her throat.

"Would you mind telling me what that was all about?" Amanda demanded the moment they stepped inside Tess's apartment. "You were downright cold to that boy."

"I know." Emotion threatened to choke her, and her voice wavered. Fighting back tears, she gave her friend a woeful look. "Oh, Amanda," she whispered wretchedly.

Without a word, Amanda's demeanor softened, and she gathered Tess close—or as close as her girth would allow—and led her toward the sofa. "All right, now. Tell me what's happened," Amanda said in a commanding but gentle voice once they were settled.

Hesitantly, Tess recounted what had transpired between herself and Ryan McCall. During the tale, Amanda's expression ran the gamut—from a haughtily raised eyebrow to a sagging jaw and finally ending with her beautiful face set in an icy mask of fury. "Do you mean that *bastard* had the unmitigated gall to accuse you—*you* of all people—of trying to seduce Mike?" she said, enunciating every word in a tight, dangerous voice. "And of using that sweet boy to get to *him?*"

Miserable, Tess nodded.

"Why that sorry, no good... And to think, I thought he was the *nice* one."

"For some reason, he seems to have taken an intense dislike to me. So you can see that I have to break off my friendship with Mike. I really don't have any other choice."

"I suppose you're right." Amanda sighed. "It's a shame though. Mike is bound to be hurt."

Tess tried not to think about that. "Yes, well... at least his father should be pleased."

Ryan was delighted. For the past three days Mike had not so much as mentioned Tess Benson. He had been spending more time at home, as well. From his son's glum mood, Ryan strongly suspected that after their talk Mrs. Benson had realized she was wasting her time buttering up Mike and had dropped him like a hot potato.

He hated to see the boy so depressed, but Ryan figured he would get over it soon. In a day or two he'd be enthused about something else and forget all about their new neighbor.

However, when Ryan entered the apartment on Friday evening, far from improved, Mike's mood had worsened. Sprawled in a chair with one leg hooked over the arm, he stared morosely at the television screen. In response to his father's greeting he mumbled something but barely spared him a glance.

"Hey, what is this? Why the long face? Cheer up, son. Things can't be that bad," Ryan teased, tweaking the toe of Mike's sneaker.

"Oh, yeah? That's what you think."

"So what's the problem?" The question brought no response, and Ryan nudged him again. "C'mon, you know you can tell me."

Mike grimaced, but finally he shot his dad a sulky look. "I don't think Tess likes me anymore. She doesn't return my calls. She doesn't answer her door. I think she's avoiding me."

Ryan's lips thinned. Impatience rippled through him and edged his voice. "It that all? So what? Forget about her."

He turned away, flipping through the mail. It contained nothing of importance so he tossed it onto his desk and sat down in his easy chair. Picking up the evening newspaper, he glanced at his son, again. To his surprise, Mike was watching him, his eyes narrowed and filled with suspicion.

"Have you eaten?" Ryan asked.

"Yeah. I had some frozen egg rolls."

"Good." He snapped open the paper and tried to ignore his son's penetrating stare.

"Dad, do you know why Tess is acting strange?"

"How the hell would I know?" Ryan barked, his conscience stabbing him.

"You didn't talk to her or anything?"

"Look, Mike. Why are you making such a big deal about this woman? She's nothing to us."

"The change in her was real quick," Mike mused, ignoring his father's question. "Like maybe somebody did something to upset her."

"So? Women get upset easily." Ryan shifted in the chair and snapped the newspaper again, scowling at the printed page without seeing a word.

Mike sat forward, his eyes widening. "You *did* talk to her, didn't you?"

Faced with a direct challenge, Ryan could not lie. He was always honest with his son. But he resented being cornered. Why couldn't Mike just let the whole thing drop? "All right, yeah, I talked to her," he replied belligerently. "So what?"

"When? What did you say to her?"

"She called and invited us over for dinner. I turned down the invitation."

"But why?" Mike wailed.

Rarely did Ryan lose his temper with his son, but the anguished question pushed him over the edge. "Dammit, Mike, you know why. I will *not* be manipulated by some man-hungry female. What's more, I resent the way the woman has been cozying up to you to get to me."

Mike leaped out of his chair. His gangly body vibrated with outrage. "Tess wouldn't do that!" he shouted. "Anyway, she's not interested in you!"

"Don't kid yourself. All women are on the make for a man. Or maybe I should say, a breadwinner."

"Not Tess. That's just plain stupid. You don't even know her. You don't know anything about her! She's nice, and…and…and she's special! And now she probably won't ever speak to me again! And it's all your fault!" he shouted, and bolted for his room.

"Mike! Mike, come back here!" Ryan called after him, springing up out of his chair. He could have saved his breath. Mike's door slammed with a force that rattled the walls.

"Damn." Spinning around, Ryan slammed his fist down on the back of the chair.

He paced back and forth across the room. This was all that damned Benson woman's fault. He and Mike had never had a serious disagreement until now.

Why was his son so taken with her? What the hell was so special about the woman?

Ryan stopped and glanced toward the bedrooms. Mike might be innocent enough to believe she had no interest in him beyond simple neighborliness, but experience had taught him otherwise. Ever since Julia had walked out on him and Mike, women had been pursuing him like hounds after a fox. Strangely, it seemed that the more he tried to discourage them, the more remote and abrupt he was, the more relentless they were. And the more devious their ploys. Tess Benson certainly wasn't the first woman who had tried to use Mike to attract his interest.

Ryan sat down on the sofa. Slumping forward, he braced his elbows on his spread knees and massaged his temples. He sighed. Maybe Reilly was right. Maybe Mike did need a mother figure in his life. That gentling, nurturing female influence that he and his brothers and sister had grown up with.

Guiltily, Ryan recalled the wistful look that sometimes came over Mike's face when he talked about a friend's mom. On those occasions Ryan had always stifled his twinges of conscience and told himself that they were doing just fine on their own. But were they? Was Mike?

Yes, dammit! Ryan shot up off the sofa and began to pace. Mike was bright and happy and well adjusted. He was doing well in school; he had plenty of friends. Just because no woman played an active role in his life that didn't mean he was deprived. He could even be better off. God knew, some women were wretched mothers. Julia certainly had been.

He wanted to forbid Mike to have anything more to do with Tess Benson, but he knew that would not be wise. Mike was at a touchy age. Ryan didn't want to push him into rebellion. No, the best thing he could do was wait it out. It might take time, but eventually Mike would get over his infatuation with their new neighbor.

At breakfast the next morning the atmosphere between the two McCall males was frosty. Mike responded to his father's pleasant "Good morning" with a curt nod and skirted around him in the small kitchen as though he weren't there, his young face stiff. Ryan's question about what Mike wanted to eat was met with an abrupt, "Never mind. I'll get it myself."

After five minutes of sitting side by side at the breakfast bar, eating their cereal in stony silence, Ryan had had enough.

"This is ridiculous," he snapped. "We have to talk about this, Mike."

Mike merely shrugged and kept on spooning cereal into his mouth.

"Look, son," he said as patiently as he could manage. "You know how I feel about women. You've always known. But, hey! Just because I don't want to be around Mrs. Benson doesn't mean you can't be friends with her."

Mike cut his eyes toward his father, his expression still sullen. "You hurt her feelings. Now she doesn't want to be friends with me."

"Well then, I guess you'll just have to try harder. Look, tell her I said it was all right."

Mike grimaced and stared at his cereal bowl.

"C'mon, son." Ryan cuffed him on the shoulder. "Whaddaya say?"

Dramatically rolling his eyes, the boy heaved a sigh. "O-*kay*," he agreed finally, in a put-upon voice that only a teenager can achieve.

"Good. So, how about it? Are we friends again?"

Mike shot him another sharp look. Ryan could see that he was struggling to hold on to his rancor, but Mike's basic good nature never allowed him to stay angry for long. In that respect he was far more like his Uncle Reilly than his father. Ryan's twin was unfailingly, at times maddeningly, good-natured and jovial, and on those rare occasions when he did lose his temper his anger never lasted long.

Finally Mike's mouth twitched in a reluctant, somewhat abashed smile. "Yeah. I guess."

By the time they headed out to do their Saturday grocery shopping and errands, the camaraderie between father and son was fully restored. Ryan's mood was buoyant... until, a mile or so from the apartment, he spotted Tess.

Her car was sitting by the side of the road with a flat tire, and she was bending over the open trunk. He couldn't see her face, but there was no mistaking that bright hair or that battered little car.

Ryan speeded up, hoping that Mike wouldn't notice her. That hope was dashed almost instantly.

"Look! There's Tess!" he shouted. "And she has a flat!" He looked at his father, his face at first eager, then crestfallen. "Aren't you gonna stop?"

Ryan opened his mouth to tell him that these days liberated women changed their own flat tires, but before he could, Tess straightened up and turned around with the jack in her hands.

Ryan's head whipped around as he zoomed past her. "What the—?" His eyes bulged and his jaw dropped.

He snapped his mouth shut then opened it again to cut loose with a stream of colorful curse words that had Mike gaping, stomped on the brake and brought the Cherokee to a screeching halt on the shoulder of the road.

He stabbed his son with an irate glare. "She's pregnant! Why the hell didn't you *tell* me she was pregnant!"

## *Chapter Three*

"*Me!*" Mike squeaked. "Why should I? I thought you knew!"

"No, I didn't know. How the hell would I kn—" Ryan stopped and raked a hand through his hair, aware that the anger he was heaping on his son was misdirected; it was himself he was furious with.

A pregnant woman, for Pete's sake. A pregnant *widow!*

"Uh... are we going to help her?" Mike asked cautiously. He watched his father, his young face puckered with anxiety and hope.

Biting off another sharp curse, Ryan turned his face away and stared out the window. He did not see the traffic whizzing by nor feel the buffeting of its backdraft.

His emotions warred. He felt guilty as hell.

But dammit! He was angry, too. He had the inescapable feeling that he was being sucked into a situation against his will. It was as though he'd fallen into a raging torrent and was being dragged inexorably toward a waterfall, no matter how hard he fought against it.

He gritted his teeth. Dammit! Tess Benson wasn't his problem. For several moments he sat ramrod stiff and stared into the distance, his face grim. His fingers clenched and unclenched around the steering wheel. A muscle along his jaw worked. Finally, as though drawn by a magnet, his gaze slid to the rearview mirror.

"Oh, what the hell!" he snapped, and reached for the door handle. "C'mon. Let's go give her a hand before she hurts herself."

"Yes! *Yes!*" Making a fist, Mike bent his arm and jerked it downward in one sharp pump of victory before scrambling out of the car and racing after his father.

With a face like thunder, Ryan stomped back toward the disabled car, his long strides eating up the ground. Mike had to break into a trot just to keep up.

When they rounded the end of the vehicle Ryan came to an abrupt halt, his frustration and fury soaring to even greater heights at the sight of Tess on her knees inside the trunk, trying to drag out the spare tire.

"Will you...come out of...there!" Grunting and straining, Tess tugged at the tire with all her might, but she couldn't budge it. Unable to reach the spare because of her girth, she had climbed up into the trunk to get closer, but she still couldn't get a good grip on the tire. Huffing and puffing, she sat back on her heels, perilously close to tears. What was she going to do?

She looked around forlornly. The traffic zipped past her as though she were invisible. Weren't there any white knights left in the world?

The thought had barely flitted through her mind when a pair of hard hands hooked under her arms from behind.

"What the *hell* do you think you're doing?" a furious voice barked in her ear. Tess let out a frightened squeal but she was plucked out of the trunk as though she weighed no more than a sack of groceries.

Just as unceremoniously, she was plunked down on her feet and released. The instant she gained her balance she spun around—and gasped.

"You!"

Ryan McCall stood before her with his fists planted on his hips, his feet spread aggressively wide, glaring down at her as though he were contemplating mayhem. "Are you crazy?" he shouted. "Don't you know you shouldn't be climbing around in the trunk of a car or trying to lift a heavy tire?"

"Of course I know," Tess fired back. "But I have a flat that needs changing. What else could I do? The nearest gas station is at least three miles away."

"You can stand by the side of the road and look helpless until a good Samaritan comes along."

"Oh really? If I waited for some big strong man to help me I'd be here all day." She gestured toward the unending stream of traffic rushing by. "In case you haven't noticed, chivalry doesn't exactly seem to be in vogue these days."

"Don't worry, Tess. Dad's real good at fixing tires. He'll have it done in no time."

Tess's head whipped around. "Mike!" She had been so stunned by Ryan's sudden appearance, she hadn't even noticed his son hovering beside her.

"Just stand back and stay out of the way," Ryan ordered, and swung around to the car.

"No, wait! Stay away from there!" Tess rushed forward and grabbed his arm. "I don't want or need your help, Mr. McCall."

"Don't be an idiot. You can't change this tire. If you won't think of yourself, at least think of your baby."

Giving her a disdainful look, he shook off her hand and, with infuriating ease, reached into the trunk and lifted out the spare. He bounced it experimentally on the ground and immediately erupted in another colorful burst of profanity.

Alarmed, Tess took a hasty step back, her eyes growing wide at the fierce expression on his face.

"This thing is flat, too! Woman, don't you have a lick of sense? Driving around on half-bald tires without even a decent spare?"

"I . . . I didn't know the spare was flat."

"You didn't know? That's no excuse. You drive the damned car—you're suppose to know what shape it's in."

"But...you see...my husband always took care of those kinds of things. I don't know anything about cars."

"Then you better learn. You don't have a husband now," he said heartlessly. He turned away and walked around to the side of the car to retrieve the jack, muttering a stream of invective and criticism.

It was too much for Tess. The tears that came so easily these days welled up. She struggled for control, but Ryan McCall was more than her overwrought nerves could take. He was the last person she had expected—or wanted—to see. Moreover, he was obviously furious and giving his assistance grudgingly.

Tess's face crumpled, and she burst into tears. *"Daaad!"*

Mike's anguished wail brought Ryan whirling around. "What? What's wro—? Aw, hell."

"Come quick, Dad! Hurry!" Mike's face wore a look of horror. His frantic gaze jumped back and forth between his father and the weeping woman. Wanting to give comfort but afraid to touch her, he hopped around Tess, shuffling from one foot to the other, his hands hovering over her heaving shoulders.

Ryan stomped to the rear of the car and threw the jack into the trunk. Tess sobbed brokenly, the sounds harsh and raw, verging on hysterical.

"I don't know what's wrong with her, Dad. All of a sudden, she just started bawling." Mike sent his father a desperate look. "Do you think she's hurt?"

"I doubt it. Women in her condition tend to be highstrung. That's probably all it is."

Tess cried harder. The sounds were piteous and unnerving and they served to exacerbate Ryan's guilt. His jaw clenched.

Mike looked distraught. *"Do* something, Dad!"

"Here." Digging into the back pocket of his jeans, Ryan pulled out a clean handkerchief and stuffed it into Tess's hands. "Now, take her back to the Cherokee, son, and try to calm her down. I'll lock up her car and bring the tires."

"Calm her down? How am I suppose to do *that?*" Mike squeaked.

"Oh, for— Here. Like this." Ryan wrapped his arms around Tess and pulled her close. He expected her to resist, but she sagged against him and burrowed her face into his chest, her fingers clutching his shirt. Her response was so urgent and wholehearted, he realized that she had no idea who held her; she was merely reacting instinctively, responding to the warmth and comfort of human touch.

Ryan's guilt deepened. He had forgotten how precariously balanced a woman's emotions were during pregnancy. Julia had been a basket case when she carried Mike. She had burst into tears if you so much as looked at her. If anyone had shouted at her, she probably would have dissolved into a puddle.

Expectant mothers needed support and reassurance. They needed to feel loved and cosseted and cared for. He had learned that much. And when you thought about it, simple physical contact and gentle words—that really wasn't too much to ask, considering what they were going through.

Staring out into space, Ryan rubbed his hands over Tess's shoulders in slow circles. He had given Julia all that. Willingly. Gladly. Hell, he'd been downright enthralled by the whole process.

He had held his wife's head and commiserated with her during morning sickness, rubbed her back when it ached, assisted her when it became awkward to rise from a chair, tied her shoes. When advanced pregnancy had forced her to make several trips a night to the bathroom he had helped her out of bed and waited outside the door to assist her back into it. Many times in the small hours of the morning he had dressed and gone out in search of whatever special food would satisfy her weird cravings.

Tess Benson was alone, with no one to do those things for her. Ryan wondered how she coped.

Despite her swollen abdomen—which he could feel pressing against his middle—she was surprisingly slender. She was a little thing, he realized. The top of her head didn't even reach his chin, and as he ran his hands up and down her back, he noticed that her shoulder blades and ribs seemed incredibly delicate, almost fragile. She was soft and utterly feminine, the kind of woman that brought out a man's most basic protective instincts. He was surprised at how pleasant it felt to hold her.

Ryan's nose twitched. She smelled good, too. Over the acrid odors of exhaust fumes, road dust and hot paving he caught an occasional whiff of the sweet, clean scent that drifted from her hair.

Mike, Ryan noticed, was watching him intently, just as he always did whenever he was learning a new skill. With a pang, Ryan realized that in the past eight years his son had not once seen him show concern or affection for any woman outside of those within their family. The boy probably truly did not know how to comfort Tess.

The thought was oddly troubling, and Ryan quickly pushed it aside and set Tess away from him.

"See, that's all there is to it. So, go on. Take her to the car," he ordered brusquely. "I'll be there in a few minutes."

Carefully, as though afraid she might break, Mike put his arm around her shoulders. "C'mon, Tess." With awkward but touching solicitude, he led her down the shoulder of the road to the waiting vehicle. Ryan watched them go, his expression thoughtful.

Tess could not stop crying; she had completely lost control. The Cherokee rocked when Ryan tossed her tires in the back and she let out a startled yelp, but still the tears came. When he climbed in behind the wheel, all she could do was bury her face in his handkerchief and gasp and choke and sob.

She was mortified. She expected him to berate her, but he merely leaned against the door and waited with surprising patience for the storm of weeping to end.

After what seemed like an eternity, she managed to pull herself together. Gulping, she wadded his handkerchief and dabbed at her eyes and nose. "I—I'm...s-sorry," she mumbled between watery sniffs. "I—I guess I over...re-reacted."

"It's okay. Don't worry about it." Ryan turned the ignition key and started the engine. "Where were you headed?"

"To the gro-grocery store," she said without thinking. Her head came up. "Oh, but...if you'll just take me ho-home, that will be fine. I'll call the garage to pick up the tires."

"It's no problem. Mike and I were headed to the store anyway. We'll drop off the tires on the way and save you a road call fee."

"But—"

"Don't worry about it," he snapped.

Tess stared at his hard profile in helpless frustration. Short of jumping out of the moving vehicle, it appeared that she had no choice.

The next hour was the longest, most miserable that Tess could recall. Despite Ryan's assistance, she was still seething over the nasty things he had said to her. During the drive to the store neither spoke. He stared straight ahead, his face so hard it looked as though it had been chiseled from granite. Tess held herself stiff and pressed against the passenger door and did her best to ignore him.

The instant he parked the vehicle, she scrambled out. She doubted that it would occur to a mannerless oaf like Ryan McCall to open her door for her, but she wasn't taking the chance of him getting that close.

If he even noticed her hasty action he gave no indication.

"We'll meet back here in half an hour," he announced when they entered the store. "If you finish first, wait for us."

"Fine," Tess replied just as tersely, and sent up a silent thanks as they parted company.

Throughout the store she constantly bumped into the McCalls. She and Ryan tried to ignore one another, but Mike made that impossible. At every encounter he greeted her with a huge grin and a barrage of silly adolescent banter. Even when they weren't in the same aisle, he darted back and forth between Tess and his father. She had the horrible feeling that to the other shoppers they probably looked like a family out for their weekly shopping.

When they met at the checkout stand, Tess could not help but notice that, other than a few staples, Ryan's cart was filled with frozen foods and microwave dinners. She experienced a pang of sympathy that anyone would have to survive on a steady diet of such tasteless junk. Then she remembered Ryan's rude and vile response the last time she had shown concern over their eating habits, and hardened her heart.

On the drive home, Tess and Ryan barely uttered a word, but Mike more than made up for her reticence and his father's tight-jawed remoteness. Sitting in the back, the boy leaned forward between the front bucket seats and chattered away about anything and everything. He was so obviously delighted to have her along, it wrung Tess's heart.

Never had she seen such a welcome sight as their apartment complex. She was all set to grab her groceries and make good her escape, but Ryan foiled her plan.

"Mike, you take our groceries up. I'm going to help Mrs. Benson with hers," he said before she could get the door open.

"I can help Tess, Dad."

"No, I'll do it. I want to talk to her. In private," he added pointedly when Mike opened his mouth to argue further.

The boy's alarmed gaze skittered back and forth between his father and Tess. "About what? You're not gonna hurt her feel—"

"That's enough, Mike." Ryan silenced him with a long look. "Take the groceries upstairs like I told you."

"Oh, all right." His young face set in a sulky pout, Mike hurtled out of the Cherokee, snatched four sacks out of the back and stomped off.

Tess and Ryan followed. She wanted to protest that she had no desire to talk to him about anything, but since he had come to her rescue she couldn't very well do that. After hefting each sack for weight, he handed her the two lightest and gathered up the rest. Side by side, they climbed the stairs without speaking, their arms laden. With every step, her dread grew.

Nevertheless, Tess always faced things head-on. If she had a dose of nasty tasting medicine to take, she swallowed it down quickly and got it over with. The instant they set the sacks on her kitchen counter, she turned to Ryan.

"You wanted to talk to me, Mr. McCall?" Her face stiff, she stared over his right shoulder, not quite meeting his eyes.

Ryan studied her, the look on his granite face inscrutable. "I owe you an apology. I shouldn't have said those things to you the other day."

The statement caught her by surprise. An apology was the last thing she expected. "No, you shouldn't have," she agreed, slanting him a cool look. "So why did you?"

"At the time, I didn't know you were pregnant. Mike failed to mention that fact. I only made that discovery when I saw you standing beside your car this morning."

Tess stared at him, her jaw slack. "So? What possible difference does that make?"

"Look, Mrs. Benson—"

"No, you look. You don't know me at all, Mr. McCall. Yet you were rude and insulting. Your nasty accusations were uncalled for, and most certainly undeserved... whether or not I happen to be expecting."

"Okay, okay. Maybe you're right. I guess I did jump to some hasty conclusions," he conceded grudgingly. "But women aren't very high on my list these days."

Tess's eyes widened slightly. Now what did that mean? Before she could ask, Ryan went on.

"Still, I shouldn't have said what I did. I apologize."

Tess merely looked at him. It would have been a lot easier to accept his apology if he had not sounded as though he were making it under duress. The terse words were correct, but he spoke them as though they left a bitter taste in his mouth.

Tess sighed. Ungracious or not, it was an apology. She supposed she would have to accept it, if only for Mike's sake. Besides, she hated strife. And it wasn't good for the baby. Unless he moved, she was going to be living next door to this man for years, so the prudent thing was to make peace.

"Very well, Mr. McCall. Apology accepted. Now, if you'll excuse me..."

Her lips curved in a stiff smile, and she made a subtle move to escort him to the door. Ryan McCall made her nervous. She hadn't noticed before just how big and overpowering he was. He dominated her small kitchen—with his height and his broad, brawny shoulders, all that brooding, raw masculinity he exuded. He was big and dark and fierce looking, and she was suddenly more anxious than ever to get him out of her apartment.

"There is one other thing," Ryan said, thwarting her plan.

"Oh?"

"Yes. It's about Mike. He's...uh...very taken with you."

Unconsciously, Tess's face softened at the mention of the boy, and her smile turned gentle. "I'm very fond of him, too. Mike's a good kid."

"He's been upset these past few days. He thinks you don't like him anymore."

"Mr. McCall—"

"Look, I understand. You've been avoiding him because of what I said to you. But...well..." Ryan rubbed his nape and grimaced. For the first time, he looked ill at ease. "It's been pointed out to me recently that Mike needs some feminine influence in his life. From his reaction to you, it's difficult to argue with that. So...I just want you to know that I won't object if you do want to befriend him. That is, if you don't mind having him hanging around?"

"Of course I don't mind. I enjoy Mike's company. And he is a tremendous help to me."

"Good. Then it's settled." He nodded brusquely and headed for the door, much to Tess's relief, but before he reached it, he turned back. "Oh, I almost forgot. I'll need your car keys."

"My car keys? Whatever for?"

Ryan exhaled an impatient sigh. "So I can drive your car home after I put the tire back on."

"Oh, no. Really, Mr. McCall. I can't let you do that. I've been enough trouble already. I'll—"

"It's no big deal," he said sharply, and Tess could tell she had annoyed him again. "Both tires should be repaired by now. I called my brother from the store. He's going to drive me to pick them up. I'll have your car back in less than an hour.''

With that settled, he stalked out. Tess locked the door behind him, then turned and leaned back against it, shaking her head, her expression bemused. What a strange man.

After that day, Mike became a frequent visitor. Though too young to be on the payroll, he often accompanied Ryan to construction sites and did odd jobs for his father and uncle. When Mike wasn't with Ryan or hanging out with his buddies, he could usually be found at Tess's apartment. On those evenings when his father worked late, she always made a point to invite the boy over for dinner.

Mike was boisterous and friendly as a puppy. And like a puppy, he was at that gangly stage where he seemed to be constantly tripping over his own feet. Filled with eagerness and boundless energy, Mike never walked; he loped. Nor did he merely sit down; he collapsed. As though he were held together by a single vital pin that someone had suddenly pulled, he would drop onto a chair or sofa like a sack of loose bones, sprawling out, long arms and legs draping over the furniture with all the rigidity of freshly cooked spaghetti.

Observing him, Tess often had to bite back a smile. She found his awkwardness endearing and viewed his guileless abandon with amused indulgence.

"If that kid ever grows into those feet of his and gets some meat on those bones he's going to be one big son-of-a-gun someday," Amanda commented on more than one occasion. "A big, *good-looking* son-of-a-gun. Just like his dad."

Though it galled her, Tess had to agree. In spite of his perpetual fierce look, Ryan was a strikingly handsome man, and Mike was the very image of him. Unlike Ryan, though, Mike had a happy disposition and a lively sense of humor.

The boy had a penchant for telling jokes—bad jokes—the cornier and sillier the better. In Tess, who possessed a slightly skewed sense of humor herself, he found the perfect audience. He constantly barraged her and Amanda with awful puns and riddles and knock-knock jokes, and when a punch line drew groans, he clutched his sides and doubled over in a fit of laughter.

Of Ryan, Tess saw very little, which did not surprise her. Despite his apology, she did not delude herself that they had parted friends. At best, they had achieved a cautious truce.

Daily, she heard his comings and goings, and once she left the parking lot at the same time he entered it, but the only acknowledgment he gave her was a curt nod as they drove past one another. They didn't exchange a word or come face-to-face until one evening about a week and a half later.

Tess and Amanda were almost halfway down the stairs when Ryan, his twin brother and Mike came pounding up them. All three McCall men carried white, grease-spotted sacks that reeked of onions, charbroiled burgers and fries.

"Hey, Tess! Amanda!" Mike called.

Ryan's head jerked up, annoyance flashing in his eyes.

Reilly grinned. "Well, well. Good evening, pretty ladies." His twinkling gaze slid warmly over Tess and zeroed in on Amanda. "This is a pleasant surprise."

Ryan didn't look pleased. His mouth flattened and he nodded. Tess had the distinct feeling that he would have kept going if there had been room on the stairs to get around them.

Her nerves fluttered. After ten days with no contact, to suddenly come face-to-face with the man was unsettling. She responded with a restrained, "Good evening." Her polite smile encompassed both men briefly, then turned warm when her gaze focused on the boy.

"Hi, Mike. How did your game go?" All afternoon he had bounced around her apartment, keyed up and nervous as a caged cat, fretting over the baseball game scheduled for that evening. The outcome of the contest was vital to Mike and his teammates, since the winner would advance to the play-offs.

"We clobbered 'em, six to three," he bragged, grinning from ear to ear.

"Congratulations. That's terrific."

"Hey! Way to go, sweetie," Amanda drawled, ruffling his dark hair.

"Yeah, it was a great game. We were just about to celebrate with double cheeseburgers and shakes." Reilly hefted the four sacks he carried and looked expectantly at Amanda. "We'd be delighted to have you lovely ladies join us."

"Reilly." Ryan practically growled his twin's name, the low tone reverberating with warning.

Reilly ignored him. He leaned closer to Amanda and gave her a heavy-lidded look. "Whaddaya say?"

One of Amanda's eyebrows arched. "No, thank you."

The frosty look and clipped tone had annihilated more than one man in the past; Reilly merely grinned wider. "C'mon, Mandy. You know you want to."

"Mr. McCall. My name is Amanda, not Mandy. And furthermore, I wouldn't have dinner with you if you—"

"What Amanda is trying to say is we're busy tonight," Tess put in hurriedly. "We're on our way to class, and if we don't hurry we'll be late as it is."

"Class?"

"Yeah, you know, Uncle Reilly," Mike piped up. "Lamaze class. Amanda is Tess's coach."

The statement drew a sharp look from Ryan. He opened his mouth to say something, then seemed to think better of it and said instead, "We won't keep you, then." He gave Mike a prod in the back. "Let's go, son."

"'Night, Tess. 'Night, Amanda," Mike said as he and his father squeezed past them and continued up the stairs.

"Ryan's right," Reilly said. "We don't want to make you late. We'll just give you a rain check on dinner. You ladies have a nice class.'' He winked and started after his brother and nephew, taking the stairs two at a time.

"Hey, wait a minute! We didn't ask for a rain check!'' Amanda yelled after him, but Reilly merely laughed and kept going.

Making a strangled sound, she whirled and stomped off down the stairs. Tess had the feeling that she had forgotten all about her.

"Amanda! Amanda, wait for me!'' she called, hurrying after her as fast as her ungainly body would allow.

By the time she reached her friend's car, Amanda was already behind the wheel, revving the engine. The instant Tess climbed inside and fastened her seat belt, Amanda rammed the floor shift into gear and sent the little red fireball of a car careening out of the parking lot.

"The gall of the man! Of all the overbearing, egotistical, Neanderthal jerks!'' she spat, taking a corner with a squeal of tires.

"Amanda, for goodness sake. What are you getting so worked up about? Reilly merely asked you to dinner. It's not as though he made an obscene suggestion.''

Amanda shot her a blistering look. "His words may have been harmless, but believe me, his thoughts were obscene. Take my word for it, that man wants a lot more than a meal and conversation. I've met his kind before. The cretin.''

Tess wanted to laugh, but she didn't dare. She had never seen her friend in such a snit over a man before. Cool, unflappable and thoroughly sophisticated Amanda had been fending off passes and winding men around her little finger since she was a preschooler. She couldn't remember a time when her friend hadn't had a whole pack of males panting after her. Amanda never so much as turned a hair over any of them. She tolerated their fawning and salivating with a blasé, almost cynical amusement. Yet a few simple words and a teasing look from Reilly McCall had shattered her insouciance and sent her temper soaring.

Studying her friend's set profile, Tess pursed her lips. What an interesting reaction.

Personally, she thought Reilly was charming. A bit of a flirt perhaps, and no doubt a rascal...but charming. It was just too bad that some of that charm and cheerfulness had not rubbed off on his dour twin.

Tess was sure that Ryan's brother meant to pursue her friend. She also had a strong hunch that Reilly would not be as easily discouraged or manipulated as Amanda's other admirers. One thing was certain; whether it was war or romance, whatever developed between those two would not be dull. Tess found that she was looking forward to witnessing the next meeting between them.

Amanda visited Tess frequently—more so than usual, now that Tess was in her last trimester—and Reilly was in and out of his brother's apartment all the time. They were certain to run into each other again soon, Tess was sure.

The next day, however, Amanda called to tell her that she was being sent overseas to cover a fast-breaking story in one of the world's hot spots. She was leaving within the hour.

"Oh, Tess, I'm so excited. This could be my big break. I'm sick to death of covering local holdups and fires and political rallies. I've just been waiting for something like this so I could show the bigwigs what I can do. And who knows, if I can get a really fresh angle on the story or ferret out an exclusive of some kind it might even lead to a network job."

"I'm happy for you, Amanda." Tess bit her lip, hoping that Amanda had not heard the catch in her voice.

Ever since they were children, Amanda had been driven by the need to prove herself, to succeed, to be the best at whatever she did. Beneath that sophisticated nonchalance was a burning ambition to make it to the top.

Amanda was very dear to Tess, and she wanted her to be happy, but the thought of her taking a network job in New York or Washington filled Tess with dread. So did the possibility of Amanda getting hurt.

"You will be careful, won't you? Things are horribly unstable where you're going. Promise me you won't take any unnecessary chances."

"Honey, taking chances comes with the territory. But I can handle myself. You know that. I'll be fine. So don't you fret about me. You hear? It's not good for junior."

"I won't," Tess lied, but Amanda must have heard the forlorn note in her voice, for she immediately sobered.

"Tess, honey, I'm really sorry about running out on you like this. But I'm sure this assignment won't last long. Three . . . four days tops. Don't worry. I'll be back in plenty of time for Lamaze class next Thursday night."

Three days passed with no word. Then four. By Wednesday Tess was almost frantic. Then that evening she received an overseas call.

"Tess, it's me," Amanda hollered over the static. "I'm sorry I didn't make it back, but things are really popping over here."

"Never mind me. Are you all right?"

"I'm fine. Great!" Even over the crackle and pop on the line and the disturbing shouts in the background, Tess could hear the excitement in Amanda's voice. "Look, Tess, I've gotta run," Amanda shouted over the worsening static. "I'll be back . . . few days if all goes well. Should th . . . ituation get wor . . . be a week . . . more. If that hap . . . I'll ca—"

The line went dead. Tess replaced the receiver with a heavy sigh and closed her eyes. Thank God, Amanda was all right.

She collapsed on the sofa, her relief so great it was some time before it occurred to her that she was now without a Lamaze coach.

She worried over the problem for a while before finally accepting that there was only one thing to do. The instructor had stressed the impcrtance of attending class during these last months. Tess had no family and no other friend with whom she felt comfortable enough to ask them to take over as her coach. She would just have to go alone.

The next evening Tess trudged down the stairs with her pillow tucked under her arm, but when she tried to start her car the engine made a sick *ump ump ump* sound. The second time she turned the key all she heard was a click.

"Oh, no. What now?" Muttering under her breath, Tess popped the hood and struggled out of the car.

With the hood raised all the way, she leaned over as far as she could and peered at the jumble of greasy auto parts, though she had no idea why or what she expected to see. It merely seemed like the correct action to take under the circumstances.

Another vehicle pulled into the parking slot beside her and immediately car doors slammed.

"What the devil is wrong now?" a familiar voice barked as Tess straightened.

She sighed, and closed her eyes. Why? Why did it have to be him?

"I . . . I don't know." She turned in time to see Ryan and Mike converging on her and the car. "It just won't start."

Sidling up to her, Mike murmured a greeting and gave her an encouraging smile.

Ryan ordered her to tell him exactly what she had done and what had happened. When she did, he muttered something under his breath, climbed inside the car and turned the key in the ignition. The result was another sickening click. Grim-faced, he stomped to the front and checked the engine.

"Just as I thought," he grumbled, retracting his brawny torso from beneath the hood. He snatched a rag out of the back of his Cherokee and started wiping the grease from his hands, his eyes boring into her. "Your battery is deader than a doorknob. When was the last time you replaced it?"

"I, uh . . . I don't know. My . . . That is . . ."

"Let me guess. Your husband took care of those kinds of things. Right?"

Tess caught her lower lip between her teeth and nodded.

"Great. Just great. Of all the irresponsible, stupid—"

"Aw, c'mon, Dad." Mike's anxious gaze skittered back and forth between his father and Tess. "If you don't knock it off you're gonna make her cry again."

Ryan clamped his jaws shut, biting off the rest of the tirade, but his taut face and aggressive stance radiated disapproval. He slammed the hood and tossed the greasy rag into the back of his vehicle, then faced her with his fists planted on his hipbones. "Were you going anywhere important?"

"Uh...yes. I was on my way to Lamaze class."

Ryan glanced around, frowning. "Don't you need a partner for that? Where's your friend? I thought she was supposed to be coaching you."

"Yes, but she's out of town." Quickly, Tess explained about Amanda's assignment. "Even so, the classes are too important for me to miss, especially now. I'll just have to make the best of it on my own."

"Say, Dad. I've got a great idea!" Mike piped up. He beamed at them, his young face alive with excitement. "Why don't you take Tess to class and be her coach?"

## Chapter Four

"What!"

"Oh, no!"

Ryan and Tess blurted out the protests in unison, their faces wearing identical appalled expressions.

"Mike...I...I appreciate your concern," Tess stammered. "Really, I do. But I can't ask your father to do that. Coaching someone in Lamaze is...well...a very, uh...a very personal thing. Your father barely knows me."

"But he'd be good at it," Mike replied, not one whit discouraged. "Dad loves kids. Don'tcha, Dad?" He looked at his father, his face alive with eagerness.

"Well...yeah. Sure I do. But—"

"Mike, for heaven's sake. Your father doesn't even li—"

Breaking off, Tess slanted a chagrined glance Ryan's way, and he realized that she had been about to say that he didn't like her. He frowned.

"That is... he doesn't really have time to be my coach. And anyway, I'll just be alone this one time. I'm sure Amanda will be back before next week's class."

"Then it'll work out great. Dad doesn't have anything special to do tonight. Do you, Dad?"

"No. Not really."

He had no idea why he had admitted even that much. Except that he wasn't comfortable with the idea of her thinking he disliked her. It wasn't true. Well... not precisely. He was down on women in general but it had nothing to do with her personally.

Tess's gaze flew to his face, her whiskey-colored eyes wide with shock. Clearly, she had not expected him to agree with Mike, not even on so minor a point. "Even so, Mr. McCall," she said with a desperate edge to her voice. "I'm sure there are other ways you'd rather spend the evening than coaching a virtual stranger in a childbirth class."

He could probably think of a hundred or so without half trying, but his son's pleading eyes would not allow him to do that. In addition, there was that niggle of guilt he still felt around this woman.

Aw, what the hell. It wouldn't kill him. It was only for one night.

"Where is this class held?" he asked, ignoring her statement.

"At the Y. But—"

"Look, Mrs. Benson, it's no big deal. Mike's right. You need a coach and I'm free tonight, so I might as well take you to the class."

"All *right!*" Mike whooped and jumped two feet straight up in the air.

Tess looked as though she might faint. "M-Mr. McCall, I really don't think this is a good idea."

Perversely, her objection made him more determined. "Nonsense. It's settled." He grasped her elbow and opened the passenger door of his utility vehicle. "Is there anything you need out of your car?"

"My... my pillow and... my purse."

Ryan looked at his son, and the boy scurried to retrieve the items while he all but stuffed Tess into the Cherokee.

"We won't be late. Keep the door locked and behave yourself," he told Mike, striding around to the driver's side.

"I will. Don't worry."

They left the boy standing in the parking lot, beaming as though he'd won the lottery and waving them on their way.

The Y was only about a mile away. They were there in less than five minutes, barely time for Tess to make one more stab at dissuading him.

"Mr. McCall... you really don't have to do this. If you'll just drop me off at the Y, I'm sure I can get a ride home with one of the other couples."

"Look, I said I'd coach you and I'm going to. So just drop it, okay."

She wanted to shriek. The very idea of this intense man performing any kind of personal service for her was ludicrous. But a *childbirth* coach? He was going to kneel beside her on the hard floor of the meeting room like all those proud fathers-to-be and guide her through the stages of labor and delivery?

Tess shivered. No. She couldn't even imagine it. The whole purpose of the exercise was to learn to relax and focus her attention away from the pain. How could she do that with those piercing blue eyes focused on her? That dark voice rumbling instructions in her ear? The very idea was absurd.

Biting her lower lip, she studied him covertly out of the corner of her eye. He had obviously just come from a construction site. Dressed in jeans, a work shirt and heavy boots, he was the picture of rugged virility, the kind of breath-stealing, larger-than-life male featured on beefcake calendars.

Tess could imagine Ryan staring into a camera lens, his arrogant stance a challenge in itself. He would have a tool belt strapped around his slim hips, his shirt opened to the waist, beads of sweat trickling through the hair on his glistening chest.

Oh, yes. Madison Avenue would love him, she thought wryly. Hours in the sun had turned his skin a deep bronze and physical labor had corded his big frame with muscle. A five o'clock shadow darkened his jaw, and his slightly shaggy black hair lay in tousled curls across his forehead and the back and sides bore marks of a hard hat. He was big, brooding, and brawny. And he was all man.

As he turned into the Y's parking lot, the setting sun gilded his profile, sharply defining those chiseled features.

Tess sighed. Absurd or not, it seemed she had no choice. She didn't want him there. She wasn't even sure she liked him. But Tess was a realist; what she couldn't control or change, she accepted. Ryan was an implacable, determined man. She had already learned that opposing him when his face had that obdurate set was futile.

The instant Ryan brought the car to a stop she reached for the door handle, but he stopped her with a sharp look. "Don't even think about it," he snapped. "This time just sit tight and wait for me."

He flung open his door and climbed out. Wide-eyed, Tess watched him stride around the hood of the Cherokee to her side. So... he *had* noticed her hasty bailout that day at the grocery store. She was surprised.

When he opened her door, Tess turned to take his hand, but instead he grasped both of her elbows. As he assisted her from the vehicle, her hands automatically closed around his powerful forearms. The sleeves of his chambray work shirt were rolled up almost to his elbows, and she experienced a faint shock at the feel of warm, hard muscles beneath her fingers and the prickly brush of crisp hair against the underside of her forearms.

She sucked in her breath, and his scent overwhelmed her—musky, dark...totally male. For an instant she felt disoriented, almost dizzy. With a faint sense of shock, she realized that it had been over seven months since she had been that close to a man. Any man.

She stepped away quickly. To her relief, he didn't seem to notice her discomfort. After retrieving her pillow out of the back seat, he slammed the car door, grasped her elbow and led her into the building without a word.

The other couples and the instructor were already there. Everyone appeared surprised to see her with a man, and they eyed Ryan curiously.

"Good evening, Tess," Cathy Greene, the instructor, greeted. "What have we here? A new coach?"

"No! Yes. That is...temporarily. Amanda is out of town on assignment. Mr. McCall is..." She stopped and bit her lower lip, her gaze darting to Ryan. She had no idea what to call him. Friend certainly didn't apply. Anything else seemed far too distant, given the circumstances.

Ryan stepped forward with his hand outstretched. "The name's Ryan McCall. I'm Tess's neighbor," he said, using her first name with the ease of long acquaintance. "She was in a bind, so I'm standing in for Amanda tonight."

There were murmurs of approval and introductions were made all around, but the speculation in the faces of the others dimmed only partially.

Cathy clapped her hands. "All right class. Take your positions and let's get started."

The couples spread out in a semicircle in front of Cathy. Following the other men's lead, Ryan assisted Tess into a sitting position on the floor and dropped down beside her. He sat casually, leaning back on one arm, the other draped over his upraised knee. The position stretched his faded jeans taut over powerful thighs.

To Tess's horror, her gaze zeroed in on his crotch and clung. Scalding heat flooded her body from the soles of her

feet to her hairline. She felt on fire. Even her earlobes
throbbed and burned. Mortified, she jerked her gaze away
and stared blindly at Cathy, heart pounding, ears buzzing.

Oh, Lord, had Ryan noticed? She could only pray that he
had not; she could not bring herself to look at him.

What on earth was the matter with her, gawking at the
man that way? She had read that pregnancy increased some
women's libido, but she had not expected it to happen to
her. And certainly not over this man.

Tess swallowed hard, forcing down the flutter of panic
and guilt. She had simply been alone too long. That was all.
That, and her nerves were frazzled by his presence. It was
nothing to get upset about.

As usual, Cathy began the class by putting them through
a few simple stretching exercises that required the coaches'
participation. They were designed not only to help the expectant mother relax but to foster a sense of partnership
between the couple. In her case, Tess knew the effort was
doomed; she felt about as relaxed as a slab of set concrete.

Gritting her teeth, she lay back on her pillow and steeled
herself for the ordeal. Ryan, listening intently to Cathy's
instructions and watching the other men, knelt at her feet.
The feel of his large, callused hands closing around her ankles sent a shock through her, and she started. If Ryan noticed he did not let it show. Concentrating on his task, he
began to methodically guide her through the exercises.

To Tess's surprise, everything went smoothly. By the time
they had finished the warm-up, she was feeling almost relaxed.

Then Cathy announced that tonight's class would be a
rehearsal of the entire labor and delivery, from start to finish.

"Coaches, take your positions," she instructed. "Now
class, this is our scenario. You have checked into the hospital. Your mother-to-be has been prepped and the two of
you are in the labor room. Dads... or rather I should say,

coaches," she corrected with a sly glance at Ryan. "It's your job to reassure your lady and to direct and assist her. To do this, you will have to monitor the contractions and begin your breathing instructions the instant one starts. Does everyone understand?

"Very good," Cathy said when they nodded and murmured assent. "Then let's get started, shall we. Coaches, place your palm on your lady's abdomen."

Ryan's head snapped up. His startled gaze shot to the instructor. Then his head whipped around, and that blazing blue stare locked onto Tess.

She bit her lower lip. She was as stunned as he was. The focus of previous lessons had been on technique; they had never actually gone through a rehearsal.

Ryan stared at her distended abdomen, and she saw his jaw tighten. For a moment she thought he would refuse.

He glanced around at the others. Then he looked back at the mound covered by the yellow maternity top and rubbed his palms down his pant legs. Slowly, he reached out his hand. It hovered over her tummy, the callused fingers spread wide. Tess noticed that it wasn't quite steady.

Finally, as gentle as a feather floating to earth, his hand settled onto her tummy.

Tess sucked in her breath. She felt the imprint of that broad palm and long fingers like a brand. She lay rigid, unable to move, or even breathe, her gaze clinging to Ryan's hard profile. He stared at her abdomen, his face set in its usual remote mask. She had no idea what he was thinking.

"Were your partner actually in labor, at the start of each contraction you would feel a definite tightening of the abdominal muscles," Cathy's voice droned on.

Through the first pretend contraction and the interval of rest that followed, Ryan dutifully kept his hand on Tess's abdomen and performed his part mechanically, his voice a monotone, his face as inscrutable as a sphinx.

After a few minutes, Cathy signaled the start of another contraction. The baby picked that instant to give a tremendous kick.

"What the—" Ryan jerked his hand back as though he had been burned with a hot poker. His head whipped around, and he stared at Tess, his eyes wide.

Hot color flooded her face. She couldn't have spoken if her life had depended on it.

His gaze returned to her tummy. He stared at it for several seconds, then—slowly, cautiously—his hand lowered once again.

The baby responded to Ryan's touch with a series of vigorous kicks and butted his head for good measure. To Tess's amazement, Ryan's face lost its granite set and his lips curved in a faint smile. He looked at her again, and her breath caught. This time his vivid eyes shone with warmth and awe and that unspoken camaraderie that occurs when two people share a special moment.

The rest of the class passed in a daze. They participated fully, both following Cathy's instructions to the letter. Ryan timed her "contractions" and gave instructions and encouragement. Tess panted and blew on cue and tried to center her attention on some outside object. Ryan even exchanged quips with the other couples. But every time the baby made a rambunctious movement, Ryan's gaze sought hers.

Tess tried to tell herself that she was imagining things, but she knew it wasn't so. Something had happened—something magical—in those unguarded moments when her unborn child had pummeled Ryan's palm. Impossible as it seemed, that small, tactile, yet moving experience had somehow forged a bond between them.

It was ridiculous. Ryan had said nothing, done nothing different. His expression was still stern. His touch was still impersonal. Yet she sensed the change. The icy remoteness was gone. So was the underlying anger. Their relationship had altered, shifted subtly without her quite knowing how or why, and she had the feeling it would never return to what it had been.

Tess was not at all sure she welcomed the change. Ryan McCall was an intense, difficult man. She had the feeling that even simple friendship with him would be emotionally wearing.

After the lesson the class members usually lingered to visit and share anecdotes and pregnancy experiences. Tonight Tess had intended to make an excuse and leave quickly, but Ryan foiled that plan. To her surprise, he responded to the other couples with an ease that left her gaping, deftly fielding subtle inquiries about his relationship with Tess without a trace of embarrassment or irritation and chuckling with the other men over tales of midnight cravings and swollen ankles and unexpected mood swings. He fit right in. Tess was certain that an outsider would have taken him for one of the expectant fathers.

During the short drive home they were both quiet. Several times Tess glanced at Ryan and wondered if he felt as unsettled as she did, but his expression was unreadable.

The air between them still pulsed with tension, but where before it had sprung from antagonism, now it resulted from different emotions—acute sensitivity, awkwardness, awareness that the gulf between them had narrowed. The taut silence held almost a sense of…of anticipation, though of what, Tess couldn't imagine.

She supposed what had happened between them during class was only natural. After all, it was difficult to maintain a distance from someone when he was holding your hand and rubbing your tummy.

Like it or not, they had become aware of each other on a personal level. No longer did they see one another solely as adversaries, but as people—people with the same basic human need for another's touch, another's warmth.

Still, it troubled Tess that the experience had felt so good. It was foolish, she knew, but having Ryan there beside her had made her feel, for a short time, as though she were like the other women in the class, as though she were part of a couple again. She had almost felt . . . cherished.

Tess sighed. Amanda was a good coach and a dear friend, but there was no denying that tonight she had drawn comfort from Ryan's masculine strength.

Which, of course, had been nothing more than foolish self-indulgence. Shifting on the seat, Tess turned her head to stare out the side window. She was alone now; she had come to terms with that—or at least, until tonight, she had thought she had. There was no man in her life—certainly not Ryan McCall. He was merely a neighbor, doing her a favor. Reluctantly, at that. She'd do well to remember that.

Ryan felt confused and surprised. He had expected the Lamaze class to be awkward, maybe even embarrassing. He hadn't expected it to be a deeply moving experience.

The thrill that had rippled through him when he'd felt those little thumps and kicks against his palm had been indescribable. He had felt humbled and awed and excited all at one time. Even now, just thinking about it made his skin tingle.

There had been more to the experience, though, than just the miracle of life. There had been the closeness of the other couples in the class. Some were expecting their first child, some their second or third or fourth. Hell, the Tolbins were having their seventh! Yet, in every case, their joy and excitement over having a baby was obvious.

He hadn't expect that, either. Logically, Ryan knew that there were couples who were happy in their marriages. His cousins, Erin and Elise and David all seemed deliriously happy with their mates. So did his younger brother, though Ryan was reserving judgment there, since Travis and Rebecca had only been married a few months. In general, however, he tended to think of marriage in negative terms. He had to admit, it felt good to know that other couples were happy together.

They were back at the apartment complex within minutes. At her door Tess turned with a polite smile. "Mr. McCall, I—"

"Call me Ryan. After what we just went through together, Mr. McCall seems a bit formal, don't you think?"

"Oh. Very well, then...Ryan. I want to thank you for all that you've done for me. I really do appreciate it. I don't know how I'll ever repay you."

"Tell you what...give me a cup of coffee and we'll call it even."

She hid it well, but Ryan knew he had surprised her. Hell, he'd surprised himself. He didn't know why he'd made the suggestion—except that he was still keyed up over the class. That, and there was something about this woman that intrigued him.

He wouldn't stay but a few minutes, he told himself. Just long enough to drink a cup of coffee and get the answers to some questions that had been nagging at him.

"All right," Tess said with a wan smile. "It hardly seems a fair exchange, but if that's what you want..."

In the living room she gestured toward the sofa. "Won't you sit down. I'll, uh...I'll just go make the coffee." Halfway to the kitchen she turned back and fluttered her hands. "Oh, I forgot. I'm afraid all I have is decaffeinated coffee. The regular kind isn't good for the baby, so I don't buy it anymore."

"Decaf is fine."

Instead of sitting, Ryan stuck his fingertips in the back pockets of his jeans and wandered around the room. While she made coffee, Tess darted several anxious glances at him over the bar that separated the kitchen from the living room, but he pretended not to notice.

The floor plan of her apartment was identical to his own, the walls the same off-white, the carpet the same neutral beige, yet hers seemed nicer. More appealing. The difference was, he realized finally, that Tess had managed to put her own stamp on the place.

In the living room a lovely old Oriental rug in mellow tones of green and cream and faded raspberry covered most of the blah carpeting. On it, her furniture—graceful tables topped with china and crystal lamps and an inviting over-stuffed sofa and chairs upholstered in soft green and cream—formed a cozy grouping. Pictures graced the walls and small decorative items were scattered throughout the room, all artfully arranged. An arrangement of dried flowers sat in the center of the coffee table and lush plants were everywhere.

She had given the place a woman's touch, and by doing so had somehow transformed a drab, run-of-the-mill apartment into a home. Next to this, his place looked downright bleak.

Tess returned bearing a tray, and Ryan joined her on the sofa. "Thanks," he said, accepting the cup she handed him. Tess smiled weakly and gazed at the shining surface of her coffee, at a picture on the opposite wall, at the toe of her shoe—anywhere but at Ryan.

"Mike tells me you're a high school teacher," Ryan said tentatively after several awkward moments.

"Yes. I teach earth science."

"I see. So, where did you go to college?"

"Texas Tech."

She looked back at her coffee, and several more seconds ticked by. Ryan's jaw clenched. So much for the subtle approach. Getting the woman to loosen up was like pulling eyeteeth. He might as well get right to the point.

"Will you answer something for me?"

Tess darted him a wary look. "I suppose so. If I can."

"What made you decide to go for natural childbirth?"

"That's easy." Her face softened and she unconsciously smoothed a hand over the swollen mound beneath her maternity smock. "Natural birth is much better for the baby."

"True. But more painful for you."

"I suppose so. But that doesn't matter. I want to be wide awake and aware of everything that's happening during my baby's birth. I've waited too long for this to miss out on a single minute."

Recalling the feelings that had shot through him when he'd felt her baby kick, Ryan immediately understood. He would have given a lot to have been present at Mike's birth.

Still, he wasn't quite sure he believed Tess. Julia had certainly not wanted any part of natural birth. Or motherhood, for that matter. Could there really be that much difference in women?

Narrowing his eyes, he studied Tess's dreamy expression and mysterious smile. Apparently so. Good Lord. The woman was almost glowing.

"You really want this baby, don't you?"

"Of course I do," she said in a shocked voice, and curved her arm around her tummy in an unconscious gesture of protection.

"Don't get upset. I only asked because a lot of women wouldn't in your position."

"You mean because I'm a widow? But that's all the more reason. When my husband died, I thought I had lost him completely. Then, I found out that I was pregnant, and I realized that part of Tom would live on through his child. It was like a miracle."

"You mean he died not knowing he was going to be a father?"

Tess nodded. "I didn't even suspect myself until almost a month after the funeral."

A sad, bittersweet smile curved her mouth. "The irony of it is, we wanted a family. But Tom and I both felt very strongly that children deserve a full-time mother, so we put off trying until we felt we were in a position for me to quit my job.

"Finally, last fall, Tom was made principal of the high school where we both taught. It was something he had been working and hoping for. We had just finished remodeling the home that I inherited from my parents, and with that expense out of the way and his salary increase we felt that, finally, we could afford for me to stop teaching and stay home and raise a family.

"We were hoping that I would become pregnant some-time before the end of the school year." She ran one finger around the rim of her coffee cup and stared at the shining surface of the liquid. "Sure enough, I did get preg-nant . . . only Tom never knew it."

"How did he die?" Ryan raised his cup to his lips and watched her over the rim.

Tess's voice dropped to little more than a whisper. "An aneurysm in his brain. One minute he was working at his desk, the next he was lying in a crumpled heap on the floor. His secretary heard the thump and rushed in, but it was al-ready too late—he was gone."

"I'm sorry. That must have been rough."

"Yes. It was." Taking a deep breath, Tess sat up straighter and blinked the moisture from her eyes. She squared her shoulders and aimed a determined little smile at him. "But after a while you realize that you have to put grief behind you and get on with life."

Only if you're a fighter, Ryan thought. And he suddenly had a hunch that Tess Benson, for all her petite build and wholesome beauty, was as scrappy as they came. She had taken a blow that had knocked her to her knees, a blow that would have done in a lot of women, but she had pulled her-self back up on her own. Somehow, he doubted that she ever stayed down for long.

"Having the baby has helped me do that. It's given me a reason to go on, something to focus my energies on, other than feeling sorry for myself."

"So what's next? Will you go back to teaching after the baby is born?"

"Not for a while."

"That's right. Mike did mention you were going to take a long sabbatical."

Tess chuckled. "I said that as a joke. Somehow, I don't think the school board would look on five years as a sabbatical."

"Five years? You're not going back to work for five *years*? How the hell will you live with no income?"

"I'll manage. Between Tom's life insurance and the money I received from the sale of my house, I figure I can make out that long. If I'm careful."

Ryan was flabbergasted. He made a restless movement and almost spilled his coffee. He set the cup down on the table beside the sofa and turned to her. "Look. I know that this is none of my business, but I think you're making a serious mistake. Any financial advisor would tell you that it's not wise to deplete your capital. You would have more long-term security if you invested that money."

"I'm aware of that. However, this is a matter of priorities. Providing emotional security for my child during the formative years happens to be more important to me than financial security for myself. Tom and I waited six years to have this baby. I'm not going to leave him or her with someone else unless I have to."

"Okay. I can understand that, but aren't there any other choices? Don't you have any family that could help?"

Tess shook her head. "My parents died in a car crash when I was in college. They were both only children, and as far as I know, I have no living relatives. I suppose I could ask my in-laws for help, but I won't."

"Why not?"

"Let's just say that I value my independence too much to give them any kind of control over me or my child."

"Independence is great, but taking a little help from family doesn't mean you have to surrender your freedom. I'm sure your in-laws are concerned about you and the baby."

"They might be . . . if they knew."

"What! Are you saying . . . you mean you haven't told them you're expecting?"

"No, I haven't. You see—"

"Man, that really stinks." His voice reeked with disgust and disapproval. So did his expression.

"I know it sounds terrible, but you see, my husband didn't get along with his family. He had all but severed ties with them, and—"

"I don't care about that," Ryan snapped. "Those people are still your baby's grandparents, and they've got a right to know about their son's child. Family is important. They may be a pain in the butt sometimes, and they may not always do and say what you want them to, but when the chips are down they're usually there for you when no one else is."

Tess bit her lower lip. Maybe that was true of most families, but from what she knew of the Bensons, she had her doubts.

She had learned from her husband to be leery of them. From what Tom had told her and her own brief experience with the elder Bensons, they seemed to equate love with control. Tom had always wanted to be a teacher, but his parents had had other plans for him. They had expected him to enter the family banking business, as his older brother, Charles, had done. At every turn they had manipulated and schemed and blocked Tom's efforts to follow his chosen career and be his own man. In the end he'd had to resort to total separation to escape their domination.

Still, the naked censure in Ryan's eyes and words raked over Tess's conscience like sharp talons. Maybe she was being unfair, judging too harshly on too little evidence. It had been a long time and people change. Surely, after their experience with Tom, they had learned by now to let go.

She sighed and grimaced ruefully. "Maybe you're right. Actually, I have been thinking about writing to them. I'll do it soon. I promise."

He studied her for several seconds, as though trying to decide if she was telling the truth. Finally he nodded. "Good. You're doing the right thing. And if they offer to help you I hope you'll accept."

"No. That I won't do." She held up her hand, cutting him off when he started to say more. "Ryan, please. I said I would let them know about the baby, and I will. But that's as far as I go." Her voice was mild, and a gentle smile curved her soft lips, but those whiskey brown eyes held an implacable glint. "Now, if you don't mind, could we change the subject?"

Ryan stared, at a loss for words. With her slight build and bright hair, those wide, innocent eyes and the smattering of freckles across her nose, Tess looked as delicate as a dandelion thistle. At that moment, however, he realized that beneath the wholesome, almost ethereal beauty, was a woman of rare strength and conviction.

A strange welter of emotions tightened his chest. He could not help but admire her. How many women would willingly sacrifice financial security and their livelihood for their child's emotional well-being? It was a loving, totally unselfish thing to do, yet he wanted to shake her for doing it.

"All right. It's your choice," he conceded grudgingly. He picked up his coffee cup and took a healthy swallow. "So what would you like to talk about?"

"Well...since you know so much about me, it's only fair that I learn more about you. Mike tells me that you and Reilly are from Crockett."

For the next half hour they talked about his family, about Mike, about his business, and the struggle it had been to keep it alive. He told her about the large tract of land that R & R Construction owned, which he and Reilly hoped to develop into a planned community. They intended to call it Wildwood, since the acreage, which was located only a few miles away, was covered with virgin forest.

Everything was cordial until Tess brought up the subject of Ryan's marriage.

"Mike told me that you and his mother were divorced," she stated innocently.

Tess knew at once that she had made a mistake. The instant the words were out she saw the curtain come down over Ryan's face. He stiffened, and his jaw grew tight.

"That's right. Eight years ago," he snapped in his coldest voice. "Houston's economy was on a downhill slide and R & R Construction was floundering. Julia couldn't stand the idea of being poor, or starting over again. She left me— and Mike—for another man. A much older man—one with money, position and power. We haven't seen her since."

Tess sucked in her breath. That a woman could walk out on her husband and child appalled her. The harshness in Ryan's voice chilled her.

Understanding, at last, the anger behind his coldness, her heart went out to both him and Mike. No wonder Ryan was so bitter and so antifemale. And that poor child; he couldn't have been more than five when his mother abandoned him.

The cup jumped and clattered in the saucer when Ryan thumped it down on the coffee table. He stood up abruptly. His face wore that cold look she had come to expect. "If you'll excuse me—"

"Ryan, wait . . . please . . ." She struggled to her feet and hurried after him. Catching up with him at the door, she touched his arm. Ryan paused and looked down at her hand, then raised his vivid gaze to her face.

Tess looked up at him, her eyes awash with sympathy. "Ryan, I know that what your wife did hurt, but you mustn't let it sour the rest of your life. Don't cut yourself off from love, Ryan. Believe me, all women aren't like that."

"Oh yeah? Tell me something? Would you have married your husband if he'd been...say...a garbage collector? Or a fry cook?"

Tess blinked, taken aback by the attack.

A nasty half smile curved Ryan's mouth. "That's what I thought. All women have their price. Some are just higher than others."

The insult took her breath away. Sympathy dissolved in a burst of indignant anger. "That's not true! Tom wanted to provide as best he could for us, and hopefully, someday for our children, but I certainly didn't marry him for his potential as a money-maker. May I remind you, Mr. McCall, that educators are not exactly on the high end of the pay scale."

She reached around him and snatched open the door before he could respond. "I won't keep you. I'm sure you're anxious to get home to Mike. Good night, Mr. McCall."

Ryan's eyes narrowed. For an excruciatingly long moment he examined her stiff expression. Finally, without a word, he walked out.

## Chapter Five

"Lamaze class? You took that cute little redhead who moved in next door to Lamaze class? Oh, that's rich." Reilly whooped. "That's really rich." He threw his head back and guffawed.

Ryan watched his twin in silence, his face impassive. Braying jackass, he thought irritably, but not by so much as a flicker of an eyelash did he show any reaction.

He should have known that Reilly would find the incident hilarious. When he'd learned that Tess was pregnant, he'd laughed himself silly and razzed Ryan unmercifully for assuming that she had her sights on him.

Ryan exhaled a small sigh. He supposed he had been lucky to have escaped his twin's teasing this long. It had been four days since he'd taken Tess to the childbirth class. The only reason Reilly hadn't found out about it before now was because Mike hadn't come to the construction site since that night. Saturday's ball game had been rained out, so they hadn't seen Reilly over the weekend.

"Gee, Uncle Reilly. What's so funny?" A puzzled frown puckered Mike's brow. "I think it's great that Dad coached Tess."

"Oh, it is. It is," Reilly sputtered. He collapsed into an easy chair and made a halfhearted attempt to control his mirth. He looked at Ryan, his eyes dancing. "It's just hard for me to imagine old stone face here, doing all that 'hee, hee, heeing.'"

Mike's frown deepened. "What's he talking about, Dad?"

"Nothing. Just some breathing exercises Tess has to practice. Don't pay any attention to him. As usual, your uncle is being a prize jerk."

"What I want to know, Hoss, is how the devil you got involved in the first place. I thought Amanda was Tess's coach at those classes."

"She is. But at the moment Ms. Sutherland's on assignment in the Middle East."

Reilly sobered and sat up straighter. "Where in the Middle East?"

Ryan told him, and his brother's expression darkened. "Isn't that the latest hot spot?"

"Right. That's usually where they send reporters, you know. Amanda is one of the team assigned to cover that border flare-up. I'm surprised you haven't seen her on the news. She's been reporting every night via satellite."

"My TV's on the blink," Reilly said absently. "That's why I came over here to watch the Astros game."

"And we thought you wanted our company. I'm hurt, aren't you, Mike?"

"Arrrggggh." The thirteen-year-old clutched his chest and staggered dramatically around the living room, finally collapsing in a sprawl on the floor. "It's a fatal wound. I may not make it," he croaked, arms and legs twitching in a death throe.

"Funny. Real funny. You two are a regular barrel of laughs," Reilly grumbled, but the beginning of a grin was already tugging at the corners of his mouth. No matter how disturbing the news or how dark a situation, it never took long for Reilly's affable spirit to reassert itself.

He nudged his nephew with the toe of his sneaker. "When you're finished emoting, Barrymore, how about fetching me a beer?"

"Okay, but it'll cost ya." Mike sat up, grinning. "Knock, knock?"

"Ah, jeez." Reilly rolled his eyes and sighed, but he dutifully responded in a long-suffering voice, "Who's there?"

"Little old lady."

"Little old lady who?"

"Gee, Uncle Reilly, I didn't know you could yodel."

Reilly groaned, and Mike dissolved in a fit of giggles. Ryan's mouth twitched.

"Out. Get out of here you miserable little twit and get me that beer."

Dodging his uncle's playful swat, Mike bounded to his feet and scampered out of the room, still chortling.

They spent the rest of the evening munching popcorn and watching the Astros win against the Padres, seven to two. Afterward, Mike hit the shower while his dad and uncle watched the evening news. The lead story was the situation in the Middle East. Barely thirty seconds into the broadcast, an image of Amanda filled the screen.

In the background an overturned military vehicle still smoldered and soldiers were making a cautious door-to-door sweep through a ravaged village. The metallic chatter of sporadic gunfire could be heard in the distance. Dressed in khaki pants and shirt, her streaked blond hair whipping in the desert wind, Amanda looked straight into the TV camera lens. With her usual panache, she gave a calm and concise account of the skirmish that had taken place between government troops and rebel forces less than an hour before.

"What the hell is she doing?" Reilly demanded in a rare burst of anger. "The army hasn't even finished mopping up. Damned fool woman. Doesn't she know how dangerous it is there?"

"I'm sure she does. But Amanda Sutherland isn't the type to sit back at command central and report on a conflict from a distance. She's running on nerve and excitement. Right now she's probably too keyed up to be scared."

"Well, she's sure scaring the hell outta me."

Ryan stared at the screen, not hearing the news anchor's report on a local bank robbery. All week he'd been troubled by Amanda's broadcasts. He couldn't help but wonder what effect it was having on Tess to see her friend in such dicey situations night after night. The two women were more than just close; they were almost like sisters. As far as he could tell, Amanda was all Tess had.

A dozen times or more, Ryan had been tempted to call or tap on her door and check on her. Guilt had stopped him.

He had been out of line the other night. She had touched a nerve and he had lashed out. Had she been any other woman, he would have meant what he'd said, but he was beginning to know Tess. It was becoming more and more difficult to see her as mercenary or manipulative.

Against his will, he was softening toward her, he knew, and that bothered him almost as much as his conscience.

"Does Tess know when Amanda is due back?"

Ryan shook his head. "I doubt it. She was expecting her days ago. I suppose matters like border skirmishes and political coups don't run on strict timetables."

Reilly grumbled under his breath and lapsed into silence.

When the news was over, he stood up, stretched hugely and headed for the door. "I'd better hit the road. Tell Mike bye for me." At the door, he stopped and looked back at Ryan.

"By the way, Hoss. Despite my teasing, I've gotta hand it to you for taking Tess to that class. A lot of men wouldn't have. And for what it's worth, I think it'd do you good to hang out with the lady more."

He winked. "Every man, even a dyed-in-the-wool woman-hater, needs the civilizing influence of a female. Without the little darlings we guys would probably revert into being a pack of belching, scratching animals.

"And you gotta admit, all things considered, Tess Benson is the safest woman we know. She's pregnant and probably still mourning her husband, so there's no chance of romance rearing its head. Not only that, she's easy on the eyes and pleasant to be around and a good influence on Mike. Face it, man. She's the perfect companion for you right now.

"So don't run her off. Okay?" Executing a two-finger salute, Reilly grinned and slipped out before Ryan could reply.

Though Ryan tried, he could not dismiss his brother's comments.

All right. Maybe—just maybe—for once Reilly was right, he conceded grudgingly. He had to admit, until the other night he had forgotten just how pleasant feminine companionship could be, forgotten all the enjoyable little things about them. Their softness. Their gentle ways. Their sweet, woman smell.

He'd been with women since Julia took off. Intellectually and emotionally he might have rejected the opposite sex, but his body had not gotten the message. When that restless itch could no longer be ignored there were always plenty of women willing to scratch it.

But that was merely sex. He had enjoyed just being with Tess. Once he'd gotten her to open up, she'd been easy to talk to. She was restful and pleasant and undemanding, and there was a gentle but determined quality about her that appealed to him.

Ryan's mouth twitched. And, as Reilly had so classily put it, she was easy on the eyes. Not drop-dead gorgeous like her friend Amanda, but Tess had her own unique kind of beauty. He thought about the way her face glowed when she talked of the baby she carried, and the twitch almost became a smile. At present, she reminded him of a cute, little broody hen.

Best of all though—as his twin had also pointed out—he could enjoy Tess's companionship without getting tangled up in any emotional strings. It was something to think about.

Over the next few days it was something he could not seem to *stop* thinking about, which did not set well with Ryan at all. At odd times—when he was ordering lumber or applying for a permit at city hall or going over blueprints— thoughts of Tess kept popping into his head, interfering with his work and his concentration. After two days of being distracted, he was so irritated, he silently cursed his brother for planting the idea in his head in the first place and swore he would have nothing more to do with Tess.

Nevertheless, Wednesday evening when he sat down to read the evening newspaper, halfway through the first article he realized that his thoughts had once again strayed to his new neighbor. Making an aggravated sound, he gave the newspaper a snap and started over at the beginning of the piece. Two sentences into it, a slow but steady *thump... thump... thump* interrupted his concentration.

Mike lay sprawled on his stomach on the living room floor, simultaneously watching television and playing a pocket electronic game. When the thuds continued, he looked up. "What the heck is that?"

"I don't know."

"Sounds like it's coming from outside on the stairs."

"Yeah, I think you're right. C'mon. Let's check it out." Tossing aside the newspaper, Ryan rose and headed for the door. Mike scrambled after him. Outside at the top of the stairs, father and son came to an abrupt halt. Mike gaped. Ryan bit off a curse.

On the seventh step from the bottom, Tess stopped to catch her breath and get a better hold on the carton she was trying to drag up the stairs. The huge, flat box was not only heavy, it was awkward to handle. Even turned on its side, she had difficulty getting a good grip on the smooth cardboard.

Balancing the thing with one hand, she gripped the railing with the other and drew in several fortifying breaths. Then she splayed her hands on either side of the carton and braced for another round of tugging.

"What the hell do you think you're doing?"

"Oh!" Tess jumped and lost her hold on the carton. "Oh no!" She watched, horrified, as the large box went thumping back down the steps and toppled over, hitting the sidewalk at the bottom with a loud *whump!*

"Now look what you've done!" Tess whirled and glared up at Ryan. "Not only did you scare me half to death, do you have any idea how hard I worked to get that box that far?"

"You've got no business trying to manhandle the thing in the first place. Hell, the damned carton is bigger than you are. Why didn't you ask for some help?"

She gave him a speaking look. He ignored it and stomped past her. "C'mon, Mike, give me a hand with this thing."

The boy aimed a sympathetic grimace at Tess and loped down the stairs. Drawing even with her, he paused and murmured out of the side of his mouth, "Hey, Tess. Knock, knock."

"For Pete's sake, Mike, not now," his father barked.

Tess shot Ryan a quelling look and turned an indulgent smile on the boy. "Who's there?"

"Ura Lee."

"Ura Lee who?"

"Ura Lee should ask for help if you need it?"

Tess's rueful gaze followed him as he took the remainder of the steps in two leaps. The corny joke was as much a reprimand as his father's caustic remarks had been, but infinitely easier to take. Maybe because it had been delivered with caring and affection.

"What's in here, anyway?" Hefting one end of the carton, Ryan signaled for Mike to take the other end, and they started up the stairs.

"A crib mattress."

Ryan halted with his foot on the bottom step, jerking his son to a halt four steps above him. He pinned her with a narrow look. "Where's the crib?"

"In another box in the back of my car."

"I suppose you were going to try to lug that upstairs, too."

Knowing her answer would only bring more recriminations down on her head, Tess turned without a word and led the way to her apartment, her chin high.

Mike and Ryan carried the mattress into the nursery and went back for the rest of the baby bed. When they returned with the second carton, they brought a toolbox with them.

"Oh, no, please. You don't have to put it together for me. I'm sure I can manage that on my own."

For an answer Tess received another dark look.

Within minutes the carton containing the crib was open and its contents spread out on the floor. The McCalls sat cross-legged in the middle of the jumble, reading the sheet of assembly directions. Feeling useless, Tess gave up and took a seat in the white wicker rocker to watch.

Father and son worked well together, she noticed. Ryan did most of the actual assembling while Mike handed him tools and the proper part or piece of hardware. He also took the time to explain to his son everything he was doing, and Mike absorbed it all eagerly.

Ryan really was a wonderful father, Tess thought. He was patient with the boy and treated him with respect, never talking down to him or berating him when he didn't understand something the first time. He wasn't reserved about showing affection, either. He touched his son often, ruffling his hair, patting his shoulder, giving him a playful sock in the arm. Warmth and love and a deep fatherly pride was in every look, every touch.

Watching the two dark heads bent close together in earnest conversation, Tess felt a touch of sadness. If her baby was a boy, who, she wondered, would teach him the practical skills that Ryan was passing on to Mike?

When the crib was assembled, Ryan gathered up his tools. Mike, following his father's instructions, picked up the packing material and cartons and carried them down to the Dumpster at the back of the complex.

"Thank you, Ryan. I really appreciate you doing this for me," Tess said, running her gaze lovingly over the white Jenny Lind style crib. She grimaced and wrinkled her nose. "I seem to be saying that to you a lot, don't I? For what it's worth, I really don't mean to be a bother."

"Yeah, I know. But it can't be helped."

Tess stiffened. She was about to remind him that she hadn't asked for his help—ever—when he snapped his toolbox shut and stood up. "What are you going to do about Lamaze class? Your friend is still in the Middle East. I saw her on the news earlier."

"I, uh…I'm sure she'll be back tomorrow. Otherwise she would have called by now."

Barely had the words left her mouth when the telephone rang. Biting her lower lip, Tess glanced toward the living room. Oh, no, please don't let that be Amanda, she pleaded silently, but she had a sinking feeling in the pit of her stomach.

She gripped the rocker arms and struggled to stand, but every time she tried to heave herself out of the chair it tipped backwards, throwing her off balance again. Finally, making an exasperated sound, Ryan reached down, grasped her hand and hauled her to her feet. Momentum carried her against him and her swollen tummy bumped his lean hips. Tess blushed furiously.

"Thank you," she mumbled, and pulled her hand free and edged around him. Self-consciously tugging at the hem of her maternity smock, she waddled out the door. Ryan followed right behind her.

On the third ring the answering machine picked up the call. They reached the living room just in time to hear Amanda shouting over a cacophony of raised voices and what sounded like a convoy of motor vehicles in the background.

"Tess? Tess, it's me. Amanda. Dearest, I'm sorry—I'm really sorry—but I won't make it back this week, either. I swear to you, when I took this assignment, everyone thought it would all be over in a few days, but things are escalating over here like crazy. In fact—I hate to tell you this—but it's beginning to look like I might be here for weeks yet. Tess, I'll try to get back before junior arrives. I'll do my very best. But maybe...well...maybe you should line up a substitute coach. You know—just in case."

For several seconds all they could hear was the roar of some sort of large truck rumbling by, then someone shouted Amanda's name. "Gotta go, Tess. I'll call when I get a chance."

The connection broke and the answering machine clicked and whirred as the tape rewound. Then there was only silence.

Tess exhaled a sigh, and Ryan watched her shoulders slump.

She turned to him, trying to appear unconcerned but the attempt was a dismal failure. Worry shadowed the wide, whiskey-colored eyes and her wan smile wobbled, despite her determined effort to control it. She shrugged and spread her hands wide. "Well...I guess—"

"I'll be by tomorrow night at a quarter till seven to take you to class," he announced abruptly, and strode across the cozy living room toward the door.

"No, Ryan, wait! I can't let you do that."

He stopped and turned back, shifting his toolbox to his other hand. He made no effort to hide his impatience. "We're not going to have this discussion again, are we? Look, is there anyone else who can take you?"

"Well...no, but—"

"Then why are you arguing? You need someone to sub for Amanda. I'm volunteering. End of problem."

"But...what if Amanda doesn't make it back in time?"

"Don't borrow trouble. You said yourself that she'll be back." He frowned and studied her shape, and Tess's blush returned. "When are you due?"

"In six weeks. Around the end of August."

"That's a long time. Amanda will most likely be back by then. But if it turns out that she isn't, we'll deal with it."

She stared at him. "Why are you doing this, Ryan? You don't even like me."

Ryan firmed his mouth, his impatience building. Dammit, why did women have to make a big deal out of everything? Why the hell couldn't she just accept his offer at face value and be done with it?

He wasn't sure himself why he had made the offer. Except that for the past week he hadn't been able to stop thinking about Tess, especially about the marked difference between her attitude toward motherhood and Julia's.

His ex-wife had hated being pregnant, had hated even more the idea of natural childbirth. She had just wanted the whole thing to be over as quickly and painlessly as possible so that she could return to her bridge parties and luncheons and tennis games at the country club.

It bothered the hell out of Ryan that this woman, who was so obviously looking forward to giving birth and being a mother, should have to go through the whole thing alone, with only a woman friend—one she couldn't even count on to be there—to help and give her moral support.

"Does it matter?" he snapped. "The point is, you need help and I'm available to give it."

He swung around and reached the door in two long strides, but he paused with his hand on the doorknob. Jaw clenched, he stared straight ahead at the wooden panel.

"I don't dislike you, Tess," he said at last, in a tight, almost resentful voice. "Maybe that was true in the beginning, but not now. Actually..." The words stuck in his throat. He swallowed hard and looked at her over his shoulder. "...I admire you for what you're doing."

He snatched the door open and stalked out, carrying with him the image of her stunned expression.

The next evening Tess was putting the finishing touches on her makeup when the doorbell rang. She glanced at her watch. Ryan was early; it was only six-thirty. Aggravated, she gave her nose one last dusting of powder and headed for the entry as fast as she could waddle.

"What are you— Oh!" Her frown turned to surprise when she opened the door and saw the postal carrier standing there. "I'm sorry. I thought you were someone else."

"I have a registered letter for Mrs. Tess Benson."

"I'm Tess Benson." Who on earth could be sending her a registered letter? She signed the sheet the man thrust at her and took the envelope. Examining the return address, she closed the door and meandered into the living room, her expression puzzled. It was from the law firm of Talmadge and Sloan in Boston. "What in the world?"

She split open the seal with her thumbnail and began to read. By the time she reached the sofa her face was pale and she sank down onto the cushions, shaking her head.

She read the letter through again, hurriedly scanning down the page to the damning paragraph, unable to accept what her eyes were telling her.

... to inform you that in addition to a bona fide birth
certificate, my clients Harold and Enid Benson, will
require blood and DNA testing of said infant at the
time of his or her birth, before they can acknowledge
said child as the offspring of their deceased son,
Thomas Geoffrey Benson, and their heir.

Therefore, to that end ...

Tess stopped reading. She didn't know what kind of reaction she had expected when she had written to Tom's
parents. She had imagined several different possibilities—
anger because she had waited so long to inform them, joy in
knowing that a part of Tom would live on in his child, subtle pressure to gain a measure of control over herself and the
baby, perhaps even an out-and-out battle for custody. She
had never once thought that they would doubt that Tom was
the father of her child.

It hurt—more than Tess had thought possible. They had
insulted her deeply, impugning her character, her integrity,
her honor and her morals. By inference, they were accusing
her of loose behavior and trying to pass off another man's
child as Tom's in order to get her hands on the Benson fortune.

Tess looked up at the ceiling and widened her eyes to hold
back the tears that filled them. "I won't cry," she vowed. "I
won't." It didn't matter. *They* didn't matter.

But it hurt. Oh, Lord, it hurt. She felt as though someone had kicked her in the stomach. Her chin quivered, and
no matter how hard she fought to hold them in check, one
by one, tears spilled over her lower eyelids and rolled down
her cheeks. A sob rose in her throat. She fought it, but the
pressure in her chest was too great, and when it broke free
she flung herself down on the sofa and gave in to the tears
of misery that came from her wounded soul.

She was still crying twenty minutes later when the doorbell rang again. She jumped at the sound and sat up, gulp-

ing back sobs, her blurry gaze zooming to the door. Ryan. Oh, Lord. She had forgotten all about him. She sniffed and struggled for control, her chest jerking with sharp little inhalations, the ragged remnant of spent tears. Getting to her feet, she headed for the door, hastily wiping her eyes and tear-stained cheeks with her fingertips.

She opened the door a crack and peered out. "Ryan, I—"

"What took you so long?" he demanded.

"I'm sorry. I should have called you. I, uh...I've decided to skip the class tonight."

He frowned and narrowed his eyes. "Why?"

"I'm...I'm not feeling well."

It was a mistake. She knew it the instant the words left her mouth. Ryan's expression immediately changed to one of concern, and he stepped forward, pushing the door open with the flat of his hand, giving her no choice but to let him in.

"What's wrong. Is it the ba—" He squinted at her averted face, then he grasped her chin and turned her head around and tipped it up. "You've been crying."

He made the statement sound almost like an accusation. "What's going on? Has something happened?"

Tess pulled her chin free and turned away, surreptitiously swiping at her swollen eyes again as she walked back into the living room. "It's nothing. I—"

"Don't give me that. You're not the type to bawl over nothing. So you might as well spit it out. I'm not leaving here until you do."

She glanced at him over her shoulder and bit the inside of her lip. He meant it. Standing with his feet braced wide, his face set, he looked about as movable as a mountain.

Sighing, Tess eased her bulk down onto the sofa, picked up the letter from where it had fallen and silently handed it to him.

Ryan cocked one brow. He looked from the letter to Tess, then back again. She watched him as he started to read. His face was set in that impassive mask he usually wore, but she knew the instant he reached the insulting paragraph. His eyes widened.

"What the hell . . . ?"

He shot Tess a sharp look. Her eyes filled with fresh tears, and she looked down at her fingers. When he went back to reading she peeped at him every few seconds. The farther he read the more his jaw muscles worked and his mouth grew so tight a thin white line formed around it.

When he finished, he slapped the letter against his thigh and singed the air with a string of curses that would have done a longshoreman proud. His sympathetic ire only made her chin wobble more, and she looked away, the painful knot in her throat nearly suffocating her.

"What the hell kind of people are these?" he snarled. "How could they do this? I thought they were family."

Tess shrugged and pressed her quivering lips together, the tears she had been straining to hold in check spilling over.

"Oh, damn." Ryan sat down beside her so suddenly Tess jumped. He put his arm around her and pulled her close, and his other hand cupped the back of her head, pressing her face into his shoulder and holding her there. "I'm sorry, Tess. God, I'm sorry," he said in his peculiar gruff, gentle way. "This is my fault. I shouldn't have talked you into writing to them. I had no idea—"

"It's all right," she mumbled into his shirt, sniffing, but she made no move to leave the comfort of his embrace. He was so big, so rock solid, so strong and warm. And it felt so good to lean on him...for just a little while. "You couldn't have known. Actually, I don't even know why I'm crying. It's not as though we were ever close."

"You're crying because you've been insulted. And you have every right to. So go ahead and bawl. Get it out of your system."

The brusque attempt at consoling filled her with warmth and raised her spirit, and she gave a watery chuckle. "I think I already have." Regretfully, she pulled out of his embrace and sat up, wiping her cheeks with the backs of her hands. "Anyway, it doesn't do any good."

"Oh, I don't know. It made you feel better, didn't it?"

"I suppose." Tess squared her shoulders and thrust out her delicate chin. "But not nearly as good as I'm going to feel."

"Why? What're you going to do?"

"I'll tell you what I'm going to do. I'm going to write a blistering reply that will burn the pants right off Mr. Roland P. Rutledge, Attorney at Law, and hopefully his clients as well. I'm going to tell Harold and Enid Benson exactly what I think of them and what they can do with their stinking money."

Ryan grinned—a full-fledged, unrestrained, heart-stopping, hundred mega-watt grin that made her heart give a little bump and stunned her into silence. "Atta girl. Give 'em hell, honey."

Tess blinked and pulled her scattered wits together. Bolstered by his support and encouragement, her determination grew and she struggled to get to her feet. Chuckling, Ryan stood and pulled her up off the sofa, but when she headed for the slant-top desk in the corner of the living room, he grasped her shoulders.

"Whoa. Not so fast. The letter can wait. Right now we've got a class to attend. If you don't get a move on we're going to be late."

"I can't go to class like this," Tess protested. She cupped her face with both hands. "My eyes are swollen and my nose is red. And I know whenever I cry my face gets all blotchy."

"Go splash cold water on your face and powder your nose and you'll be fine."

"*Ry-an!* I look a fright."

"You look adorable." He put his forefinger under her chin, tipped her face up, and kissed the tip of her nose. He drew back a few inches and his eyes crinkled at her at close range. Tess stared back, her own eyes big as saucers. "Now hurry up and make yourself presentable. You know how crabby Cathy gets when anyone is late." He turned her around, pointed her toward the bedroom and gave her a little shove.

Dazed, Tess went, docile as a lamb.

## Chapter Six

If someone had told Tess that she would end up with Ryan McCall as her Lamaze coach she would have laughed in their face. If they had said that she would grow accustomed to the taciturn man, even grow to like him and feel comfortable around him, she would have thought they were crazy. Yet, she had.

She wasn't quite sure how it had happened. Her expression bemused, Tess gazed at the television, barely aware of the game show on the screen as she pondered the matter. The rocking chair continued to move at a steady, placid rhythm that matched the clack of her knitting needles.

It had been a month since Ryan had declared his intention of taking over for Amanda. At first they had been stiff and ill at ease with each other, but once the class started, they forgot about everything but the baby and the awkwardness disappeared. There was no time for self-consciousness when you were working together to bring a new life into the world, even if you were merely rehearsing the event.

With each succeeding day Ryan had seemed less angry, more approachable, and she had realized finally that he was making an effort to establish a rapport between them. True, he had remained reserved and wary, and at times he was still shockingly abrupt, but the tension between them had faded. So much so that Tess had even risked another dinner invitation.

"I only want to thank you," she had tacked on anxiously before he could misinterpret. "You're doing so much for me. At least let me repay you with a home-cooked meal."

He had not responded with cutting insults, but he'd still been reluctant to accept.

"You shouldn't be standing on your feet cooking a big meal," he said, scowling at her. "That's too much work for someone in your condition."

"Don't be silly. I'm in perfect health. It may take me longer to do things these days, but I'm not an invalid. Actually, you'd be doing me a favor. Do you have any idea how difficult it is to cook for one? And to tell you the truth, I get tired of eating alone."

At the last, understanding and empathy flashed in his eyes for a fraction of a second, and for the first time Tess wondered if Ryan was as lonely as she was. Whatever, the tack proved to be the right one.

Delighted to have someone to cook for, she outdid herself that night. Ryan and his son enjoyed the meal so much that after that she had no difficulty getting him to accept a dinner invitation, provided she allowed him to purchase the groceries for the meal. Soon, much to Mike's delight, the three of them were eating together two or three times a week.

The dinners had helped to ease the tension between them, but the real breakthrough in the relationship had occurred two weeks ago when she had entered her ninth month.

The knitting needles ceased their clicking, and Tess's hands fell idle in her lap atop the tiny half-finished garment, a wry smile tugging at her mouth at the memory of that morning.

With a feeling of dread eating away at her, she had knocked on his door. Seconds later, he jerked it open, bristling with annoyance, but at the sight of her his scowl vanished and one brow arched.

"Tess. What're you doing here so early?" His frown returned. "Is something wrong?"

Tess didn't reply. She did not even hear him. All she could do was stare.

Ryan was barefoot and bare-chested, his sole article of clothing a pair of unbuttoned jeans, which he had obviously pulled on in haste on his way to the door. He held a damp towel in his hands, using it to dab blobs of white foam off his face. He smelled of soap and shaving cream. Ringlets of wet hair hung across his forehead and beads of moisture clung to the dark curls on his chest.

Tess stared helplessly at a droplet that trickled down through that silky pelt. Mesmerized, she tracked its darting path downward over his flat, muscle-ridged belly where, at last, it settled in his navel.

Staring in that indentation with its surrounding swirl of dark hair, Tess tried to swallow, but her mouth was so dry it felt like cotton.

"Dammit, Tess, answer me! What's wrong? Are you sick? Are you hurt?"

She jumped, and her cheeks pinkened. She dragged her gaze away from his torso and forced herself to meet his glare. "N-no. No, I'm fine."

"Then what the hell are you doing here at seven o'clock on Saturday morning?"

"I...I wanted to catch you before you left. I, uh...I was wondering if I could get a ride with you to the grocery store today when you go?"

His eyes narrowed. "All right. Out with it. What's wrong with your car this time?"

"Nothing!"

"Nothing, huh? Then why do you need a ride?"

Her blush deepened. She did not want to tell him her reason, but he obviously would not be satisfied until she did. She looked away from that intense blue stare, only to encounter his bare chest again. Jerking her gaze to the side, she stared down the passageway. "There's nothing wrong with the car. I just can't drive it."

"What the hell does that mean?"

Tess sighed. She glanced at him out of the corner of her eye, and her mouth turned down sourly. "It means I can't fit behind the wheel anymore. Not without pushing the seat all the way back. And when I do that I can't see over the darned hood."

Ryan gaped at her. His gaze dropped to her now enormous belly, then returned to her sulky face. His lips began to twitch.

Tess spotted the movement and gasped. "Don't you *dare* laugh!"

The admonition had the opposite result. Ryan leaned weakly against the doorframe and let loose with a rich, full-throated laugh that sent goose bumps over her flesh.

She was so startled by the sound coming from him and the transformation that laughter brought to his face, for an instant all she could do was gape. Recovering herself, she snapped her mouth shut, her shock turning to affront.

"Oh! I should have known better than to come to you! Just forget it!" She spun on her heel and started to flounce off, but she had barely taken a step when he snagged her arm.

"Whoa, there. Don't run off mad. I didn't mean to upset you." Grinning, he pulled her to stand between his spread legs, so close that Tess had to brace her hands against his bare chest.

She heard the laughter in his voice and knew she should pull away, but she kept her gaze lowered and stared at his collar bone, intensely aware of the warm flesh and crisp hair pressing against her palms, the clean male scent that assailed her nostrils.

Ryan draped his forearms over her shoulders and tipped his head to one side, giving her a coaxing look. "C'mon, Tess. You've got to admit, it *is* funny."

"I'll do no such thing. This is serious, Ryan. I nearly hit a pedestrian yesterday. If the poor man hadn't jumped back onto the curb I would have run him down."

Ryan's mouth worked and his eyes danced even more. Tess tried to look stern but she could not quite manage it. He was so incredibly handsome with his face alight with good humor, it took her breath away. His mirth was contagious as well. After a moment her own lips began to twitch.

She tried to hold back, but when Ryan's grin widened, a sound somewhere between a snort and a giggle broke free and she was lost.

"Atta girl," Ryan whooped, and when he rested his forehead against hers, she leaned weakly against him as their laughter blended.

Tess shook her head at the memory and picked up her knitting again, a smile tugging at her lips. That morning had marked a change in their relationship, put them at ease with each other in a way that was oddly comforting.

Ryan had not only taken her to the grocery store, and to the pharmacy and the dry cleaners and on any other errand she needed to run, last week he had driven her to the obstetrician's for her regular checkup.

Mike, of course, was in heaven. He was so elated over the turn things had taken that he almost balked at spending the last few weeks of summer vacation with his grandparents. It was something he had done every summer for the last eight years. He had been looking forward to the visit for weeks, and Tess could tell that he wanted to go, but he was torn. He had still been hesitating when he climbed into his uncle's truck for the drive to Crockett.

"But I want to be here when the baby's born. What if I don't get back in time and I miss it?"

"You won't miss it," his father assured him for the hundredth time and slung his bags into the back.

Grinning, Reilly ruffled Mike's hair. "Hey, don't sweat it, sport. It's only a two-hour drive from Crockett, and babies always take longer than that to get born. So even if something happens we can give you a call in plenty of time for Gramps to get you here for the big event."

"Mike, don't worry," Tess assured him. "The baby isn't due until the end of the month. You'll be back and in school before then."

"You sure?"

"Yes, I'm sure. Now go."

Chuckling, Tess shook her head. He had been gone barely ten days and he had already called five times. Mike was almost as excited about the baby as she was.

A shrill beeping drew Tess's gaze to the television, and she was surprised to see that the regular program had been interrupted. The man on the screen, a meteorologist with the National Weather Service, advised solemnly that Hurricane Homer, which had been expected to go ashore on the eastern coast of Mexico during the previous night, had changed direction and was now threatening the Texas coast.

"If the storm continues on the same northeasterly course it will come on shore to the west of Galveston on a direct line with Houston. If that becomes likely we will recommend evacuation.

"At its current rate of speed, Homer is expected to make landfall around ten o'clock tonight. However, please be advised that winds are increasing and the storm is picking up speed as it moves over the Gulf of Mexico, so that estimate will probably be revised.

"Hurricane Homer could change direction again at any time. We here at the National Weather Service are tracking it constantly and will keep you informed of any developments as they occur."

The man went on to advise of safety precautions that should be taken and what supplies to have on hand in case of a power outage and various other emergency situations. Tess listened in a daze, the first stirring of anxiety tightening her chest.

Her gaze went to the window. The night before and all morning it had rained off and on, sometimes in gusty, wind-driven sheets, but that was not unusual for the Gulf Coast, especially when a tropical storm was brewing offshore. When she had watched the evening news the night before, the weatherman had been confident that the hurricane would continue its westerly course and miss the U.S. completely.

It took almost five minutes, but finally Tess struggled out of the rocking chair and waddled to the window. The rain had stopped for the moment but the trees around the apartment complex were whipping and swaying in the wind like frenzied dancers and the sky had an unnatural greenish tint that made her uneasy.

Her first instinct was to call Ryan, but she stopped herself in time. While she was glad of their new amiable relationship, she still was not comfortable about imposing on him. She was not Ryan's responsibility, after all. She could not keep running to him every time she had a problem.

Besides, it was early yet. Barely noon. There was plenty of time to take action if it became necessary. These storms were unpredictable. Homer might not come anywhere near

Houston. By evening it might even be headed in a totally different direction. There was no reason to panic.

The rain started again, lashing against her window with a sudden savageness that made her jump. Tess looked at the telephone. Biting her lower lip, she crossed her arms over her swollen abdomen, hugging herself tightly, and fought the urge to run to the instrument and dial R & R Construction.

"This bulletin just in from National Weather Service. As of six o'clock this evening Hurricane Homer was located less than one hundred miles offshore and taking dead aim at Houston."

Across the width of the R & R Construction office, Ryan and Reilly exchanged a worried glance but neither spoke. Their faces taut, they listened carefully to every word coming from the battered radio that sat on top of the filing cabinet.

"...hundred and fifty miles wide. At present, Homer has sustained winds of one hundred and forty-five miles an hour, but that speed is expected to increase. Homer is moving in our direction at a current speed of twenty-four miles per hour. The National Weather Service and the Bureau of Civil Defense is advising all residents to evacuate the city or move to designated shelters in your area. I repeat—"

"Well, that cuts it." Ryan stood up and switched off the radio. "We can't wait any longer hoping it will change course. Even if it veers off now, which seems damned unlikely, we'll still catch the edge of it."

"Yeah, you're right." Reilly hauled himself to his feet, took a rain slicker from the coatrack and shrugged into it. He had already protected his Stetson with a clear plastic hat cover. "I guess we'd better go batten down as best we can and hightail it outta here. An apartment is sure as hell no place to ride out a hurricane." His gaze swept the interior of the trailer that served as the on-site office, and he grimaced. "This place will probably get blown into the next county."

For the next hour they worked in the driving rain to secure their equipment and materials at Wildwood. They had received approval on their loan three weeks before and clearing had already started on the property. They made several trips, hauling the heavy earth-moving equipment and concrete mixers back to the storage barn on a flatbed trailer, where they chained them to rings in the concrete foundation. Thankfully, little in the way of building material had been delivered to the development yet, just a load of bricks and some beams for the entrance marker. Those they covered with a tarp and anchored it with stakes and chains and crossed their fingers that the force of the wind would not make flying missiles out of the lot.

"Okay, that does it," Reilly hollered over the howling wind and rain when they had finished. "Let's head out. We're closest to my place. It won't take me but a few minutes to throw some things together, then we'll swing by your apartment and you can do the same. I assume we're going to head for the folks' place."

"Right. I've got a few valuables I want to take along, too, but that won't—" Ryan stopped in midsentence. "Good Lord! Tess!" He looked at his brother, his eyes wide. "She's all alone. She can't even drive herself anymore. We'll have to take her with us."

"Hey, no problem. Mom won't mind. She'd skin us both if we didn't."

"C'mon, let's hurry it up. Tess is probably scared to death by now."

Tess's hands shook as she folded a smock and added it to the suitcase. Another gust of wind hurtled rain against the side of the building. It lashed and drummed against the structure with a roar that was deafening. Warily, reaching for another nightgown, she glanced out the window. Now even the greenish pewter sky was obliterated. All she could see were the solid sheets of water. It was barely seven o'clock, but it was so dark outside that the streetlights had been on for the last hour.

The sudden banging on the front door nearly made her jump right out of her skin. She gave a squeal and dropped the nightgown, her hands flying to her mouth.

"Tess! Tess, are you in there?"

*Ryan.* She sagged against the bedpost and closed her eyes. Thank God.

"Tess?"

Ryan's fist hammered again, and she pulled herself together and headed for the door as fast as she could waddle, her heart pounding in her throat. "I'm coming. I'm coming."

The instant she opened the door, Ryan burst through and grasped her shoulders. "What took you so long? Are you all right?"

Tess gave a shaky laugh. She never thought she'd be so glad to see that fierce scowl. "Yes. Yes, I'm fine. I was just—"

"Good. Go pack what you need. You're coming with us."

He grabbed her hand and started toward the bedroom. Tess tried to hang back but he towed her along with him. "Go-going with you? But... where? And who is us?"

"Me and Reilly. He's next door packing some things for me. We're getting the hell out of here. Ah, good, you've already started," he said with satisfaction when he spotted the half filled suitcase on her bed.

"Ye-yes. I was going to call a taxi—or the police if I had to—to take me to a shelter."

"Shelter, hell. I'm taking you to my folks' place."

"Ryan! I can't let you do that. I'm not going to impose on your family that way. They don't even know me."

"Believe me, you won't be imposing. They have a big barn of a house and Mom loves having company. Anyway, by now Mike has told them all about you."

He scooped up the remaining items she had laid out on the bed to take and stuffed them into the case. "Is this all you need?"

"Yes, but—"

"No buts, Tess. If you think I'm leaving you here alone when you're just a couple of weeks from dominoing, you're crazy. You're coming with us, and that's final." He snapped the locks and straightened with the suitcase in his hand. "Is there anything else you want to take?" The determined look on his face warned her that arguing was useless.

Tess told herself she should refuse anyway. She wasn't his responsibility. She wasn't even family. Why should Ryan be burdened with looking after her? It wasn't right.

But, heaven help her, she was glad he had come for her. She had been so frightened. Somehow, in the last month she had come to depend on Ryan, on his strength, his steadiness, his rock solid dependability. She had complete confidence in him. With Ryan she felt safe.

Biting her lower lip, she looked at him uncertainly and tried to work up the gumption to refuse, but she couldn't. Finally she gave in with a guilty sense of relief.

"Well . . ." Tess gestured toward the overnight case sitting beside the dresser. "There is the bag I've kept packed to take with me to the hospital. Perhaps—"

"Hell, yes, we'll take it."

"Hey. You two ready to hit the road?" Reilly stuck his head in the door, grinned at Tess and murmured a cheerful, "Hi, darlin'," before turning to his brother. "I locked your place and tossed your stuff in the Cherokee. It's getting hairy out there, Hoss. We'd better get a move on."

"Right. Here, take this." Ryan shoved the smaller of Tess's cases into Reilly's hand. He picked up the other one, grabbed her elbow and hustled her out with a speed that made her head spin.

Though only a few miles away, it seemed to take forever to reach Interstate 45, the main highway that led north out of Houston to Dallas and beyond. Every car in the city appeared to be heading in that direction. On the other side of the wide median, the southbound half of the freeway was eerily empty. Ahead, to the north, the highway was an unbroken ribbon of red taillights, behind, a necklace of glaring headlights, stretching out in both directions as far as the eye could see.

The bumper-to-bumper traffic crept along at an erratic stop-and-start pace, like a long, slow-moving parking lot. Which was just as well, Tess thought. The wind had picked up even more and was buffeting the Cherokee so hard that Ryan had to fight the steering wheel constantly to keep control.

Sitting in the back seat, Tess stared out at the almost horizontal wall of rain that lashed and pounded with a demented fury. It sheeted the windows, overpowering the furiously thumping wipers. Visibility extended mere feet in front of the vehicle. Thick woods lined the freeway on either side, and the trees were blurry shapes, swaying and whipping with wild abandon, like a troupe of crazed dancers. The frenzy and power of the approaching storm was awesome, and this, Tess knew, was merely the forward edge.

Yet, strangely, she was not afraid. Not anymore. She was apprehensive about barging in on Ryan's family. But the tight, fizzy feeling gripping her chest was excitement and fascination over the impressive display of nature's force. Her fear had fled the instant that Ryan had pounded on her apartment door.

It took them almost two hours to travel the fifty miles to the Highway 19 cutoff, just south of Huntsville. Once they left the interstate they began to make better time, though they were unable to drive at anywhere near the speed limit.

The traffic was not quite as congested, but it remained bumper-to-bumper, and though they were pulling ahead of the storm, they were still on the forward fringes of it and the rain and winds continued to batter them. A hurricane of the size and power of Homer created squalls for hundreds of miles in every direction beyond the actual storm center.

Occasionally the brothers exchanged a few quiet words, and now and then Ryan would glance in the rearview mirror at Tess and inquire if she was okay, but otherwise they said little. Driving under such harrowing conditions required all of Ryan's concentration.

They were fifteen or so miles beyond Huntsville when Tess felt the first twinge of pain. She didn't think much of it; all day she'd had an ache in her lower back and this was only slightly more severe.

Ten minutes later, her eyes widened and she went utterly still when the aching tightness returned and spread from her back around to her abdomen. The sensation lasted only seconds, so quick she could not be sure it had been a contraction. Tess looked out the window into the pitch darkness as the Cherokee's tires thumped noisily over the Trinity River bridge. She hoped not; they were in the middle of nowhere.

There had been no reoccurrence of the discomfort when they drove through the small town of Trinity a few minutes later, and Tess began to relax. Dr. Baxter had warned her that she might experience twinges of false labor during the last couple of weeks.

Barely five minutes north of town another pain grabbed her. This one was no twinge but a full-blown, excruciating contraction. The cramping pain rippled from her back around her belly like clawing talons. Tess gripped the edge of the seat and gritted her teeth to keep from crying out.

When the spasm passed she slumped back against the seat and panted, unaware until then that she had been holding her breath. Oh, Lord. This couldn't be happening. Not now. Please, God, not now. But deep inside, she knew that it was.

What should she do? She wondered if she ought to alert Ryan and ask him to turn around and go back to Trinity, but she wasn't sure whether the little town even had a hospital. And she didn't want to add to Ryan's problems unless she had to. He had his hands full already.

She knew for certain that Crockett had a hospital. Mike had told her about breaking his arm last summer and having it set in the emergency room. When they reached the outskirts of town she would tell Ryan... if she made it that far.

The thought that she might not sent fear skittering through her, and she licked her suddenly dry lips. Don't panic. Just stay calm, she cautioned herself. Stay calm.

When she looked up Ryan was watching her in the rearview mirror. ''Is something wrong?''

''Uh...no. I uh...I was just wondering. How far are we from Crockett?''

''About twenty-five miles, give or take a mile or so. But at the rate this traffic is moving, it'll take forty-five minutes or more to get there.''

Forty-five minutes. That wasn't too bad. The pains seemed to be about ten or twelve minutes apart. And Dr. Baxter had said that first labors were usually long.

The next contraction, however, occurred a mere six minutes later. It caught her unawares and was agonizing and endless. In the middle of it, though she bit down hard on her lower lip, Tess couldn't hold back a moan.

The sound drew the attention of both men. Reilly whipped around and stared at her, and Ryan's gaze snapped to the rearview mirror. ''What is it? What's wrong?'' they said in unison.

Caught in the torturous grip of the contraction, Tess could not answer. She barely heard them, barely registered the looks of shock and horror that slid over their faces.

"Tess? Tess, for Pete's sake, are you in labor?" Ryan demanded.

"Ye-yes!" she gasped when the pain began to release her.

"Sweet Jesus," Reilly whispered.

"Dammit, Tess! Why didn't you say something? When did the pains start? How far apart are they now?

"It . . . it hasn't been long. Just about . . . forty-five minutes," Tess panted weakly. "They started after we left the interstate."

Ryan bit out a vicious curse.

"But the last two were only— Oh! Oh! Oh my goodness!"

The terrified cry sent an icy trickle down Ryan's spine. His gaze shot back to the mirror. "What? What? Dammit, Tess, answer me!"

She seemed incapable of speech. Her stunned gaze locked with his in the mirror, staring back at him like a terrified rabbit, her eyes enormous in her pale face. "I . . . my water broke."

"Holy hell!" Reilly groaned, but Ryan didn't hear him.

He felt his heart skip. Terror had him by the throat. He could barely breathe.

He had to do something. But what? He couldn't think.

Then Tess whimpered, and the tiny sound galvanized him into action.

"Get back there and help her," he yelled at his brother. "I don't think she'll make it to the hospital."

"*Me!*" Reilly yelped. "I can't do that! I don't know anything about delivering a baby!"

"One of us has to do it."

"Well, it sure as hell isn't going to be me. Hey! What're you doing? You can't pull off in this driving rain! Somebody'll plow right into the back of us!"

"All right then . . ."

"Wha . . . Man, are you *crazy!*"

Ignoring his brother's outburst, Ryan turned on the emergency flashing lights and brought the Cherokee to a stop in the middle of the highway. "Here. You drive."

He unfastened his safety belt, twisted around and squeezed between the bucket seats.

"Holy— Watch it, will ya," Reilly growled when Ryan's foot almost caught him in the head. Behind them, horns blared and a few cars began to pull cautiously around them. Reilly quickly shifted over into the driver's seat and buckled up.

"All right, all right, we're going. Jeez, give us a break," he muttered, casting a disgusted glance in the mirror at the line of stopped cars. "We got an emergency here, for Pete's sake." He put the vehicle in gear and stepped on the gas so hard that the tires spun. Within seconds they had caught up to the traffic ahead.

"Oh, Ryan—!" Tess grabbed his arm the instant he joined her.

"Easy. Take it easy, honey. We'll get through this. First I'm going to help you into the back. Then I'll lower this seat so you'll have room to lie down. Okay?"

"O-okay."

The cramped quarters made movement difficult for Tess. In the end it proved easier for Ryan to simply pick her up in his arms and lift her over the back of the seat. He had barely climbed over after her when another hard contraction hit.

Scooting on his knees, Ryan got behind her and supported her back against his chest. "Take shallow breaths, Tess. The way we practiced. C'mon, you know how to do it. That's it. That's it. Breathe. Breathe. Atta girl."

When the pain ebbed, Ryan set to work like a madman. He ordered Reilly to turn on the dome light, and with frantic haste he shoved all the luggage to one side and to the rear. Then he lowered the back of the rear seat and gave silent thanks that the surface of the resulting cargo bed was covered with a thick carpet. Reaching into the front, he snatched up the newspaper he had brought with him that morning and spread it over most of the back. Then he eased Tess down onto it.

When she was stretched out on her back, he took her hand and squeezed it gently. "Honey, I know this is awkward and embarrassing, but...I'm going to have to take off your panties. Will you help me?"

Tess closed her eyes and gave a distressed moan, but she nodded.

"Good girl," Ryan said, and when he slid his hands up under her billowing tent dress, she lifted her hips.

"How's it going back there?"

At that instant Tess clutched her belly and cried out.

"Ah, jeez," Reilly moaned. "I had to ask."

Kneeling between Tess's knees, Ryan placed his hand on her abdomen. His eyes widened when he felt the rippling movement against his palm. "Easy honey. Easy. Go with it. Remember what we learned in class."

Tess's gaze met his. Her eyes were wide with apprehension but she choked back the moan that was building in her throat and nodded gamely. She began to pant, making desperate little *hee-heeing* sounds.

When the pain subsided, Ryan squeezed her hand. "You did great, Tess. Just great."

"Uh...I don't know much about these things," Reilly put in. "But wasn't that a little quick?"

Ryan checked his watch. "Yeah. The contractions are down to less than four minutes apart."

"Ah, man." Reilly shook his fist at the line of cars ahead. "Can't you people go any faster, dammit!"

"My guess is it wouldn't matter if we had a clear road and a police escort. You still wouldn't be able to get us to the hospital in time. This baby wants to be born *now*."

"Jeez, man. Did you have to tell me that?"

"Ry-Ryan. In my hospital bag…there's a small bottle of alcohol, and…and some manicure scissors. And some moist towelettes, too."

"Right." Ryan scrambled on his knees to the rear of the vehicle and opened the overnight bag. He rummaged through the contents with no regard whatsoever for their neatness and located the items. He also discovered a nightgown trimmed in eyelet lace that had a narrow pink satin ribbon running through it. Ryan stripped the ribbon from the eyelet and put it into his pocket. Slinging the gown over his shoulder, he picked up the other items and hurried back to Tess.

When he took up his position between her knees again another hard contraction was building. He glanced at his watch and frowned. Two minutes.

Fear clawed at Ryan when he glanced up at Tess's face. She was drenched in sweat. Her bright hair was darkened with it and plastered to her scalp. Arms raised above her head, she gripped the strap across the back of the front passenger seat and pulled and strained, writhing from side to side. Pain ravaged her lovely face. Her eyes and jaws were clamped shut but tiny sounds of distress came out with every breath.

"Concentrate on your breathing, Tess. C'mon, honey. Take short, quick breaths through your mouth."

The pain had caught her in its grip. Ryan wasn't even sure that she had heard him. Her moans quickly built into a hoarse scream that tore from her throat and her back arched off the cargo bed as her belly tightened into a tortuous hard ball.

"Don't fight it, Tess," he instructed when the agonized sound faded away. "Pant with the pains and relax in between. C'mon, honey. Don't tell me we went through all those lessons for nothing."

His feeble attempt at humor brought a wan smile to her lips as she sagged with exhaustion.

When the next pain hit a minute later, Tess tried, but toward the end her breathless pant dissolved into a high, keening wail that made the hair on the back of Ryan's neck stand on end and drew a string of frightened curses from his brother.

Three more contractions came in rapid succession before Ryan cried out, "I can see the head!" He looked up at Tess and grinned. "It won't be long now."

The undulating contractions were coming so close together that Tess had only scant seconds of respite in between.

"You're doing fine, sweetheart. Just fine. Okay, here comes another one. You're going to have to push now, Tess. Push! *Push!*"

Tess gulped in air and strained with all her might as the wrenching pain twisted her insides. Her face turned an alarming purple-red with the effort. She dug her heels in and pushed, and pulled at the strap above her head—so hard she ripped one end of it right out of the upholstery.

Reilly glanced over his shoulder and paled.

Ryan's gaze went to that dangling strap, still held in her grasp. Her knuckles were bone white and the tendons in her neck, shoulders and arms stood out like taut wires.

He stared and swallowed hard. *Jesus!*

Gritting his teeth, Ryan forced his gaze back to the birth area, and his eyes widened in delight. "Here it comes! The baby's coming!" He sucked in his breath. "Oh, man...this is really something," he murmured as the head emerged.

"You're doing terrific, Tess. Just a little more. There, that's it. That's it. Oh, sweet heaven," he murmured in an awed voice as he caught the slippery newborn in his hands.

He stared at the tiny flailing scrap of humanity cradled in his palms. Emotion filled him. It swelled in his chest and thickened his throat. He looked up at Tess, his heart so full he could barely speak.

"Well, little mother, you have a daughter." His deep voice was rough and scratchy with emotion, not quite steady. "A beautiful little daughter."

"A daughter," Tess repeated dreamily. Tears of relief rolled from the corners of her eyes. Her face glowed with such profound warmth and feeling, the painful band around Ryan's chest tightened even more. "Is she all right?"

"Oh, yeah." He looked down at the infant again and swallowed hard. "I'd say she's about as right as they come."

The baby choked, then squalled lustily.

"One thing is certain. She's got a healthy set of lungs," came Reilly's quip from the front seat, breaking the spell, and they all chuckled in relief.

However, a few seconds later when Ryan had dealt with the cord and laid the infant on her mother's stomach, all the suffocating emotions came rushing back and he found himself blinking back tears.

Tess lifted her head wearily to look at the baby and touched the tiny quivering chin with one finger. "Oh, Ryan. She's so perfect."

Before he could agree, her face contorted again. Ryan bent quickly.

The contraction was mercifully brief. "There. That's it." He wrapped the afterbirth in the newspaper. Looking up at Tess, he smiled. "Feel better now?"

"Yes."

"I'm afraid this will have to be sacrificed to the cause," he said, holding up her nightgown. Without waiting for her consent, he used the manicure scissors to make two small cuts in the bottom edge of the soft batiste and with quick, efficient movements, he ripped the garment neatly in two.

The baby howled and squirmed on her mother's tummy. Ryan lifted her carefully and cleaned her as best he could with the moist towelettes, which made her squall all the louder.

"Holy cow, Hoss. What're you doing back there? Killing the kid?"

Ignoring his brother, Ryan wrapped the shivering, squirming, squalling babe in half of the gown, and laid her in her mother's arms. She quieted at once, the howls turning into a series of tiny squeaks and grunts.

"Oh, Ryan." Tess's voice quivered. She looked up with a beaming smile. Joy and wonder lit her face and her eyes brimmed with such love and pride it brought a pain to his chest and made his throat close up again. "Look at her. Isn't she beautiful?"

"Yeah," he managed in a rough voice. "She looks like you."

Tess barely heard him. She was too enthralled. Folding back the edges of the soft cloth, she inspected tiny fingers and toes, the scrawny, flailing legs and arms, ran a fingertip down the velvety skin. When she discovered the pink satin ribbon Ryan had used to tie off the cord, she flashed him another smile. The baby made a mewling sound and rooted against her. Cuddling her close, Tess nuzzled the pale peach fuzz on her daughter's head and tenderly kissed the pulsing soft spot.

She was so entranced, she barely noticed when Ryan pressed the pad he had made of the other half of the nightgown between her legs and pulled her dress down.

Ryan leaned over mother and daughter. "How're you doing?" He touched the starlike hand waving above the swaddling. His heart bumped when the tiny fingers clamped around his calloused forefinger with a surprising grip, and his gaze met Tess's.

Her face was pale with exhaustion but joy sparkled in her eyes—joy she invited him to share. "Oh, Ryan. I have a daughter. A beautiful, perfect little daughter." She stroked the rosebud mouth. "I can't believe it."

"What're you going to name her?"

"Molly. Molly Clare Benson."

"It suits her." He stroked his thumb over the tips of the matchstick fingers, marveling at the minuscule nails, and struggled with the sweet pain that swelled his heart.

They were both so intent on the baby, neither noticed that Reilly had brought the Cherokee to a stop outside the hospital emergency room. When he tore open the door and bailed out of the vehicle as though it were on fire, they were both surprised.

Within seconds a swarm of orderlies and nurses descended on them. Tess, with Molly in her arms, was gently lifted from the back of the Cherokee and placed on a gurney. Ryan walked beside her, holding her hand, but once they were inside, he was not allowed to go beyond the admitting desk.

"You'll have to stay here, sir, and fill out the papers while your wife and daughter are being examined," one of the nurses ordered brusquely.

Ryan felt a queer sensation in his chest.

"Oh, but he's not—"

"That's all right, Tess. I'll take care of it."

She reached out to him again, and when Ryan took her hand, she said softly, "Thank you, Ryan. For everything."

The impatient staff began wheeling Tess and Molly away. Feeling useless and anxious and strangely bereft, he watched until they disappeared through the double doors at the end of the hall.

## Chapter Seven

"Tess?"

"I think she's asleep," Reilly whispered.

She lay still in the hospital bed, one arm resting on the pillow beside her cheek, the other draped across her waist on top of the covers. Her bright hair glittered under the bedside light, a swath of flame against the sterile white pillowcase. She looked exhausted, but her faint smile was one of utter peace.

"I think you're right," Ryan agreed, and found himself battling a sharp stab of disappointment.

Tess's eyelids fluttered open. "Ryan? Is that you?" Sleepy fatigue slurred her voice and made it husky.

"Yeah, it's me." He stepped closer to the bed and took her hand. "How do you feel?"

"Like I had a baby in the back of a moving truck."

"I'll bet," Ryan said with a wry grin.

"Hey. I'm here, too, you know. Aren't you going to say hello to me?"

Smiling sleepily, Tess held out her other hand. "Hi, Reilly. Sorry. I didn't see you standing there."

"Ah, well. That's okay." He glanced across the bed at his twin, and his mouth twitched. Ryan's eyes had not left Tess since they entered the room. "I understand."

Her sleepy gaze went back to Ryan. "Molly? Is she all right?"

"She's fine. We just saw her in the nursery. They put her in an incubator just to be safe, but the doctor assured us that she's fit as a fiddle. No problems at all."

"May I see her?"

"When you've rested. You just had a baby, remember."

She chuckled weakly. "Right now, it's kind of hard to forget." Her eyes started to droop, then they popped back open. "Oh. Did you have any trouble admitting—"

"Everything's fine. Don't worry. I found your insurance card in your wallet. Other than the usual aggravation of endless paperwork, that got you and Molly checked in without much fuss."

"Thank you, Ryan. You've...been..." A huge yawn cut her off, and when it ended, she grimaced. "Sorry. They gave me a shot for pain and it's making me drowsy."

"C'mon, Hoss," Reilly whispered. "We'd better go and let her get some rest."

Ryan shot his brother a dark look. "I'm not leaving until she's asleep."

He hated to leave her at all. If he had his way, he'd stay right there all night, but that battle-ax in the nurses' station down the hall had already warned them to keep the visit short. She looked capable of throwing them out bodily if they disobeyed.

"I'd say she already is."

Reilly nodded toward the bed, and Ryan saw that Tess's eyes were closed and her breathing was deep and slow. He sighed and released her hand, tucking it beneath the cover. When he had adjusted the blanket more snugly around her shoulders, he touched her cheek and whispered, "I'll be back."

Sitting propped up in the bed the next morning, Tess gazed out the window at the softly pattering rain, the tail end of Homer. One of the nurses had told her that after hitting Houston, the hurricane had veered in a more eastward direction, staying roughly parallel to the coast.

In an abstract sort of way, Tess wondered if her apartment had been damaged, but she was too happy at the moment to worry about it. Not even the gray skies could dampen her spirits.

She had been awakened at six, when a nurse had brought Molly to her for her first feeding. The feel of that rosebud mouth tugging at her breast had been the most profoundly beautiful and moving experience of her life. The rush of love Tess had felt for her child had been almost painful.

The door pushed open, and she looked around in time to see Ryan walk in. She became immediately and excruciatingly self-conscious. Beneath the covers, she felt her body heat up.

Last night the urgency of the situation had nullified modesty and inhibitions. She had simply been too grateful that Ryan had been there to deliver her baby. She still was. Only now that the crisis had passed, she was filled with embarrassment.

When she thought of the incredible intimacy of that harrowing half hour, the things he had done for her, she wanted to squirm. If she hadn't been so sore, she would have.

She had only a muzzy recollection of Ryan visiting her the night before, but this morning she had woken with a clear head, and she had been dreading this meeting ever since. She wanted to run and hide, but that was impossible, so she hid her humiliation behind a cheery facade.

"Ryan! My goodness. You're up early."

He frowned at her overbright tone. "I thought you might be feeling lonely. But if I'm too early I can come back later."

"No. No. This is fine. Really." She had to face him sometime so she might as well get it over with. Postponing the inevitable wouldn't help.

His appearance had rattled her so, she had not noticed until that moment that in one hand he carried a vase filled with an enormous bouquet of yellow roses and in the other a fuzzy teddy bear.

"These are for you and Molly. I hope you like roses." He set the flowers on her bedside table and handed her the stuffed animal.

"I love them. But you shouldn't have," she protested, then blushed when she realized how trite that had sounded. "I mean . . . you've done so much for us already."

"Since I was the first one to hold her, it seemed only right that I give Molly her first present. I couldn't very well leave you out, now could I?"

He made the statement with a straight face, but that stern mouth slowly curved into one of his rare, heart-stopping smiles, and Tess experienced a moment of acute shock when she realized that Ryan was teasing her.

Flustered, she looked down at the teddy bear and fiddled with the bow around its neck. "Well...it was sweet of you, anyway. Thank you, Ryan." She plucked at the stuffed animal's fluffy ears, not knowing what else to say.

Astonishment and something close to panic slammed through Tess when he sat down on the side of the bed and took her hand. The expression on his face was one she had never seen before. He was so close she could make out the faint shadow of whiskers beneath the surface of his freshly shaved skin, each individual eyelash, the slightly darker streaks of blue that rayed outward from his pupils. Drops of moisture clung to his dark hair and splotched his pale blue cotton shirt. He smelled of rain and soap. And maleness.

"I came early because I couldn't wait any longer to be sure you were okay."

Despite its deep timbre, his voice was husky and infinitely gentle, and Tess felt a lump form in her throat. What was the matter with her? It seemed this morning the least little thing produced extreme emotion. She wondered if new mothers were always so sensitive.

"I'm fine. Couldn't be better, in fact," she said in her perkiest voice.

"Are you sure?" Absently, he stroked the tender skin on the back of her hand with his thumb. He watched the action for a moment, then looked into her eyes again. "I worried all night that I might have bungled things and done you permanent damage."

"I'm perfectly all right. Really. The doctor who checked me over last night was in first thing this morning. He gave me a clean bill of health."

Her stomach fluttered. She was acutely aware of his hip pressing against hers, so tight she could feel his heat through the covers. His nearness, his clean masculine scent, his intensity, overwhelmed her. Unable to hold that steady stare, she looked down, but the sight of their joined hands sent her gaze skittering out the window. Her twanging nerves set her tongue in motion.

"So. Tell me," she said brightly. "How is your family? And Mike? I'll bet they were relieved to see you and Reilly. They must have been terribly worried. Hurricanes can be so destructive. I'm really looking forward to meeting—"

"Dammit, Tess. Why are you chattering like that? And why the hell won't you look at me?"

"I . . . I . . ."

"Tess?" Hooking his finger beneath her chin, he turned her face toward him. He stared at her flaming cheeks. "Good Lord. Don't tell me you're embarrassed?"

More scalding heat rushed to her face and spread over her chest and shoulders. She stared at the teddy bear, still clutched in her hand, and nodded.

"Look at me, Tess."

The gentle command brooked no denial, and slowly, reluctantly, her eyelids lifted. Her heart skipped a beat. Never had she expected to see such warmth and caring in that hard face, those vivid blue eyes.

Cupping his callused palm against her cheek, he looked deep into her eyes. "There's no reason to feel embarrassed, Tess. Delivering Molly was the most beautiful thing that has ever happened to me. I wouldn't trade the experience for anything in the world. Believe that.

"Somehow we've become friends." The corner of his mouth twisted ruefully. "I'm not quite sure how it happened, but there it is. And, honey, there's no need for embarrassment or shyness between good friends." He tipped his head to one side and gave her a coaxing half smile. "Agreed?"

Tess was so relieved she went limp. She smiled sheepishly and sagged back against the pillow. All the tension drained out of her like air escaping a balloon. "Agreed."

"That's my girl." He leaned down and brushed her lips with his.

Tess was sure that he had intended it to be merely a soft salute of friendship, but at the first touch the kiss set off sensations that took them by surprise.

Her breath caught. Her heart stumbled, then took off at a gallop. She tingled all over. The pleasure was intense, like a shower of sparks cascading through her. She felt the shudder that rippled through Ryan's big body and knew that he was experiencing the same feelings.

Slowly he pulled back partway. In the taut silence they stared into each other's eyes, bewildered, mesmerized. Neither moved nor spoke. The air around them throbbed and hummed.

His breath puffed between parted lips, erratic and shallow, feathering her cheek. A pulse beat rapidly in his temple.

Tess's heart hammered painfully against her ribs, then jumped right up into her throat when Ryan's gaze dropped to her parted lips. He leaned forward, slowly, and her eyelids drifted shut.

Before their lips could touch, the door burst open and Mike sang out, "Hey, Tess! Look who I brought to meet you. My grandma and grandpa McCall."

Ryan sprang off the bed as though the lumpy hospital mattress had suddenly caught fire. He recovered himself quickly, however, and when he turned to his family his face wore its usual indifferent expression. Only his eyes revealed any emotion; they glittered a silent warning at his brother.

Reilly's wicked smile merely grew wider. "Nice roses," he drawled, flicking a yellow flower petal.

Tess was so mortified she wanted to curl into a ball and hide under the covers. Good Lord, what on earth was the matter with her? What would Ryan's family think? A fiery blush swept over her from the soles of her feet to the roots of her hair, suffusing her body with heat.

If Ryan's parents noticed the intimate scene they had interrupted or Tess's discomfort they had the good manners to pretend otherwise. With an aplomb that Tess thought astounding, Ryan made the introductions, and Maggie and Colin McCall came forward, greeting her with smiles and warmth.

"Tess, my dear, we're so happy to meet you, at last." Maggie took Tess's hand in both of hers. "Mike has told us so much about you."

"Yes, indeed. All we've heard is Tess, Tess, Tess ever since the boy arrived. But in all that chatter, he neglected to tell us how lovely you are," Colin said gallantly. "Although, I must admit, I'm not really surprised. We McCall men have always had a fine eye for feminine beauty."

"Awww, Grampa," Mike groaned, rolling his eyes and turning pink to the tips of his ears.

Grinning, Colin rumpled the boy's hair, his pale gray eyes twinkling with devilment and sheer enjoyment of life.

Ryan and Reilly may have inherited their black hair and blue eyes from their mother, but it was apparent to Tess that Reilly at least had his father's personality and easygoing nature.

"I'm just sorry we had to meet under these circumstances." Maggie gave Tess's hand another squeeze. "It must have been horrible for you, my dear, giving birth in the back of that cluttered Jeep in a storm. Why, you must have been terrified."

"I was, at first. But then things started happening so fast there wasn't time to think of anything except having the baby." Faced with Maggie's open friendliness and warmth, Tess began to relax, her embarrassment dissipating.

"Yeah, and I missed it." Mike shot his father and Tess a surly look. "I told you I shouldn't have come here. I wanted to be there when Tess had the baby."

"Trust me on this one, sport. You lucked out. That was the most hair-raising ride of my life. I can't remember ever being that scared. I tell you, pal, my heart may never be the same. Of course, luckily for Tess, I kept a cool head and handled myself well."

"Oh, yeah. Right." Ryan snorted.

"Hey! I did my part." Reilly gave his brother a wounded look. "I'll have you know it took nerves of steel to drive with all that going on in the back."

"I'm sure it did. And here I haven't even thanked you yet." Fighting back a chuckle, Tess took his hand and gave it a squeeze. "Thank you, Reilly, for all that you did for me. I really do appreciate your help."

"Anything for you, gorgeous." Reilly slanted his brother a smug look and brought her hand to his lips for a kiss. "Anyway, it was nothing."

"You got that right," Ryan muttered.

Mike looked at his father, his expression changing from belligerent to awed. "Gee, Dad. Did you really deliver Tess's baby in the back of our Cherokee, like Grandma said?"

"Tess was the one who did all the work. I just helped out a little."

"Wow. Wait'll I tell the guys."

"Well, I for one am thankful that my sons were there to help you when you needed them." Maggie gave Tess's hand a pat. "Are you feeling all right now? I hope you're not suffering any unpleasant aftereffects from the ordeal."

"No, I'm fine. Actually, I feel wonderful. So does Molly."

"So it's Molly, is it? Och, a beautiful name for a beautiful colleen," Colin said in an Irish brogue that rolled from his tongue with the ease of a mountain brook flowing over smooth stones. Grinning, he rubbed his palms together. "What do you say we go down to the nursery and have a look at the little darlin'?"

"Can we, Dad?"

"Sure."

"Certainly you can." Tess sat up gingerly and reached for her robe. "Just give me a minute and I'll go with you."

"You'll do no such thing," Ryan barked. "You're staying in that bed where you belong."

"Don't be silly, Ryan. A Dr. Tuttle came by first thing this morning and checked both Molly and me over. He says we're doing fine. He even encouraged me to walk around. He said it was the best way for me to regain my strength."

"Huh. What the hell does he know? I've known Joe Bob Tuttle all my life, and believe me, he's nothing but a snot-nosed, know-it-all jerk with the brains of a flea. I wouldn't trust a dog to his care."

"I have to side with Ryan on this one," Reilly put in. He looked pale and shaky at the mere idea of Tess getting out of bed. "Look, honey. Maybe you ought to just lie back and take it easy for a while."

"Don't pay any attention to these two. They haven't liked Joe Bob Tuttle since they were all in the third grade together," Maggie said, helping Tess into her robe.

"And with good cause. Don't you remember? He chopped down our tree house."

"Only because you and Ryan were behaving like typical nasty little boys and refused to let him join your club. He was hurt and upset, so he retaliated."

"Yeah, well, we didn't want the jerk in our club." A satisfied grin spread over Reilly's face. "But Ryan got even. Bloodied his nose good."

"Wow. Did you really, Dad?"

"Reilly McCall, you will not talk about such things in front of this child. You hear me? I don't want him to grow up thinking that the way to solve a problem is with his fists. And as for you, young man. Don't you go letting your uncle give you any ideas. I'll have no hooligans in this family. Is that clear?"

"Yes, ma'am," Mike agreed in a subdued voice.

"Good...now let's go see Molly."

When Tess eased out of bed, Ryan was there to slip his arm around her waist. His sudden nearness made her pulse flutter, nevertheless she leaned into him, grateful for his support. She was a lot shakier than she had thought.

She took small, tentative steps. He tried to shorten his long-legged stride to match her shuffling gait, but the effort caused him to wobble comically.

Tess looked down at her well-manicured toes peeking out of the white satin slippers, and the large well-worn cowboy boots clumping along beside them. It was heaven to see her feet again at last. She only hoped they survived this walk.

"Are you sure you should be doing this?" Ryan questioned. "You're not too steady on your feet, you know."

"Would you be if you'd just had a baby?" his mother asked dryly.

"My point, exactly."

"Ryan, please don't fuss. I really am fine. Not only did Dr. Tuttle say I could walk around, he gave me permission to travel back to Houston any time I wanted. I explained that you and Reilly would probably be in a hurry to return, now that the worst of the storm has passed."

She felt Ryan shrug. "No hurry. Things are in such a mess down there it's chaos. I heard on the radio that power is still out over most of the city. Anyway, after all the rain, it'll take the ground at the site at least a week to dry out enough for us to move the heavy equipment back in."

"But what about our apartments? What if they're damaged?"

"Same thing. With so much damage all over town the contractors will be swamped with jobs. It'll probably be a week or more before the owner will even be able to get bids. We're here—so we might as well spend the weekend."

They found Mike, who had run ahead, at the nursery with his nose pressed against the glass. They came to stand beside him, but Ryan didn't remove his hand from Tess's waist. She told herself he was just being helpful, lending his support, but her heart thumped wildly anyway.

Tess knew she was being foolish, considering what they had been through together, but she couldn't help it. She was much too aware of the hard strength in the big body pressed against her side, of his heat seeping through her gown and robe, of his tantalizing male smell—much more aware than she had any business being, she told herself severely.

Molly had been taken out of the incubator and placed in a bassinet, but it was at the back of the room. When the nurse saw Tess, she waved and grinned, and hurried over to pick up the sleeping infant and bring her to the nursery window.

"Gosh. She sure is little," Mike murmured.

"Little! I'll have you know she weighs five pounds and four ounces. That's a very respectable weight, especially considering she was two weeks premature."

"How come she's all red and wrinkly?"

"Mike!"

"Well, she is."

"She's no such thing. She's adorable."

"Grandma's right. She's a beauty, just like her mother," Colin said, and Tess beamed with pride.

"Son, you'd be red and wrinkly, too, if you'd gone through the ordeal she did last night. Just give her a week or so—she'll pretty up."

Tess looked up to thank Ryan, but the words flitted right out of her mind and her breath caught. His intense gaze was fixed on the baby, every trace of harshness and indifference gone from his face. His expression now held so much warmth and tenderness, it brought tears to her eyes.

He's such a complex man, Tess thought. So hard and cold on the outside. Yet, when it came to babies and small children, he was a marshmallow. A faint smile tugged at her mouth. *And*—luckily for her—pregnant ladies.

Molly began to fret. She puckered up to cry, flailing her arms in building outrage. By accident, she found her thumb, and the tantrum ended abruptly as she gave a little shuddering sigh and began to suck.

Everyone laughed, including Ryan.

Tess watched the crinkles form around his eyes, watched those chiseled lips stretch wide with merriment and affection, and she felt a sharp pain in the region of her heart.

No, he was not really complex, she amended. And certainly not cold. Just wounded. He had loved once, deeply, had trusted a woman with his heart, only to have it stepped on. Now he worked hard at keeping people—women especially—away and guarding himself against more pain. But inside . . . inside he yearned for the very love he spurned.

The nurse unwrapped Molly, and she released her thumb and stretched and yawned.

Mike laughed. "Lookit her scrunch up her face. And look, she's got legs like a frog."

"Michael Patrick McCall! Shame on you. If you keep making remarks like that Tess is going to forbid you to get anywhere near her baby."

Mike flashed a cocky grin. "Naw, she wouldn't do that. Me'n Tess are pals. Aren't we, Tess?"

"Yes, we are," Tess agreed, biting back a grin. "But I'm warning you, *pal,* you're skating on thin ice. So watch it."

Mike chuckled and gave her a dig in the ribs with his elbow.

"Oh, hey, would you look at that. She's smiling. Ahh, aren't you a cutie," Reilly crooned with a sappy grin. "You're gonna break a ton of hearts one of these days, Molly girl." He cocked his head and gave a wistful sigh. "You know... I wouldn't mind having a kid myself."

"You? A parent?" Ryan snorted. "Oh, yeah. Right."

"Hey. I resent that. I happen to think I'd make a pretty darn good father."

"Say, Uncle Reilly. That reminds me of a joke. Do you know what the tuba calls his father?"

Reilly rolled his eyes. "Oh, Lord. I know I'm going to regret this but, what the hell, I'll bite. No, Mike, I don't know. What does a tuba call his father?"

"Uoom pah pah."

Making a sound somewhere between a groan and a growl, Reilly hung his head. Then he lunged and hooked his arm around the giggling boy's neck. "Can I choke him, Ryan? Pleeeese. Just a little?"

"Sure. Be my guest. But I'm taking Tess back to her room now. She's been on her feet long enough." He looked around and frowned. "Where's Mom? She was here just a minute ago."

"You know your mother. She probably saw someone she knew and wandered off to talk. She'll show up," Colin said without a trace of concern. "Go ahead and take Tess back. We'll stay here and admire Molly a while longer."

No sooner had Tess settled back into the bed when Maggie breezed through the door waving a piece of paper. "Pack Tess's bags while I go check her out of here. I saw Joe Bob making his rounds and I talked him into signing her release. She's coming home with us."

"What!"

Tess was so floored by the announcement, she gaped at the other woman. By the time she found her tongue, Maggie had shoved the paper into her son's hand and was pushing him out the door. "On second thought, you go take care of the paperwork while I pack her things."

"But Mrs. McCall—"

"Did Joe Bob give you any argument about this?" Ryan paused in the doorway long enough to ask.

"Humph. A little, at first, for all the good it did him. I reminded that young man that when he was small I used to wipe his nose and that I'd paddled his rear end a time or two as well, *and* I told him I wasn't going to stand for any foolishness out of him now. I pointed out that if Tess could travel all the way back to Houston, she could certainly come home and stay with us."

Ryan shook his head and gave Tess a dry look. "Joe Bob didn't stand a chance. And neither do you. You might as well give in." Without waiting for a reply or the outcome of the discussion, he disappeared down the hall.

"Mrs. McCall, I appreciate your offer, but I really can't impose on you this way."

"Nonsense. It isn't an imposition at all. We'd love to have you. And, please, call me Maggie."

"But, Mrs . . . uh . . . Maggie, I can't—"

"Now, child, there is absolutely no reason for you to pay money to stay in this depressing place all alone, when you can come home with us and be taken care of properly."

"But—"

Maggie turned from the closet with one of Tess's nightgowns in her hand. "Don't tell me that you'd *rather* stay here?" she asked with a touch of hurt in her voice.

"Oh, no! It's not tha—"

"Good. Because you'll certainly be more comfortable in my guest room. The food's better, too."

"But—"

"Good heavens, child, why are you arguing? You came up here in the first place to stay with us."

"But... that was before I had Molly. A new baby is a lot of work and trouble. I can't ask you to take that on."

"Oh pooh. If that's all that's worrying you, just put it right out of your mind. Why, heavens. Don't you realize that Molly is half the reason I want you to stay with us? To tell you the truth, I can't wait to get my hands on her. It's been too many years since there was a baby in our house."

Tess opened her mouth, then shut it again. With a defeated sigh, she sank back against the pillows and watched the older woman bustle around the room. Ryan was right; she hadn't stood a chance.

A half hour later, Ryan turned the Cherokee into the driveway of his parents' home on the outskirts of Crockett. Sitting far off the country lane, nestled in a stand of huge oak and pecan trees, the rambling Victorian house reminded Tess of an elegant old dowager.

Through the tinted, rain-splattered windows, she got a blurry view of wraparound porches trimmed with gingerbread and bordered by nandina and rosebushes. There were brick walkways and colorful flower beds of petunias and begonias, battered and drooping now under the heavy downpour. In the yard she caught a glimpse of a white lat-

ticework gazebo, an old-fashioned two-seater glider swing
and an overflowing birdbath.

Ryan brought the vehicle to a halt under the porte co-
chere at the side entrance. Over his objections, Tess climbed
out unassisted and followed his mother, who was carrying
Molly, into the house.

Matching her slow pace, Ryan walked beside Tess in silence, his face set in its usual remote mask. Since leaving the
hospital, he had barely spoken to her. She knew he was
probably thinking about that kiss they had shared. How
could he not be? The memory of that sizzling exchange had
been hovering in the back of her mind ever since it occurred, tormenting her, raising questions.

Had that kiss changed things? Ruined their fledgling
friendship? And most disturbing of all; what would have
happened if his family hadn't arrived when they did?

She glanced at Ryan out of the corner of her eye. Was he
angry? Did he blame her for what happened? From his expression it was impossible to tell, but she had a feeling that
he was not pleased that his mother had insisted she stay at
their home.

They reached the foyer, but when Tess started to follow
Maggie upstairs, Ryan bit out a curse.

This time he didn't ask; he simply swooped her up in his
arms and started up the steps.

"Ryan!" she shrieked, and flung her arms around his
neck, clutching him frantically. "What are you doing? I can
walk."

"Not up stairs, you won't."

"But—"

"Save your breath. I'm not putting you down."

The side door banged, and a few seconds later, Mike
skidded to a halt in the entrance. Holding Tess's suitcase
with both hands, he gaped. "What are you doing with Tess,
Dad?"

His uncle and grandfather walked into the foyer in time to catch the question. Reilly grinned up at them, his eyes dancing wickedly, but he put his hand on Mike's shoulder. "Now what do you think he's doing, sport? He's giving her a lift upstairs. Tess just had a baby. Remember?"

"Do you feel bad, Tess?" the boy asked anxiously.

"No. No, of course not. Your father is just being overly cautious. That's all."

Ignoring the exchange, Ryan continued up the stairs without pause.

"You mean he's showing good sense," Reilly called after them.

Tess strove to look unaffected and tried to pretend that her nerves were not fluttering. She couldn't remember ever being so aware of a man.

Ryan's body felt like warm steel. She had always known that he was strong, but being held snugly against that broad chest brought home to her just how much raw power he possessed. He carried her with ridiculous ease. He wasn't even breathing hard, for heaven's sake.

Tess stared at the swirls in his ear, the stubby ends of the trimmed hair that brushed the top. This close, she could see the pores in his skin and each individual eyelash—even the faint brush marks in his hair. His clean male scent surrounded her and made her sightly light-headed—or perhaps it was just the result of being swept off her feet.

When they reached the top of the stairs, she glanced at him and said politely, "You can put me down now."

He gave her a sardonic look and kept walking. "What's the point? We're almost there."

He carried her to a room at the end of the hall. Maggie turned from folding back the covers on the bed and smiled when she saw them.

"Just put her down right there, son," she said unnecessarily, as Ryan strode across the room and lowered Tess onto the mattress.

The four-poster bed, with its lacy crocheted canopy and patchwork bedspread in shades of lavender, cream and silvery green, dominated the high-ceilinged room. Braided rugs in the same colors lay scattered across the glossy heart-of-pine floors, and tiny violets dotted the cream wallpaper in a random pattern. Ivy trailed from a hanging copper pot beside the window, where gauzy Priscilla curtains framed the rain-washed panes.

"I think you'll be comfortable here." Maggie shifted the baby to her other arm and reached around Tess to help her slip out of her robe.

"It's charming." The room smelled of lemon furniture polish and the floral potpourri in the china bowl on the dresser. "I can't imagine not being comfortable here. Thank you, Maggie, for having us."

Tess glanced around, and her gaze met Ryan's. He stood just a few feet away, watching her in that unnerving, intent way of his. "Are you all right?" he asked.

"Yes. I'm fine." Self-conscious, she eased her legs onto the bed and pulled the covers up over her breasts.

Ryan hesitated, as though he wanted to say more. Then his jaws clenched and he dipped his chin in an abrupt nod. "Good. Then I'll leave you in Mom's hands. I'll send Mike up with your things."

Tess watched him stride out the door and wondered why she felt so desolate...so...abandoned.

Lord, what was happening to him? Halting in the hallway outside the guest bedroom, Ryan leaned his back against the wall and closed his eyes.

What was it about Tess that made him feel so damned protective? So...possessive? Just because he'd delivered her baby, that didn't mean that she was his, or that Molly was his child.

But, heaven help him, that was exactly how he felt. Anxious and proud and happy and scared all at once.

He didn't want to let Tess out of his sight. He'd had to make himself leave her room. That scared the living hell out of him.

And there was that kiss. What had he been thinking of? Ryan dragged his hand down over his face and exhaled wearily. That was the trouble; he hadn't been thinking at all. He had let himself get caught up in the emotion of the moment and responded to her softness, her sweetness.

The storm of feelings the simple kiss had set off had taken him by surprise. Recalling the startled look in those wide, whiskey-colored eyes, he knew it had surprised Tess as well.

He had to nip this thing in the bud. Now, before it got out of hand.

Eyes closed, Ryan leaned his head back against the wall and grimaced. But dammit! He liked Tess. He liked being with her. For the first time in eight years he was enjoying a woman on more than just a physical level. He didn't want to give that up.

He opened his eyes and looked around at the familiar old house. Maybe that was it. Maybe it was just the forced intimacy of being there together under his parents' roof. Once they were back in Houston, in their own apartments, living separate lives, things would be back in perspective and their relationship would return to what it had been before this trip.

In the meantime, he would back off a step or two.

## Chapter Eight

By Sunday Hurricane Homer was merely a memory. The sun blazed down from a cloudless sky and the smells of barbecuing chicken and fresh mown grass hung in the air.

Tess sat alone on the veranda. The porch swing creaked as it swayed back and forth. Absently, she nudged the floor with her toe to keep the lazy motion going and sighed, her wistful gaze on the action in the yard.

Wearing a chef's hat and an apron emblazoned with the words, Insult the Cook at Your Own Risk, Colin manned the barbecue grill. The rest of the clan were playing softball.

At the pitcher's position, Ryan's cousin rubbed the ball in his mitt and flexed his broad shoulders, getting ready for the windup. David and his wife, Abby, had been visiting his parents for the past week. They had intended to leave on Friday, but when they learned that Reilly and Ryan had arrived, they stayed for the weekend.

David reared back and fired a pitch over the plate.

"Strike!" Dorothy called.

Reilly lowered the bat and shot his aunt a dark glare. "In a pig's eye."

She held her ground, unperturbed by his opinion of her call.

On the next pitch the bat cracked against the ball. Shouts erupted and Reilly took off for first. At second base, Ryan made a leap for the ball, but it sailed over his head just out of reach. Exhibiting surprising agility, Maggie raced up from the outfield, caught the ball on its second bounce and tossed it to Ryan. Reilly changed his mind about stretching the hit into a double and pulled up at first, calling a taunt to his twin.

Tess laughed at his exuberance, but the sound had barely died when, against her will, her gaze drifted back to Ryan.

For the past two days she had seen little of him. She told herself that he was busy with his family, that he was giving her time to recuperate, but deep down she didn't really believe any of it. Ever since that kiss, things had changed between them. She had the uneasy feeling that he was avoiding her.

He looked terrific. A lock of ebony hair hung across his forehead and his bronze skin glowed with a sheen of perspiration. Wearing a pair of cutoffs and a loose muscle shirt that showed off his broad chest and impressive shoulders, he stood with his legs spread wide, the epitome of a healthy, virile male.

"Hey, look who's awake."

Startled, Tess glanced over her shoulder. "Rebecca. I didn't see you there. Why aren't you playing?"

"I am. But I'm last in the batting order so I came in to get a drink. While I was in the kitchen I heard this little sweetie pie fussing." Ryan's sister-in-law pushed open the screen door and stepped out onto the porch, carrying Molly cradled in one arm and a glass of iced tea in her other hand. "I tried to quiet her but she wasn't having any of it. I think she wants her mommy. She was soaked through, so I changed her diaper and her gown.''

''You didn't have to do that. You should have called me.''

''I didn't mind. Actually, I enjoyed it.''

Rebecca's response was typical. Ryan's family fussed over Tess and pampered her as though she were visiting royalty. For the past two days she had not been allowed to lift a finger except to eat the delicious meals and snacks that Maggie prepared, or to feed Molly. Her daughter had merely to let out a peep and someone was there to change her diaper or rock her or whisk her away to be cooed over and cuddled.

Molly quieted the instant she felt her mother's arms enfold her. Tess held the baby close for a minute, inhaling her sweet scent, then she laid her in her lap. She fingered the lace trim on the gown Rebecca had chosen and smiled, touched anew by the warmth and generosity of these people.

Molly's early arrival had caught Tess totally unprepared. The nursery in her Houston apartment was stocked with every conceivable item needed to care for a newborn, but all she'd had with her was one tiny infant's gown that she had packed for the baby to wear home from the hospital. The problem had seemed gigantic to Tess, but she hadn't counted on Maggie.

In no time at all a crib and dressing table had been brought down from the attic and set up in the guest room, Ryan had been dispatched to the local pharmacy with a list of supplies, and Maggie had started calling friends. By noon that first day, four women had stopped by to drop off boxes of baby clothes.

A burst of shouts and whistles drew their eyes back to the game.

Wearing a pair of skimpy shorts and a halter top, Abby stood over the garbage can lid that served as home plate, her gorgeous long legs spread wide in a batter's stance.

"Strike!" Dorothy called when David burned one past her.

*"Strike!"* Abby whirled on her mother-in-law. "What do you mean, strike? The ball was a mile wide. It's not fair. You're partial because he's your son."

Dorothy shrugged, unfazed. "So sue me."

Eyes narrowed, Abby thrust out her chin. "All right. If that's the way you wanna play..."

She started to take up her stance again, then fluttered her eyelashes innocently. "Wait. Why, I do believe my laces are loose." Taking her time about it, she turned her back on her husband and bent from the waist to retie her shoe.

"Uh-oh, cuz. You're in trouble now," Travis taunted from the sidelines.

David stood stock still, staring at the shapely bottom stuck up in the air, while from all around him came catcalls and whistles.

Straightening, Abby blew David a kiss.

Tess chuckled and shook her head, but the sound came out wistful and a bit lonely.

"I know the feeling. They're really something, aren't they?"

Looking up, Tess saw that Rebecca was gazing at her in-laws, her lovely face soft with love.

"Yes. Yes they are. I don't think I've ever known such a close-knit clan. I hate to admit it, but I'm envious. I had a very happy childhood, but being around this family makes me realize how much I missed, being an only child."

"Mmm. I know what you mean. I spent most of my life wishing I could be one of them. And now I am," Rebecca said softly. "At times I can still hardly believe it." She took a sip of tea, her adoring gaze drifting to where her husband stood on the sidelines, jeering at David and encouraging Abby's antics.

Tess followed her gaze. This McCall brother had come as something of a surprise. She had expected him to be a younger version of Ryan and Reilly, but Travis had taken after their father in every way. Not only had he been blessed with Colin's disposition and personality, he had the same blond hair and sexy, silvery gray eyes. Though totally opposite in looks and coloring, he was every bit as handsome as his older brothers.

He also seemed to be the wildest, the most unconventional. Which was why it had come as a surprise to learn that he was the only one of the McCall or Blaine offspring who had settled down in Crockett. The previous year he had quit his job with the FBI and joined his father and uncle in their law firm. He and Rebecca lived just a ten-minute walk from his parents' home.

"Oh, my goodness, would you look at that," Rebecca hooted. "Watching her now, no one would ever guess that when David met Abby a little over a year ago she was a shy little thing."

The count was three and oh, but Abby was still doing everything she could to rattle her husband. She preened and posed provocatively. She adjusted her halter top. Fanning herself, she lifted her hair off her neck and arched her back.

"Way to go, Abby!"

"Oh, yeah, baby. Work it. Work it."

Her teammates kept up an encouraging chatter. Their opponents groaned and yelled "foul" and "unfair tactics."

"Don't let her get to you, son," Joe Blaine called from the outfield.

When Abby finally assumed the batting stance again, she blew her husband another kiss, braced the bat over her right shoulder... and wiggled her bottom.

In a daze, David released a pitch.

"Ball four!"

Abby's teammates cheered. David's groaned.

"All right, you shameless hussy—take your base," Dorothy ordered, laughing.

Making a show of it, Abby dropped the bat, dusted off her hands, and sauntered to first base.

The two women on the porch laughed along with everyone else.

"Oh, I love it," Rebecca crowed. "She is going to lead David a merry chase until they plant him in the ground."

Ryan's sister was up next. Tess's own hair was carroty but Meghan's was a pure bright red. The curly mane sticking out of the back of her baseball cap glittered like fire in the sunshine.

On the second pitch Meghan caught a piece of David's curve ball and popped a high one. Ryan backpeddled a few steps, snagged the ball out of the air and rifled it to Mike, who was playing catcher.

Reilly tagged third at a dead run and kept going.

"Slide! Slide!" his teammates yelled as he pounded for home.

The ball drilled Mike's glove, and Reilly's muscles bunched. He came in low under his nephew's reaching arm and they both went down in a tangle of arms and legs.

"Safe!" Dorothy yelled.

A brouhaha erupted instantly.

Every member of the family came running to the plate, shouting and gesturing. Reilly bounded to his feet and stood nose to nose with David. Meghan whipped off her baseball cap and swatted Ryan with it. He responded by snatching it out of her hand and returning the favor. Even Maggie and Dorothy were shaking their fists and yelling at one another.

"Oh, my," Tess murmured, but Rebecca merely laughed.

"Don't worry about it. Give them five minutes and they'll be laughing and hugging. One thing about this family, they may squabble and tease, but they love one another fiercely. Let one of them need help, and they all come running." Rebecca slanted Tess a sidelong look. "Of course, they do sometimes tend to be a bit overprotective, as I'm sure you've noticed. If they've seemed a little ... well ... pushy and inquisitive, please don't take it personally. It's just that they care about Ryan."

Tess blinked. "I... I'm not sure I understand."

Rebecca studied her blank expression. "Don't tell me you didn't realize you were being checked out?"

"Checked out?"

"Of course. That's why David and Abby extended their visit. And why else do you think Meghan cleared her schedule and hotfooted it down here as soon as her mother called and told her about you?"

Stunned, Tess looked at the group in the yard. The altercation had been settled, and as the players resumed their positions, her appalled gaze locked on the petite redhead returning to the sidelines.

Meghan had come barreling up the driveway in her snappy yellow sports car only the night before while they had been eating dinner. At the time Tess had thought that the trip from Dallas was a long one to make for just an overnight visit, but she assumed that Meghan had merely been lonesome for her family.

"But... this is terrible."

"Don't be upset, Tess. We're all happy about you and Ryan. Oh, I'll admit at first when we heard that you were pregnant we were a little concerned, but now that we've met you, we're delighted. The whole family has been so worried about Ryan. We were beginning to give up hope that he would ever care for another woman, after Julia."

"But you don't understand. Ryan and I are just friends."

Rebecca merely smiled.

Tess had no more luck convincing the other women.

The softball game was halted temporarily in favor of lunch, and afterward, when the men wandered off to look at Joe's new pickup truck, Tess broached the subject, for all the good it did her. Abby laughed as though she had told a huge joke, and Maggie and Dorothy merely humored her.

"We understand, my dear. If you say that you and my son are just friends, then of course we believe you," Maggie assured her, but Tess saw the sly look that passed between the sisters.

Meghan was more blunt.

"Just friends? Oh, pul-leeze. Who're you kidding? I've seen the way Ryan looks at you. The man practically devours you with his eyes, for pity's sake. It's downright embarrassing."

Nothing Tess said had the least effect. By the time the softball game resumed, she had tried every tack she could think of, short of getting Ryan to set them straight, and she doubted even that would help. She was so frustrated, she wanted to scream. There was just no talking to some people.

Picking up on her mother's tension, Molly began to fret. Tess held her against her shoulder and patted her back. "There, there, sweetheart. Everything's okay," she murmured into the baby's ear as she watched the play from the porch.

They were wrong, of course. The idea that Ryan could be interested in her romantically was absurd. That the two of them were even friends was a minor miracle, given their beginning.

For a moment she debated about actually discussing the matter with Ryan but quickly rejected the idea. He would only be furious, which wouldn't help their relationship any. Heaven knew, it was shaky enough as it was.

"Eventually his family will just have to accept that they were wrong," she whispered to Molly, patting her tiny diapered bottom.

"Are you sure you won't reconsider and stay?" Maggie asked one last time, hugging Tess goodbye.

"Thank you, Maggie, but I can't. I really should get back."

The offer was tempting. Maggie could have no idea just how tempting. During the past four days Ryan's relatives had all taken her under their collective wing as though she were one of them. As an only child, she had never known the special security and sense of belonging that comes from being part of a large, loving family. For over nine years she had not even had the comfort of her parents' love. She was an adult, it was true, an independent woman with a child of her own now, but still . . . it had been quite wonderful to be, if only for a little while, on the receiving end of the Mc-Calls' warmth and protection and Maggie's maternal cosseting.

Too wonderful, actually. It would be entirely too easy to get used to that sort of thing, and that would be foolish. As comforting as the past four days had been, as much as she adored Ryan's family, the truth was she had no place in their lives.

She and Molly were alone. She was responsible for the two of them—no one else. Certainly not Ryan. He had stumbled into her life against his will and been coerced into helping her by his son and his own strict conscience. The only reason she was here with him now was through a quirk of fate. Or perhaps, more accurately, good fortune on her part.

The wisest thing to do was to return home and begin her life with Molly.

"At least promise me you'll come back soon for a visit," Maggie insisted, looking longingly from Tess to Molly. For a moment Tess thought the older woman was going to cry.

"I'll try," she hedged. Privately, though, she thought that a very unlikely possibility.

"Here now, you two. None of that weepy stuff. C'mon, Mom, give us a hug so we can be on our way." Reilly wrapped his brawny arms around his mother and swung her in a circle.

"Reilly, you big oaf! Put me down," Maggie whooped, but her incipient tears turned to squeals of merriment.

Amid laughter and good-natured teasing, goodbyes were said all around. Molly was fussed over and nuzzled by everyone, then handed to Tess when she had settled into the back seat of the Cherokee beside Mike. She buckled the baby into a borrowed car seat, then they were on their way. As they drove down the long drive, Tess looked back at the crowd of waving people standing in the yard, a heavy feeling in her heart.

The ride home was uneventful and much easier than Tess had anticipated. Molly, bless her, slept like an angel all the way, and if any disturbing undercurrents lingered between Tess and Ryan, they were defused by the presence of Reilly and Mike.

On the outskirts of Houston they began to see evidence of storm damage. The destruction became more apparent with each passing mile—signs down, light stanchions and utility poles snapped, trees uprooted, their broken branches and other debris strewn everywhere, houses and small buildings demolished, traffic lights still inoperable, snarling traffic. Even so, Tess was not prepared for the sight that greeted them when they reached their apartment complex.

Mike's eyes bugged out. "Wow! This is awesome!"

"I'll say. This place looks like a war zone, Hoss."

Tess could only stare.

The front two buildings of the complex were all but leveled. Other's had broken windows and roof shingles missing, stripped right down to the bare tar paper. A few buildings—those tucked in the center of the complex—were relatively unscathed. Luckily, Tess and Ryan's was one of the latter.

Her car, however, had not fared so well. One of the few left in the parking lot, it had been blown completely over into a corner of the brick fence. Trash and storm debris covered most of it. The little compact reminded Tess of a dead bug lying on its back.

Ryan inspected Tess's apartment first. A window had been blown out in the living room. The draperies and carpet were ruined and the wind had blown over a table and shattered a lamp. The roof had leaked in a couple of places. One, luckily, was over the bathtub but the other had collapsed a section of the kitchen ceiling and the rain pouring in had buckled the tile floor.

Standing in the middle of the living room with Molly in her arms, Tess forlornly surveyed the mess while Ryan moved through the apartment, checking the telephone for a dial tone, flipping light switches, turning faucets on and off.

"The phone's out but at least the power has been restored. You're a little waterlogged in places and it's not too pretty, but it's livable. I think you can manage for a few days until the repairs are done."

"Ryan's right." Reilly patted Tess's shoulder. "Cheer up, sweetheart. I know it looks bad, but it won't take a good contractor long to put things right."

"I wouldn't drink the water, though, until we get it tested," Ryan added. "As soon as we unload the truck, I'm going to go get some glass to reglaze that window. While I'm out I'll pick up some bottled water and whatever else you need. Why don't you make a list while I go check out my place?" Motioning to his son and brother, he started for the door. "C'mon, Mike, and give Reilly and me a hand with the luggage."

"Ryan, you don't ha—"

He halted and looked back at her, one eyebrow cocked, and she bit her lower lip. She had been about to say that he didn't have to keep looking after her, but then she realized that she had no idea how she would cope on her own.

The trip from Crockett had exhausted her. She was going to have her hands full just taking care of Molly. Had she been lucky enough to still have a car in operating condition, she was certainly in no shape to drive, or to go running around looking for drinking water or window panes. Even if she could manage that much she didn't have the foggiest idea how to reglaze a window. She could tell by the look in Ryan's eyes that he knew it, too.

"That is...I...uh..." Tess exhaled a defeated sigh. "Thank you, Ryan."

"Don't worry about it." His gaze flickered over her, taking in her sagging shoulders, and his expression gentled. "On second thought, forget about that list. Why don't you just go get some rest and let me take care of things for now."

She smiled wanly. "Thanks. I think I will."

When the door closed behind him, Tess trudged into the bedroom. She didn't bother to put Molly into her crib but curled up on her bed with the baby, sighing as her head touched the pillow.

Where had she gone wrong? It had all seemed so simple when she had made her plans. She was a mature adult, fully capable of coping on her own. She and her baby would lead an independent, self-reliant life. Now her apartment was a wreck, her car was demolished and she was totally dependent on her macho neighbor for the tiniest thing. Worst of all, at the moment she didn't even care.

Sighing again, Tess burrowed her face into the pillow. Tomorrow. Beginning tomorrow, she would start working on being independent. Right now, she was just too tired.

"When we finish here and take a look at my place, you want to go check out the site and the equipment barn?" Reilly asked as he followed Ryan into his apartment.

"Maybe later. First I'm going to take a look around the complex and work up an estimate on the repairs and rebuilding."

"What for?"

"So we can bid on this job."

"What! Hey, I thought we weren't going to take on any more small jobs like this now that we've got the development project going?"

"Yeah, well, you're forgetting that I live here. I want to make sure the work is done right."

"Ahh, I see. Good point." Reilly eyed his brother shrewdly, his lips twitching. "And, of course, if you're here all day overseeing the work, you'll also be able to keep an eye on a certain little redhead and her baby. Right?"

The narrow-eyed look Ryan shot him would have made any other man back off. Reilly grinned.

"So? You got a problem with that?"

"Me? Heck no."

"Somebody has to give her a hand. At least for a while, until she's stronger," Ryan muttered, stalking through his apartment. "And she's too damned proud to ask for help."

"Hey, Hoss. You don't have to convince me."

Amanda returned from her Middle East assignment two weeks later. Her surprise over Molly's early arrival was nothing compared to her reaction when she learned the circumstances. She stared at Tess, flabbergasted.

"Ryan McCall? Your hunky neighbor? *He* coached you in Lamaze? And delivered your baby in the back of that . . . that thing he drives? In the middle of a hurricane?" At Tess's nod, she sank down onto the sofa. "Good grief."

"Calm down, Amanda. I know it sounds horrendous but everything turned out all right. Molly and I are both doing fine."

"Thanks to Ryan," Amanda stated emphatically. "Thank God he was around when you needed him. I take back every bad thing I've ever said about the man."

Her revised, highly exalted opinion of Ryan did not extend to his brother, however. Whenever Reilly came anywhere near Amanda—which seemed to happen with amazing regularity—she bristled like a junkyard dog.

Tess had assumed that her contact with the McCall brothers would dwindle once Molly was born, but instead over the next few months she saw more of them than ever—particularly Ryan.

R & R Construction was awarded the contract to rebuild and remodel the apartment complex, and since Ryan was on-site supervising the work himself, he frequently dropped in on Tess during the day.

At times Tess felt guilty about relying so heavily on Ryan, but she honestly didn't know what she would have done without him those first months. While she was without a car, he did her shopping for her and ran errands. When her auto insurance finally came through, he went with her to purchase a used car to be sure she did not get stuck with a piece of junk. He took her and the baby to the pediatrician and the obstetrician for checkups, he gave her advice on caring for Molly and helped her through the new mother jitters.

He was still gruff and sometimes brutally frank, but whenever she needed help or just a shoulder to lean on, Ryan was always there for her.

Tess also recognized that daily both Ryan and Mike were becoming more attached to Molly. Every afternoon Mike hopped off the school bus and raced upstairs, detouring by his own apartment just long enough to drop off his books before making a beeline for Tess's. He would still be there when Ryan stopped by at the end of his workday, a practice that had become a habit with him. Even when they were in their own apartment, the least squawk out of her daughter brought Ryan or Mike—often both—to Tess's door.

For her part, Molly kicked and crowed and smiled with delight at the sight of either father or son. Tess knew that any move on her part to withdraw and stand totally on her own feet would only cause pain. Besides, when compared to the special bond they had all forged, being self-reliant and independent no longer seemed so important, or even that desirable. She enjoyed being close to Ryan and Mike. They were almost like family.

To Tess's relief, since their return to Houston there had been no repeat of that madness in the hospital or any of the other weird feelings she had experienced while in Crockett. She had come to the conclusion that those moments had been an aberration, merely the result of the heightened emotions surrounding Molly's birth.

Molly was a healthy happy baby. Except for an occasional cranky spell, she gave Tess little trouble or cause for concern. Then one night, after an unusually fussy evening, Molly awoke crying in the small hours of the morning.

Tess was out of the bed and across the hall to her daughter's room in a blink. "There, there, precious. What's the matter?" she crooned, patting the baby's back. "It's okay. Mommy's here."

The reassurance did not help. Neither did anything else that Tess tried. She changed Molly's diaper. She tried to give her a drink of water, but the baby merely spit out the nipple and cried louder. Tess rocked and swayed and jiggled. She sang lullabies and rubbed Molly's back but the distressed cries continued at full volume. Her little body stiffened, and she drew her knees up sharply and shrieked so loud and hard her face turned a mottled purple. The tiny veins on her head stood out alarmingly as her flailing fists pummeled her mother's shoulder.

Real alarm began to tighten into a hard knot in Tess's chest. "Shh, shh. It's okay, sweetheart. It's okay," she crooned. She walked back and forth across the living room, bouncing Molly and rubbing her back, but nothing worked. She was frantic and close to tears herself when the knock sounded on the door.

"Tess, it's Ryan. Let me in."

At the first soft rap Tess knew who was at the door, and she reacted like a drowning man who had been thrown a lifeline. She was fumbling with the locks before Ryan finished speaking.

At the sight of him she nearly sagged with relief. He stood there, sleepy-eyed, his dark rumpled hair hanging over his forehead. He was barefoot and wearing only a pair of faded jeans, which he had obviously stepped into so hastily he hadn't even bothered to button them all the way. Tess didn't care; she had never been so happy to see anyone in her life.

"Oh, Ryan," she wailed. "I'm sorry if she woke you, but—"

"Never mind that. What's the trouble?"

"I don't know. I've done everything I can think of but she just keeps crying."

He stepped inside and kicked the door shut with his bare foot. "Here, give her to me," he said, plucking the infant from Tess's arms.

"Hey, sugarplum, what's your problem? Hmm?" He cuddled the baby against his shoulder, one big hand cupping her diapered bottom, the other splayed over her back, completely covering it. "C'mon now, sweetie, it can't be that bad."

Ryan strolled into the living room, crooning into Molly's ear. Tess followed right on his heels, wringing her hands. "What do you think is the matter?" she asked anxiously, raising her voice to be heard above the baby's screams.

"My guess would be colic." Molly's cries went up in pitch when he cradled her in one arm and massaged her lower belly with his other hand. "Yep. You can feel how hard her tummy is."

"Colic?"

"Gas. Indigestion."

"But...what caused it? She's never had anything like this before."

"Did you feed her anything new yesterday?"

"Yes. I took her in for her three-month checkup. The pediatrician said I could start giving her peas and green beans. I gave her pureed peas tonight for dinner. She seemed to like them."

"Maybe so, but they don't seem to like her much."

"Oh, dear. What can we do for her?"

"What worked best on Mike was a little heat." He undid the drawstring at the bottom of the baby's nightgown and shoved it up under her armpits. Then he put her to his shoulder again, but this time he pulled her legs down until her tummy was flat against his naked chest. She shrieked louder and tried to draw her knees up again, but he held her pressed tightly to him not allowing the maneuver. In the nursery he pulled a light blanket from her crib and wrapped it around her. Keeping up a low, consoling murmur, he walked the floor, giving the infant his caring and his heat.

It took almost an hour, but finally the fractious baby quieted. When Ryan eased her into the crib his chest hairs were matted with sweat, but Molly slept in peaceful innocence, her long lashes fanned out over cherubic cheeks.

Tess tucked the light cover around her, and she and Ryan shared a relieved look. They tiptoed out, pulling the door partway closed behind them.

In the dimly lit hallway, Tess turned to Ryan and exhaled a long sigh, all the tension draining out of her. "Thank goodness."

"Mmm," he grunted in agreement and braced his hand against the wall above her shoulder. "She wore herself out. She ought to sleep a good long while."

"I hope so. It's almost dawn." Tess smiled wanly. "Thank you. I don't know what I would have done without your help."

He did not reply. He simply stood there, looking at her, his face serious and taut. Beneath half-closed lids his eyes glittered.

Without warning, the air in the dimly lit hallway came alive with a different kind of tension. It crackled around them like heat lightning, making breathing difficult.

Tess nervously fiddled with the full sleeves on her robe, conscious suddenly of how she must look with her hair mussed, her face scrubbed clean of makeup. Unable to meet Ryan's intense stare, she lowered her gaze, only to encounter his broad chest and the wedge of damp black curls that covered it. She looked aside, and nearly moaned when her gaze locked on the tuft of hair beneath his arm. She had never been so acutely aware of a man in her life. He was so big, so beautifully made, so blatantly male.

Standing this close, she inhaled his wonderful male scent with each breath she took—dark and slightly musky, tinged with some citrusy smelling soap. And incredibly erotic.

Her eyes dropped to the unbuttoned waistband of his jeans, and she swallowed hard. He was almost naked. She tugged the front edges of her robe together, conscious all at once that the insubstantial garment and the thin silk gown it covered were all she wore. Immediately her nipples puckered against the silk.

Tess told herself to move, but her muscles seemed to have stopped working.

"I, uh . . . it's late. I know you must be ti—"

Ryan leaned down and captured her mouth with his, cutting off the words.

Tess's heart leaped. Pleasure, fear, excitement—all exploded inside her at once. She moaned, and her hands fluttered uncertainly. A part of her wanted to push him away. Another part wanted to cling to that warm, hard body and never let go. Which instinct would have won she never had a chance to discover, for when her fingertips grazed Ryan's bare chest, he grasped her waist with both hands, backed her against the wall and pressed his body tightly against hers.

Sensations overwhelmed her. She felt her unbound breasts flatten against the solid wall of his chest, the ticklish brush of hair against her skin above the scoop-neck gown and robe, the rigid evidence of his desire pressing into her abdomen.

Hot and hungry, his mouth rocked over hers, urging her lips apart. She obeyed the ravenous urging with no thought of resistance. With quick, sure strokes his tongue thrust into her mouth, telling her of his impatient need, setting fire to her own.

Tess's womb tightened. A searing heat spread outward from that intimate core. Feelings she thought had been buried with Tom, passions she hadn't ever expected to feel again, came surging to the surface. She shivered and made a desperate sound. Somehow—she didn't know when—her arms had found their way around his neck, and she clung to him, straining to get closer, desire coiling through her.

The thin layers of silk between them were at once an unbearable barrier and no protection at all against erotic sensations. She squirmed, and Ryan made a low, savage sound at the rub of her hardened nipples against his chest.

The burning kiss went on and on, neither aware of anything beyond their need for one another. Then, without warning, Ryan jerked away from her.

An involuntary whimper of protest shuddered from Tess, but before her rubbery knees could give way beneath her, he swooped her up in his arms and strode into her bedroom.

He lowered her to the mattress and followed her down in one quick movement, covering her body with his. "Tess. Tess." He muttered her name like a litany, his breath hot and moist against the side of her neck. "I can't fight this any longer. I've tried, but I can't. I won't," he declared in a low guttural voice. "I want you too much."

His teeth nipped her flesh, and she gasped and arched her neck in silent supplication. "Say you want me, too?" he demanded. He raised up partway, and in the faint glow of light seeping in from the living room she saw the hard glitter in his eyes. "Say it."

Tess was on fire. Frantic. She clutched his bare back, her fingers digging into the hard muscled flesh. "Yes. Yes, I want you. Oh, Ryan—"

She was given no time to say more. His mouth fused with hers in a kiss so rawly possessive, Tess knew a moment of panic. Then the fire flamed higher and reality fled. In its place was only sensuous pleasure and the pounding urgency of desire.

The feel of Ryan's rough hands gliding over her smooth skin was so erotic that Tess was only remotely aware of the wispy gown and robe being stripped away. When those same calloused palms cupped her breasts, her back arched and she held her breath in anticipation. For a moment nothing happened, and she knew a twinge of disappointment. When her heavy eyelids lifted she saw that he was staring at her, and the feverish look in his eyes held her spellbound.

"God, you're beautiful," he whispered, fondling her gently. "So full, and soft and—"

She sucked in her breath as his thumbs grazed across the pebbled hard crests.

"Tess. Sweet, sweet Tess." A heartbeat later, his lips closed over a distended bud. The pleasure was so great, she cried out. Of their own volition, her hands clasped his head, holding him against her. His flicking tongue stroked and circled and nudged. The savoring torment almost drove her wild, and just when she thought she could bear no more, he drew on her sweetly. With each gentle tug she felt her womb contract.

With a curse, Ryan rolled away and sprang off the bed. Shivering, her heart pounding, Tess watched him snatch open the few fastened buttons on his jeans. In mere seconds he had shucked out of the denim pants and kicked them aside. Then he was back, and Tess sighed at the first touch of his warm flesh against hers.

His mouth found hers again, and for long moments the only sounds in the dimly lit room were sighs and low moans, the rasp of labored breathing.

Ryan pulled back. He cradled her face between his palms and seared her with a look so ardent her heart skipped a beat. "Tess. God, Tess, I have to have you. Now."

"Yes. Yes," she gasped, clutching him to her.

"Sweet—"

They froze at the shrill ring of the doorbell. It was followed almost at once by three soft raps on the door.

"Dad? Are you still there?"

## *Chapter Nine*

The sound of Mike's worried voice snapped them to their senses as effectively as a douse of cold water.

Biting out a string of vivid curses, Ryan sprang from the bed. He snatched up his jeans and shoved his legs into them, hopping on one foot, then the other.

Tess started to rise too, but he stopped her with a gruff, "Stay there. I'll handle this."

He paused in the act of buttoning his jeans, his eyes flickering over her. Belatedly Tess remembered that she was naked, and in a reflexive move she crossed her arms over her breasts. Her entire body flushed scalding red. Frantically, she reached down to the foot of the bed where the covers lay in a bunch, grabbed the sheet and pulled the thin covering over her body. As she tucked it securely under her armpits, she felt Ryan's eyes on her, but she couldn't bring herself to look at him.

The knock sounded again. "Dad?"

Without a word, Ryan stomped out of the room.

Tess sank back onto the pillow. Clutching the sheet to her, she curled into a ball and stared into the darkness, appalled and shaken. She heard the door open, heard the murmur of Ryan and Mike's voices. Then the door clicked and there was only silence.

Squeezing her eyes shut, she bit her lower lip. Oh, Lord. How could she have been so foolish? She should have done something—said something—to stop what was happening before it got out of hand. Beneath his hard exterior, Ryan was a good man. One word from her, the least sign of resistance, and he would have backed off.

But did she do anything to discourage him? Tess gave a bitter little laugh. Oh, no. Not her. At his first touch she had practically melted and run all over him.

Recalling those torrid moments in Ryan's arms, she moaned and buried her face in the pillow. Even now, just thinking about those callused hands sliding over her skin made her tingle all over and brought another rush of embarrassed heat.

What was happening to her? Her behavior had been shameless. Wanton. But, heaven help her, it had felt so wonderful to be held in Ryan's arms, crushed against that magnificent body. And the things he had made her feel. She had never experienced pleasure that intense before...not even with Tom. And she had loved him.

Tess sucked in her breath. Eyes growing wide, she pressed her fist against her mouth. No. No, she wasn't falling in love with Ryan. She couldn't be. He was nothing like her gentle, sweet Tom, and she had loved him dearly. She still did, she vowed. She *did!*

She squeezed her eyes shut and tried desperately to visualize Tom's face, but the image would not form. Instead it was Ryan's dark, brooding visage that swam in her mind's eye.

An anguished cry tore from Tess and she pummeled the pillow. No! No! It couldn't be! But deep inside, she knew that it was true. She had committed the most foolhardy act of her life; she had fallen in love with Ryan McCall—an angry, embittered man whose heart was encased in ice.

Fool! Fool! Fool! How could you be so stupid? she berated herself, swiping at the tears that streamed down her cheeks.

For the next hour, Tess tossed and turned, but her thoughts continued to torment her and sleep would not come. When the first pale light of dawn began to seep through the window, she gave up and tossed the sheet aside.

Climbing from the bed, she looked at the gown and robe that lay on the floor in a crumpled heap. Unable to bear the thought of putting them on again, she stuffed the silk nightwear into the hamper and dressed in an old pair of jeans and a baggy sweater.

After checking on Molly, who was still sleeping peacefully, Tess went into the kitchen and made a pot of coffee. She was standing at the sink, sipping a mug of the fresh brew and staring listlessly out the window at the sunrise when she heard the soft tap on the door.

She jumped and looked toward the sound, her expression pained. At that hour of the morning the caller could only be Ryan. She wasn't ready to face him. It was too soon. She still felt too raw, too vulnerable. For a moment she thought about ignoring the summons, but she had no choice. Ryan knew she was there.

With a feeling of dread, she went to the door and opened it.

He stood there staring at her, his vivid blue eyes intense and brooding. Tess's heart began an erratic beat. For several awkward moments, neither spoke. On the humid morning air the combined scents of soap and after-shave, along with a faint whiff of laundry starch, drifted to her, and she realized that he had shaved and showered. In freshly laundered jeans and a chambray work shirt, his still damp hair slicked back from his face, he looked bandbox clean . . . and so ruggedly handsome and appealing the sight of him made her ache.

Ryan shifted his feet. She crossed her arms defensively over her middle. Exhaling a sigh, he folded his lips together in a thin line and looked away to one side. Tess's gaze swept over the potted plants down in the courtyard, the pink-tinged sky, then dropped and fixed on the toes of her sneakers as though she found them fascinating. The awkward silence was broken by only the distant hum of traffic and the twitter of sparrows in search of an early morning tidbit.

"Look, I'm sorry about what happened," Ryan snapped in a terse voice that made her flinch. "It was a mistake. We were both worried about Molly and tired from lack of sleep and not thinking straight. I guess you could call it midnight madness."

Though Tess had expected him to say something of the sort, each word stabbed her aching heart. Nevertheless, she somehow kept her expression impassive. She even managed a wan smile. "I understand. And I'm sure you're right."

"It won't happen again. I just wanted you to know that."

"No. I'm sure it won't." She hated the stilted, polite way she was speaking, but at the moment it was all she could manage.

"Good. I'm glad we got that settled."

The awkward silence returned. Tess glanced down and was surprised to see that she still held the coffee mug in her hand. She looked back at Ryan and gestured behind her. "I just made a pot of coffee. Would you like to come in and have some?"

"No thanks. I need to go to Wildwood today. I've got some paperwork to tend to before the crew gets there."

It was a transparent excuse and they both knew it. Ryan rarely left for work before eight.

"I see. Well then, I guess I'll see you later."

For an instant, his eyes glittered and his jaw tightened, but then he jerked his chin in a curt nod. "Yeah, sure."

To his credit, Ryan did try. They both did. Work was winding down on the apartment rebuilding and all the repairs were done, so he began spending more and more time at the development site, but he still dropped by her apartment every evening. His attachment to Molly did not diminish; if anything, his love for her daughter deepened by the day. He treated her as though she were his own and took all the mess and inconvenience that came with babies in stride, never raising a hair when she spit up beets on his boots or when a leaky diaper left a wet spot on his shirt.

If at times Tess caught him staring at her intently, she ignored the leap of her pulse and pretended not to notice. There was no future in loving Ryan; he would never open his heart to a woman again.

At least they had managed to salvage their friendship. Sort of.

Ryan and Mike still came to dinner two or three evenings a week. She still saw them as much as before. Ryan still gave her a hand when she needed one. He had even baby-sat for her once or twice. Even so, despite Mike's exuberant presence and her and Ryan's determined efforts to forget that night, there was a strain between them now, a fine coil of tension that ran just beneath the surface that neither mentioned but of which both were aware.

It revealed itself in small sad ways. In the determined friendliness of their conversations, the way they jerked apart whenever they accidentally touched, the way they both avoided direct eye contact or being alone together or any situation that could possibly bring them closer.

Such as the one that arose at Thanksgiving.

Ryan dutifully passed on his mother's invitation for her and Molly to join the family for the holiday weekend. Tess longed to accept, but she knew it wasn't wise. When she de-

clined with a made-up excuse, she could tell that he was relieved.

The four days that Ryan and Mike were in Crockett were
the loneliest that Tess could remember since that awful period right after Tom's death.

Amanda was out of town that weekend, also, visiting her
mother in Arizona, so Tess was all alone. It seemed foolish
to cook the traditional feast for herself. She thought about
going to the local cafeteria for a turkey dinner, but even that
seemed like too much effort. In the end she had warmed-
over chicken and dumplings for her holiday meal and spent
most of the weekend either watching television or doing
busywork to fill the time, things like polishing silver and
reorganizing perfectly straight dresser drawers.

On Sunday evening when she heard Ryan and Mike clump
up the stairs and enter their apartment, she felt ridiculously
relieved and happy. That night she slept like a rock, something she hadn't done the previous four.

The next morning her euphoria faded when it occurred to
her that the long weekend was a taste of what her life would
have been like had she not met Ryan and his son—what it
would be like if she lost them. Bleak and empty and lonely.

The thought was disturbing, especially when she allowed
herself to consider how unlikely it was that they would still
be neighbors ten years from now, or even five. These days,
long-term friendships were difficult. People flitted in and
out of your life with such frequency that many didn't even
bother to get to know their neighbors; they could be gone
tomorrow.

If their relationship ended it would be doubly painful, for
she would lose both Ryan and Mike, and she loved them
both, father and son. However, even with her optimistic
nature, Tess could not deny that their eventual parting
seemed inevitable.

Their lives slipped back into the same pattern of uneasy friendship it had followed for the past few weeks, and Tess tried not to think about the future.

One afternoon, a week after Ryan and Mike's return, she was powdering Molly's bottom when the doorbell rang. "Who in the world could that be?" she muttered, glancing at the clock. Her daughter pumped her legs and squealed. Hastily, Tess fastened the diaper and scooped the baby up.

The bell rang again before she reached the door. "Hold your horses. I'm coming," Tess muttered. In the entry she looked through the peephole and her jaw dropped.

"Oh, my word." She looked down at her daughter and huffed indignantly. "Do you believe the nerve of some people?"

Molly gurgled and flashed a toothless grin.

Checking her appearance in the hall mirror, Tess groaned. Her blouse was askew from Molly's twisting and their recent play session had left her hair a mess. She ran her fingers through the tangled strands and straightened her blouse as best she could, retucking the tail and patting the crumpled collar point that had fallen victim to her daughter's fat little fist. She rubbed ineffectually at the damp blotch of drool on the shoulder of the garment before giving up with an exasperated hiss. "Oh, who cares, anyway."

Molly bounced and crowed her agreement.

Hitching the baby a little higher, Tess set her jaw, stepped to the door and snatched it open. She stared coldly at the tall, blond man. "Hello, Charles."

An ingratiating smile lit her brother-in-law's handsome face, but his eyes were wary. "Tess. How nice to see you again."

"Really? I'm sorry I can't say the same."

He flushed and had the grace to look chagrined. "I can understand that. You have every right to be angry and upset. My parents handled this situation poorly. They realize that now. That's why I'm here."

"Situation? Molly is not a *situation*, Charles. She's a person." Instinctively, Tess's arm tightened around her child and her chin came up a notch higher. Molly took exception to the confining hold and let loose a shrill whine.

Charles Benson's gaze dropped to the infant for the first time. "So. You had a girl. She's lovely, Tess."

"What do you want, Charles?"

"I'd like to talk to you."

Her icy demeanor did not thaw by so much as a degree. "I don't think so."

"Please. Just hear me out, Tess. Give me a chance to set things right. That's all I ask."

She tried to steel herself against him, but the earnest plea and the contrition in his eyes tugged at her. Tess thought of the warmth and closeness the McCalls and Blaines shared. The Bensons might never offer her daughter that kind of familial comfort and love, but they were the only family Molly had. Tess knew, only too well, how dreadful it felt to be all alone.

She sighed. She supposed she owed it to Molly to at least listen to what he had to say. "All right. I guess you can come in," she said, and stepped back, motioning him inside.

"Well ... actually..." His gaze flickered uncomfortably to Molly, whose fretting was increasing in volume and intensity. "It would be better if we could go somewhere, just the two of us. Perhaps I could take you to dinner tonight. Somewhere nice and quiet where we could relax and talk with no interruptions."

"I don't know—"

"Please, Tess. This is important."

"Well ... maybe I could get my neighbor to baby-sit."

"Splendid." Charles brightened at once, his smile full of urbane charm. "I'll pick you up at seven."

The minute Ryan and Charles set eyes on one another, Tess could feel the hostility between the two men. During her introduction they shook hands and muttered curt hellos but the antipathy in their eyes and body language spoke volumes. They bristled like two savage male animals, circling in on one another for the kill.

Fearing they would come to blows, Tess hustled her brother-in-law out as quickly as she could.

"Do you really think that man is a proper baby-sitter for Molly?" he questioned the minute they left her apartment. "He seems a trifle rough around the edges if you ask me."

As annoyed as Tess was with Ryan, she was not about to let anyone, especially an elitist snob like Charles Benson, criticize him.

"But then, I didn't ask you, did I, Charles? However, just to set the record straight, let me assure you that Ryan McCall is a decent, kind man. There is no one in the world I trust more."

No fool, Charles read the warning loud and clear and adroitly changed the subject.

After that, the tension eased and Tess began to actually enjoy herself. Though Charles lived in Boston, he came to Houston often enough on business to know all the best places to dine. He took her to Tony's, an exquisite French restaurant on South Post Oak Lane, where the ambience was elegant, the service excellent and the food superb.

The conversation over dinner was pleasant but general. Charles turned out to be a sophisticated and entertaining companion. He possessed a quick intelligence and a smooth wit, and by the time coffee was served, Tess was pleasantly relaxed. It was then that Charles finally broached the subject they had come there to discuss.

"Tess, I want you to know that my parents feel simply terrible about the way they responded when they learned of the baby. It's just that... well... they had not fully recovered from losing Tom and when your announcement came out of the blue like that..." He shrugged and spread his hands. "It caught them so completely off-guard they responded with a knee-jerk reaction.

"Now that they've had time to think things over, they realize how wrong they were. They asked me to convey their sincere apology, and to assure you that they're delighted to have a granddaughter. I talked to them after I saw you this afternoon and told them about Molly. They were thrilled, Tess."

"I see." Tess's smile was noncommittal. She doubted that Harold and Enid Benson's sudden acceptance of Molly had as much to do with cooler thinking and an attack of conscience as the shocking discovery that Tess wasn't interested in their money.

"They're hoping that you will forgive them." Charles reached across the table and took her hands between his. He looked deep into her eyes, his expression at once persuasive and pleading. "Do you think you could do that, Tess? It would mean so much to them."

She hesitated. His parents had insulted her on a deep, personal level. That was not easy to forgive. Still, Tess knew it was the only way they would ever mend the rift between them. She sighed. "I suppose I can try—for Molly's sake."

"That's great." Charles gave her hand a squeeze and his eyes grew warm. "They'll be so happy. Mom and Dad want to see Molly, become a part of her life."

"That might be a bit difficult. But I suppose that we could come for a visit now and then when she's a little older."

"Actually...we were thinking—hoping, at any rate—of something more than just a visit."

Tess was instantly on guard, but when she started to withdraw her hands from his he held them fast. "Tess, we would like for you and Molly to move to Boston. That way we can take care of you. As Tom's family, we feel a moral obligation to look after his wife and child, now that he's gone."

So...that was it. Her instincts had told her there was more to this evening than met the eye.

Her smile was polite but this time she firmly withdrew her hands from his grasp. "I appreciate the offer, Charles, but—"

"Please, Tess, don't give me your final answer just yet. This is a very important decision. Give yourself time to think about it. Consider all the advantages there would be— for Molly and yourself. At least promise me you'll do that much."

It was a reasonable request. Tess knew that time would not change her mind, but it seemed churlish to refuse outright. "All right. I'll think about it."

"Great. I'm glad. You know...Mother and Dad, of course, are anxious to get to know their granddaughter." His gaze trailed over her hair, her neck and shoulders, then moved to her lips and lingered there. A slight smile tipped up the corners of his mouth, and his voice dropped to a husky pitch. "I, on the other hand, have my own reasons for hoping you will make the move."

Tess would have to be a fool not to know that Charles found her attractive. The warm gleam in his eyes and his fulsome compliments had made that obvious all evening.

Nor was she totally immune to him. Charles was handsome and charming, after all. And it had been a long time since any man had shown that kind of interest in her. Ryan certainly did not. He desired her, but he resented doing so. In her brother-in-law's gaze there was only admiration and pleasurable anticipation, and she had to admit, she was flattered.

However, Tess knew that nothing would ever come of it. No matter how good Charles was for her ego, he was not Ryan, and it seemed her heart would accept no other.

For that reason she merely smiled and let the remark pass without comment. Disappointment flickered in Charles's eyes, but he wisely did not pursue the subject.

A short while later outside her apartment door, he gave her a chaste kiss on the cheek and left her with a reminder that he would be back in a month or so and they would talk again.

She found Ryan watching the news on television.

"Hi," she called from the entry. After hanging her coat in the closet she walked into the living room and smiled when he looked up.

His expression was set, but his eyes raked slowly over her, from the top of her swinging pageboy, down over the simple black sheath dress all the way to the black pumps on her feet. The silent inspection set off a fluttering in her stomach but Tess ignored it and settled into the Queen Anne chair.

"Ahh, that feels wonderful," she groaned, slipping off the high heel shoes, and wriggling her toes. "I hope Molly didn't give you any trouble."

"None. She's sleeping like an angel." He punched a button on the remote and the TV screen went blank. "So? How did the talk go?"

"Fine. Charles apologized profusely, said his parents were sorry and wanted to be friends and get to know Molly. So for her sake I accepted," she said, giving him an expurgated version.

"And that's all there was to it?"

"Well...not exactly. Charles and his parents want Molly and me to move to Boston."

Five full seconds of silence ticked by. "I see," he said finally in a voice like steel.

"I'm not going to, of course."

"Did you tell him that?"

"Yes . . . well . . . I did agree to think about it. But only to pacify him," she tacked on hastily when something flared in Ryan's eyes. "It seemed easier than arguing. The next time he comes to town I'll tell him my decision is definitely no."

"And you think he's going to just accept that?"

"Why wouldn't he?"

"Because the man wants you, dammit." Tess could not control the blush that swept over her face, and Ryan's eyes narrowed. "But then, I see that you already knew that didn't you?"

"No! At least, not until tonight. And anyway, why are you angry with me? I'm not responsible for Charles's feelings."

"If you didn't want the man panting after you, then why the hell did you wear that damned dress."

"What?" Flabbergasted, Tess looked down at the simple black sheath. "What's wrong with this dress?"

"Nothing, if you're trying to raise a man's blood pressure. And it sure worked on good old Charlie, didn't it. When he walked in and saw you in that little number, his eyes nearly popped right out of his head."

Tess was both hurt and resentful. It had been over a year since she'd had an opportunity to dress up and go out to dinner in a nice restaurant. She had worked hard at trimming down and firming up since Molly had been born and it felt good to know that she looked nice. The dress was form fitting but it had long sleeves and a simple scooped neckline. It was elegant and classy and she felt feminine and attractive wearing it, but it certainly was not a blatant come-on, as Ryan had implied.

Her chin jutted, but before she could give voice to the angry reply forming on her tongue, Ryan went on.

"Was that what you were hoping for? That you'd catch Charles's attention? What's the deal, Tess? Does he resemble Tom? You can't have your dead husband back so you'll settle for his brother? Is that it?"

She gasped and shot to her feet. "That's a rotten thing to say!"

Ryan sprang up as well, bounding off the sofa like an un-coiling spring. "What's the matter, did I hit too close to the truth?"

"Certainly not! Just because you don't like my dress and you and Charles clashed for some idiotic, macho reason that totally escapes me, that's no reason for you to insult me. I am *not*—in any way, shape or form—interested in my brother-in-law. Nor did I do anything to encourage him, and I resent your nasty accusations!"

In her stockinged feet Tess was barely five foot three, a good foot shorter than Ryan, but the disparity in their sizes in no way intimidated her. She stood with her feet spread, hands on her hips, brown eyes flashing—one hundred and five pounds of quivering, indignant woman.

"You sure as hell didn't do anything to discourage him. That guy's as slick as snake oil, with his smooth smile and his manicured nails and his custom-tailored silk shirt!" Ryan shouted, waving his arms. "I'll bet he's never done a hard day's work in his life. And dammit! I never said I didn't like your dress!"

By the time he'd finished, Tess was so worked up she barely heard the last. "I don't have to take this!" She whirled, stomped into the entry and jerked the door open. Jutting her chin, she stabbed him with a cold look. "I think you'd better leave."

Ryan closed the distance between them in four long strides. "I'll leave all right. But first..." He slapped the door with the flat of his palm and slammed it shut, jerking it right out of her hands. At the same time he hooked her waist with his other arm, hauled her against his chest and fastened his mouth on hers.

It was like setting spark to tinder. The banked coals of desire that for months had glowed and crackled just below the surface ignited into flame at the first touch of their lips. All the anger and frustration that had been building inside Ryan instantly fueled the rough kiss into a roaring inferno.

After her initial start of surprise, Tess caught fire as well. Making a desperate sound, she went up on tiptoe, locked her arms around his neck and kissed him back with equal intensity and heat. For several seconds they clutched one another, straining to get closer, their mouths hot and hard and hungry.

Then as though by mysterious design, everything changed.

The conflagration settled into a steady, consuming blaze. Hands that had grasped and clutched began to stroke. Taut bodies grew languid. Dueling tongues touched and tasted. Lips softened, rubbed, clung. Miraculously, the turbulent kiss turned to one of melting sweetness that suspended time and made them ache.

Finally, their lips parted. Breathing heavily, their thunderous heartbeats roaring in their ears, they drew back and stared at one another, their faces slack with shock and confusion.

After several taut seconds, Ryan snatched open the door and slammed out.

Tess didn't move. She closed her eyes and pressed her lips together to keep them from trembling. Perhaps . . . perhaps she was being a fool. Perhaps she ought to honestly consider the Bensons' proposal. She obviously had no future with Ryan.

Ryan pounded on Reilly's door with his balled fist. He waited only a second, then pounded again. On the other side of the oak panel, the sounds reverberated through the darkened town house like thunder.

"All right. All right, already," Reilly grumbled. "I'm coming!" He jerked the door open, and grimaced wryly.

"Jeez, Hoss. What're you trying to do, knock my door do—"

"I've got to talk to you." Ryan brushed past him and strode inside.

"Uh...look man, can this wait? I mean...well the truth is...you've kinda caught me at a bad time. You see—'' Reilly glanced toward the living room, which was lit only by the glow of the crackling blaze in the fireplace, but when his gaze returned to Ryan he frowned. "Damn, Hoss. What's wrong? You look like hell."

"That's what I—"

"Reilly, honey? Did you get rid of whoever was at the door?" a feminine voice called.

"Who the—" Ryan's head whipped toward the sound, then back to his twin. Belatedly, he noticed Reilly's mussed hair and the lipstick smudges around his mouth. He was shoeless, and his shirt was unbuttoned and pulled partway out of his jeans.

Ryan grimaced. "Damn. I'm sorry, man. I didn't realize you weren't alone. I'll go."

He started for the door, but Reilly stepped in front of him.

"No, don't. I don't know what's buggin' you, Hoss, but I can see it's important. Look, just give me a few minutes. I'll send Sheila home in a cab, then we can talk."

"I don't know—"

"I do."

"Reilly? Where are you, sugar?"

Reilly turned his brother toward the back of the town house, giving him a little shove. "Go on back to the kitchen. I'll be right there."

For what seemed like an hour, but in reality was no more than fifteen minutes, Ryan paced back and forth across the small kitchen. He heard the voices from the front of the house. The woman's was raised and strident, screeching obscenities and insults. Mingled in between now and then came Reilly's placating murmur. Something crashed, shattering against the marble floor of the entry. At once, the voices increased in volume.

Ryan grimaced. He felt bad about the situation. But dammit! He had to talk to Reilly!

Without conscious thought, he had headed straight for his brother's place the instant he left Tess. He and Reilly might not have quite the telepathic link like that which existed between their twin cousins, Erin and Elise, but there was still a powerful connection between them. At the first hint of trouble or crisis, each instinctively sought the other.

Finally the front door slammed. Seconds later, Reilly strolled into the kitchen. He shot Ryan a sheepish look. "Sorry about that."

"No, man, I'm sorry. I shouldn't have—"

Reilly stopped him with an upraised hand. "Hey, don't sweat it, Hoss. To tell you the truth, Sheila wasn't doing a lot for my blood pressure anyway, so you did me a favor. And what a temper! I had no idea the woman was such a shrew."

Opening the refrigerator, he pulled out two beers. "You look like you could use a stiff drink, but this is all I've got," he said, handing one to Ryan.

Leaning back against the counter, Reilly crossed his bare feet at the ankles and flipped back the tab on the can. He had pulled his shirt completely out of his jeans, and the wrinkled tail of the unbuttoned garment hung around his hips, leaving a wide strip of bare chest and belly visible. A halfhearted attempt had been made to wipe away the lipstick smudges but a few smears remained and his hair still stuck out at all angles.

He took a long pull on the beer and watched Ryan's restless pacing. "So. You wanna tell me what's eatin' at you, Hoss? Or did you just come over here to wear out my linoleum?"

Ryan halted and raked a hand through his hair. "It's Tess."

"Somehow, I figured that."

That earned Reilly an annoyed look, which he ignored. After a moment Ryan sighed heavily and started pacing again. "She was waiting for me when I got home..."

In jerky, agitated sentences, Ryan told him the whole story. He left nothing out and was brutally honest about his part in both the quarrel with Tess and the disturbing kiss that had followed.

"It was all my fault. I shouldn't have goaded her," he said reasonably, then ruined it by exploding, "But, dammit! I was upset!"

He was more than just upset. Over the last few months Ryan had come to think of Tess and Molly as his, and the thought of them moving away, out of his life, was unbearable. The thought of that damned Charles sniffing around her made him feel murderous.

"Are you worried she'll change her mind and take them up on their offer?"

"Maybe. I don't know. No! No, of course she won't." Ryan absently took a sip of beer. "I'm probably just being paranoid. She said herself she was going to turn them down. When she does, that'll be the end of it."

"Mmm. I wonder?"

"What does that mean?"

"Just that people like the Bensons can be tenacious as hell. And if this Charles is as interested in Tess as you seem to think, I wouldn't count on him giving up that easily."

"If Tess turns him down, he'll have to."

Reilly gave him a long, level look and cocked one eyebrow. "Would you?"

For several seconds Ryan stared at him, his jaw clenched and working. Finally he bit out a curse. "Dammit. I've got to do something. And fast. But what?"

"Ah, c'mon, Hoss." Reilly's deep chuckle brought Ryan's dark glare down on him, but he didn't turn a hair. Crossing his arms over his brawny chest, he smiled. "I think you've known the answer to that all along."

\* \* \*

Tess was still awake when her doorbell pealed. She glanced at the bedside clock and made a distressed sound. At a quarter till five in the morning it could only be Ryan.

She wasn't ready to face him, but she threw back the covers and reached for her robe. He would only keep ringing that bell until she answered it. As it was, the chime sounded two more times in rapid succession before she reached the entryway.

"For heaven's sake," she hissed, jerking the door open. "Will you kindly remember that there's a sleeping baby in here!"

"We have to talk, Tess."

Tess gazed at him, her heart aching. He was unshaven and bleary-eyed and he looked as strung out as she felt. The blue-plaid flannel shirt beneath the sheepskin coat was the same one he'd had on last night, and with a pang, she realized that he had not been to bed.

She gripped the edge of the door with trembling fingers and shook her head. "No. Please, Ryan," she pleaded in a shaky whisper. "Just go away and leave me alone. I can't take any more. Please."

"Neither can I. That's why I'm here." He paused, staring at her, his vivid eyes burning. "I think we should get married, Tess."

## Chapter Ten

"What?" Tess's heart skipped a beat, and her hand fluttered to her chest. "You . . . you can't be serious."

"I've never been more serious in my life. Now will you let me in?"

Wordlessly, Tess stepped aside, and when he strode past her into the living room she shut the door and followed in a daze. In the middle of the floor he turned to her. Tess came to a stop behind the Queen Anne chair and gripped the high back for support.

"Are you all right?" Ryan questioned, searching her pale face.

"Yes. That is . . . I don't know. Ryan . . . this is crazy. You don't really want to get married. You told me yourself that it wasn't high on your list."

"I believe what I said was 'women' weren't high on my list. They still aren't, but you're an exception. And I do want to marry you."

She could not doubt the sincerity in his voice or the serious look in his eyes. Still, she was confused. There was no affection there. No tenderness. Merely hard determination. "But...why?"

"This isn't a decision I reached lightly. I drove around most of the night thinking about our situation. Marriage seems the most sensible answer."

"*Sensible?*" Tess almost laughed, except that she knew if she did she would start crying. She shook her head. "There's nothing in the least *sensible* about it."

"It seems to me to be the most logical solution to a number of problems. First of all, we can't keep ignoring this thing between us. We've tried that and it doesn't work. The chemistry is too strong."

Tess blushed and looked down, unable to meet his gaze. Undeterred, Ryan came around the chair and stood beside her. She could feel him watching her but she kept her eyes fixed on her fingers, plucking nervously at the green-and-cream-striped upholstery.

"Soon, Tess—very soon—we're going to wind up in bed together, married or not," he murmured almost in her ear. "All the good intentions in the world won't stop it."

Her head whipped around. "Ryan!"

"Why are you shocked? It's the truth, and you know it." He ran the back of his forefinger down her burning cheek, his eyes following the path. His voice dropped, becoming soft and gravelly. "When you walked out of the bedroom last night wearing that damned dress that showed off every delectable curve, I wanted to throw you down on the floor and make love to you on the spot. I still do."

"*Ryan!*"

"I hated watching you walk out of here with that damned snob, Charles," he went on in the same low voice. "I hated the thought of him hovering over you, touching you. I could see in his eyes that he wanted you, and I wanted to kill him for even thinking of you in that way."

"Oh, Ryan." This time his name came out in a breathy murmur, thick with feeling. Tess stared at him, her eyes wide. His words were so shocking, so full of primitive passion it took her breath away.

"I don't want to have to endure another evening like that. I don't want to have to worry that you might move to Boston, or that some other man might come along and steal you and Molly away. I couldn't stand that," he admitted with such raw emotion and vulnerability that her chest contracted painfully. She felt as though her heart were being squeezed in an iron fist. She stared at him in amazement, scarcely able to breathe.

"You're not the type for an affair. Even if you were, I have Mike to think of. That's not the kind of example I want to set for my son. So it seems to me that marriage is the obvious route."

"I see."

It was all that Tess could say; her mind was so numb she could barely speak. He could have no idea what he was doing to her. With each word he spoke, her heart broke a little more. What woman wanted a man to marry her because it was the "logical" thing to do? She was in love with him, for heaven's sake!

"Either we get married, or we have to part," Ryan went on. "And quite frankly, the thought of that tears my guts out."

Surprise widened her eyes. Her heart pounded and hope began to soar, only to plummet with Ryan's next words.

"Molly means the world to me. You have to know that. Maybe when you help bring a baby into the world, when you're the first one to hold that new life in your hands, a special bond forms. Hell, I don't know. All I'm sure of is, I couldn't love her more if she were my own. It would kill me to lose her."

That startled a painful little laugh out of Tess. "You want to marry me because you love my daughter?" she choked in a disbelieving voice.

"You know it's not just that. I . . ." Ryan looked away. A muscle in his jaw jumped. He looked back at Tess and scowled. "I care about you, too."

"But you don't love me." It was a statement, not a question, her voice toneless.

It seemed to annoy him. He grimaced and raked a hand through his hair. "Love isn't something I have to give. Or want."

"I see."

"But I do want you, Tess. I want you very much." He stepped closer and touched the side of her neck, trailing his rough fingers over the smooth flesh. Tess shivered.

"Ryan," she said, faintly shocked at her body's powerful reaction to even that slight touch.

"You see—you want me, too. Don't deny it."

She didn't even try.

"Look, Tess. You and I got off to a bad start, but somehow we've become friends. Good friends. Hell, I never even thought I'd hear myself use that word in connection with a woman. It's more than a whole helluva lot of people have going for them. Can't it be enough?"

"Oh, Ryan, I—"

"We can make it work for us, Tess. We like each other and we get along well. God knows, we desire each other." Tess blushed scarlet again, but he ignored her discomfort. "You know how I feel about Molly, and I think you like Mike."

"I love Mike."

"There you go, then. Molly needs a father and Mike needs a mom. We could give them that. We could be a family, Tess."

It wasn't fair. It simply wasn't fair. With the instincts of a wily street fighter, he had zeroed in on her weakness, hitting her with the argument she found hardest to resist.

Family had always been important to Tess, especially so after losing her parents. She and Tom had planned to have a large family of their own. Then she had lost him, too, and she had resigned herself to living alone, just her and Molly. Now Ryan was offering her another chance.

In addition, there was Ryan's family. For someone like Tess, just the thought of becoming a part of the large and boisterous McCall-Blaine clan was an inducement. The strongest temptation of all, however, was her love for Ryan.

She tried to resist. She told herself that he didn't love her, that she would be a fool to accept his proposal, that she was setting herself up to be hurt—worse than she had ever been hurt in her life. It did no good. Her head might urge caution, but her heart wanted Ryan.

"Marry me, Tess," he urged, sensing her wavering. The hand at her neck slipped beneath her silky pageboy and cupped her nape. Giving a little tug, he brought her closer, and Tess's hands came up automatically to rest on his chest. He looked deep into her eyes, his handsome face serious and intent. "We can have a good life together. Give us a chance, Tess."

She searched his face, her lower lip caught between her teeth. She couldn't bear never to see him again. Yet if she accepted his proposal she could very well be sentencing herself to a loveless marriage.

No. Her optimistic nature would not allow her to accept that possibility. Ryan could come to love her someday. Anything was possible when two people shared a passion as strong as theirs. She had to believe that, because, heaven help her, she could not lose him.

"What's your answer, Tess?" Ryan asked in his usual straightforward way.

She looked at that dear face, at the fierce intensity in his beautiful blue eyes, longing and fear thrumming through her. Finally, gathering her courage, she sent up a silent prayer, drew a deep breath, and nodded. "All right. I'll marry you."

On Christmas day, they were married in Crockett, in the church that Ryan had attended all his life.

The simple ceremony, which was held immediately after the Christmas service, was a private one just for family.

They were all there, every last one, including a couple of old maid great-aunts, Eula and Clara Mae Monahan, who lived thirty-five miles away in Palestine. This time Tess even got to meet Erin and Elise, Ryan's infamous twin cousins, about whom she had heard so much when she was there in August.

Erin and Elise and their husbands, Max Delany and Sam Lawford, had intended to celebrate Christmas at their homes in Santa Fe, New Mexico, since they had come to Crockett for Thanksgiving, but the minute they heard about the wedding the sisters had started packing for the trip to Texas. When they couldn't get airline tickets at that late date, they talked their long-suffering husbands into hiring a private plane to fly them.

"We certainly couldn't let one of our favorite cousins get married without us," Erin defended staunchly when the others razzed her and Elise. "Besides . . . any woman who could get Ryan McCall to the altar, we *had* to meet."

The pair lived up to their reputations. Arriving in a whirlwind of commotion, they no sooner said hello to their family than they turned their attention on Tess.

Elise greeted her with a smile and a warm embrace. Her lovely face was alive with curiosity but her gentle, unassuming nature held it in check.

Erin was not hampered by such inhibitions. "So. You're Tess," she said, boldly looking her over. She shot Ryan a twinkling look. "Another redhead, huh? That's just what this family needs. And definitely a mark in her favor," she said with a droll smile. Erin and Elise's hair was the same flame red as their cousin Meghan's, a feature all three had inherited from their maternal grandmother, Maureen Monahan.

With the pleasantries out of the way, Erin ignored her husband's groans and the reprimands of the rest of her family and proceeded to grill Tess with a series of pointed questions.

"Hmm. I have to say, you're not what I expected," she said when done. "For one thing, I never knew my cousin went for wholesome beauty. It's good to know his taste is improving. You look about as tough as a spring lamb, but I guess you've got guts, if you're willing to take on this bad-tempered brute." She pursed her lips and studied Tess through narrowed eyes.

Tess shifted, uneasy under that penetrating stare. She had the feeling that, for all her feistiness and daring, Erin Blaine Delany was an exceptionally bright and perceptive woman. That steady gaze seemed to see right into Tess's soul to her innermost secrets.

Evidently satisfied with what she found, she finally nodded and pronounced audaciously, "Yes. Yes, I believe you'll do just fine."

All of Ryan's relatives shared the sentiment, though most expressed their approval and delight over the match in more diplomatic terms.

His parents were overjoyed. Maggie, who had made all the arrangements for the rushed wedding, was in her element, bustling around giving orders, organizing events and her family, not only for the wedding but the holiday. In between, she fussed over Molly.

Reilly, of course, took full credit for the match, claiming he knew from the start that Tess and his twin were perfect for each other.

Mike was over the moon. When Tess and Ryan had broken the news to him, he responded with an ecstatic, *"Aw right!"* During the trip to Crockett and the holiday weekend preceding the ceremony he was so excited, he drove everyone crazy, constantly getting underfoot during the frantic preparations, and cracking corny wedding jokes to anyone who would listen.

The only person who had any reservations about the match was Amanda.

"Tess, are you sure you know what you're doing?" she had questioned with obvious concern when Tess broke the news to her. "Have you thought this through?"

"Yes, of course I have."

"Don't you think you ought to at least wait a while to be sure this is what you want? Why be in such an all-fired hurry?"

"Amanda, calm down. It will work out. You'll see. Why are you objecting, anyway? I thought you liked Ryan now?"

"I do. I think he's a great guy, and I'll be eternally grateful to him for what he did for you, but...well...he's obviously still carrying around some serious baggage from his first marriage. That's bad enough, but you told me yourself that he doesn't love you."

"I know," Tess replied quietly. "But the thing is...I love him."

Amanda groaned. "Oh, Lord, I was afraid of that. But don't you see, that's all the more reason to exercise a little caution. You've been hurt so much already." She took Tess's hands, her eyes worried and beseeching. "Oh, Tess. Honey, I know you're a fighter, but I'm afraid if you get knocked to your knees again, all the optimism and determination in the world won't get you up this time."

Tess was afraid of that, too, but she loved Ryan too much not to take this chance at happiness, no matter how slim.

Amanda continued to express her doubts and concerns all week, but when time for the wedding came, she put them aside and stood beside Tess at the altar.

Mike was Ryan's best man. Dressed in his Sunday suit, he stood tall and proud, beaming throughout the exchange of vows, while behind them, Molly burbled and cooed in her new grandmother's arms.

Tess was so nervous she could barely concentrate on what Reverend Dixon was saying. Panic almost overtook her as Ryan repeated the solemn vows that would bind them together, his deep baritone firm and sure. Her own voice came out a quavery whisper, and during the exchange of rings, her hands shook as though she had the palsy, but somehow she got through it.

Then, suddenly, it was over. As Tess went into Ryan's arms for their first kiss as husband and wife, she thought, *"It's done"* and she sagged against him, her heart caroming in her chest.

The next couple of hours passed in an blur for Tess. They were immediately surrounded by family. The men thumped Ryan on the back and they were both kissed and hugged and showered with well wishes.

From the church they went back to Maggie and Colin's home for a sumptuous combination Christmas dinner and wedding feast. Dorothy and Joe Blaine's dining table had been brought over and butted up against the McCalls'. Together, the long linen-covered tables stretched from the dining room through the double sliding doors all the way into the middle of the parlor.

Conversation around the table was lively and boisterous, with everyone talking at once—except for Ryan and Tess.

He weathered the toasts and affectionate teasing of his kin with his usual stoicism, responding now and then with a raised eyebrow and sardonic look, an occasional terse comment. Tess was so nervous she barely heard a word that was said. She did little more than pick at her food and nod and smile vaguely whenever anyone spoke directly to her. Had her life depended on it, she could not have said what was on her plate.

Almost before she knew it, the cake had been cut and duly eaten, pictures had been taken, the bouquet had been caught—reluctantly by Meghan, who had been jostled into position by her sisters-in-law and cousins. Then it was time to go.

"Are you sure you won't leave Molly here with us for a few days? Mike is staying for a week. If you left the baby, too, you and Ryan could have some time alone, maybe take a trip," Maggie wheedled while she helped Tess pack the last minute items into the baby's bag. "You could go to Erin and Elise's beach house on Rincon Island. They were serious when they offered to let you use it for a honeymoon. I promise you'll love it there. It's such a beautiful place, and so secluded and romantic."

"I'm sure it's lovely," Tess said with a regretful smile. "But I'm afraid that won't be possible. Wildwood is beginning to take shape and Ryan is swamped with work. He can't get away right now."

Even if he could, given the practical and prosaic reasons for this marriage, a romantic honeymoon in an island paradise would be awkward. Deep down in her lovelorn soul Tess might long to walk hand in hand with Ryan down a moonlit beach, to experience warm, silken nights of sensuous delight in his arms, fun-filled days totally absorbed with one another to the exclusion of all else, but she tamped down on the feelings, knowing she might as well wish for the moon.

"Nonsense. Reilly can look after things for a few days. I swear, that eldest son of mine doesn't have a romantic bone in his body. Maybe if I talked to h—"

"No! Don't do that," Tess said, putting her hand on Maggie's arm. "It's all right. Really, Maggie, it is. Besides, it's not just Ryan's schedule. The truth is, even though

Molly is weaned to a bottle now, and I know that you would take excellent care of her..." Tess's mouth twisted in a rueful grimace. "You're probably going to think I'm silly, but... I can't bear to be away from her just yet. Not even overnight."

"Ahh, I see. It's new mother separation anxiety, is it? Well, I can certainly understand that. When mine were babies I didn't want them out of my sight." She patted Tess's shoulder. "Maybe when Molly's a little older and you feel more comfortable about leaving her, you and Ryan can take a delayed honeymoon."

"Maybe," Tess mumbled, ducking her head again.

But Maggie was much more astute and observant than Tess realized. When she zipped the diaper bag and straightened, her mother-in-law was watching her with compassion and concern. She searched Tess's face and looked deep into her eyes. "You love him very much, don't you, my dear?" she asked gently.

Tess felt exposed. She had never been good at hiding her feelings. She stared back helplessly and fought the urge to cry. "Yes. I do," she murmured.

"Good. I'm glad. Ryan needs a good woman to love him." With a sigh, Maggie pulled Tess into her motherly embrace, hugging her tight. "Don't give up on him, Tess. He'll come around. You'll see."

They arrived home a little after nine that evening. Molly, who usually slept like an angel in a car, had been cranky throughout the entire trip. For Tess, the two-hour drive had been fraught with nervous anxiety, and she was sure her daughter had picked up on her jitters, but at least trying to soothe the fussy baby had kept her busy and helped her ignore the awkward tension.

That was no longer possible once they reached the apartment complex. During the climb up the stairs Tess's nerves wound tighter with each step. By the time they walked through her door, they were twanging like a plucked string on a cheap guitar.

She stopped in the middle of the living room and glanced uncertainly at Ryan, holding the baby to her like a shield. "I, uh . . . I'll go put Molly to bed," she said, gesturing vaguely toward the nursery.

Ryan watched her. "Fine. While you do that I'll go check my place. But first I'll put these bags in our bedroom."

Blushing, Tess nodded, ducked her head and almost ran from the room. In the nursery she took several restorative breaths and listened to Ryan moving around in her bedroom—*their* bedroom—across the hall. Had the remark been deliberate? A pointed reminder of their changed relationship? She suspected it had. If so, who could blame him? She had been acting like a skittish virgin ever since the ceremony.

Tess had no idea why she was so nervous. It was ridiculous. She hadn't been this jumpy when she married Tom, and she *had* been a virgin then.

She jumped at the sound of the front door closing, and quickly set about readying her daughter for bed.

Molly's eyelids began to droop as Tess bundled her into a warm gown. When she placed the baby onto her tummy, Molly assumed her bottom-in-the-air sleeping position and drifted off before Tess had laid the blanket over her. Smiling, she kissed the downy head, tucked the blanket in all around and left the room, pulling the door partway closed behind her.

Tess was in the kitchen, rinsing out the empty baby bottle she had taken from the diaper bag when she heard Ryan come in. Her nerves had settled to a low hum but they immediately began to jangle.

Sensing his presence, she glanced over her shoulder. He stood in the doorway, one shoulder propped against the jamb, watching her.

He had discarded his suit coat and tie and the white dress shirt was unbuttoned halfway to his waist, the sleeves rolled up over his powerful forearms. His face was unreadable, but there was a glitter in his eyes that made her pulse jump. She knew his indolent pose was deceptive. He looked big and gorgeous and utterly male . . . and dangerous. Like a big jungle cat, waiting for the chance to spring.

"I'll be through here in just a minute. If you don't rinse the formula out right away these things are the devil to clean." Oh, Lord, now she was babbling.

"Is Molly asleep?"

"Yes. She went out like a light. It's hours past her bedtime and she wore herself out on the way home."

Tess stuck the bottle under the faucet again. It was almost full when Ryan's hand settled on either side of her waist.

She gasped and jumped.

"You've rinsed that bottle about ten times already. Don't you think that's enough?" His voice was a low rumble, a rough, tender sound tinged with a hint of amusement.

"I, uh . . . you can't be too careful."

She felt him step closer, felt his heat all along her back. He nuzzled her temple. The baby bottle overflowed and water poured over her hand and into the sink in a steady stream. She didn't notice.

"I think you're stalling." His breath stirred her hair, its moist warmth seeping through to her scalp, making it tingle. "What's the matter, sweetheart? Are you nervous?"

"Yes. No. Yes! That is . . ." Tess groaned, and Ryan chuckled.

"There's nothing to be nervous about, honey. I promise." He buried his face in the fall of silky hair at the side of her neck.

Tess sucked in her breath. The plastic baby bottle slipped from her fingers. It hit the sink with a dull *thunk,* bounced three times and wobbled to a stop, water gushing out of it.

"Ry-Ryan, wait." She tried to infuse her voice with stern command, but it came out breathless and wobbly. "I . . . I was going to shower and . . . and put on a pretty gown."

"Why? I'd just take it off. And we can shower later. Together."

Tess gasped, faintly shocked, yet excitement zinged through her. She hunched her shoulder against his marauding mouth, but a quaking had begun deep inside, robbing her of both strength and will.

"Relax, honey. You know you like it when I do this." Nuzzling aside her fragrant hair, he nibbled her neck and her shoulder, as far as the neckline of her wedding suit would allow. He worked his way back up to her ear. "And this." He nipped her lobe, then batted it playfully with his tongue.

A shuddering breath fluttered through Tess's parted lips. Her head lolled back and she closed her eyes. "Ryan . . ."

"This, too," he whispered, pressing his open mouth over the delicate shell.

Hot breath filled her ear. Then the tip of his tongue traced each delicate swirl, and a delicious, prickling sensation rippled over Tess's skin.

Ryan's hands slid around her and splayed across her abdomen, pulling her back against him. She felt his arousal pressing against her bottom and made a helpless little sound somewhere between a moan and a sigh.

She grasped his arms with the half-formed intention of removing them. Instead, her forearms came to rest on top of his and her fingers flexed around the wide wrists. His flesh was warm and hard, the silky hair on his arms an erotic abrasion against her tender skin.

"Feel what you do to me," he whispered huskily, moving his hips against her.

"Oh, Ryan." This time his name came out on a sigh.

Tess's head fell back against his shoulder. She felt weak, her body burning with a delicious lassitude.

"I've been going crazy for the last few months...wanting you...fighting wanting you," he growled. "This last week I've barely been able to keep my hands off you."

A shiver rippled through Tess at the evocative words, and she felt some of the tension drain out of her.

Since he proposed, over a week ago, Ryan had been even more distant. Other than to put a guiding hand at her elbow or the small of her back when they walked together, he had not touched her. He had not offered so much as a chaste kiss on the cheek. In addition to her other doubts and worries, she had begun to fear that he no longer desired her. His strong attraction to her and the possibility that it could grow into something deeper was the only hope she had for their marriage. It was a relief to find she had been wrong.

Sighing, she relaxed and gave herself up to the sensations coursing through her. At that moment all her worries and fear about the future flitted right out of her head and she surrendered willingly to the sweet rush of passion. She was passive in his arms, absorbing his heat, his strength, greedily breathing in the heady masculine scent that surrounded her, reveling in the exquisite assault on her senses.

Her breasts were heavy and aching, and when Ryan cupped them, Tess spread her hands over his and pressed them closer. His thumbs swept back and forth over her nipples, and they peaked, pebble hard. Moaning, Tess rocked her head on his shoulder. He growled softly.

"Come here," he whispered, turning her in his arms.

He stared down at her, his face taut. Desire glittered in his blue eyes as he studied her flushed face. Tess was so aroused she was shaking. She clutched his shirt and leaned against him for support, aware that her slumberous gaze and bemused expression betrayed her longing—perhaps even more—but she was too entranced to care. Her chest rose and fell rapidly with each shallow breath that hissed through her parted lips, and when the tip of her tongue stole out to glide in a swift circle, something hot flared in his eyes.

The water still gushed into the sink. Never taking his eyes off her, Ryan reached around her and turned it off. In the pulsing quiet that followed, Tess was sure he could hear her heart thudding.

Wordlessly, he cupped her cheek. His thumb brushed over her chin, her lower lip. Then, with slow, sure movements, he pulled her closer, tilted her face up and lowered his mouth to hers.

The first touch sent excitement streaking through Tess like summer lightning. She moaned and pressed closer, her arms sliding up to encircle his neck of their own accord. Her heart overflowed with love and her body thrummed with desire. Oh, Lord, she hadn't known how much she wanted this. Needed it.

The kiss was unrestrained, hot and hungry, unleashing in both of them the fierce passion so long held in check. He parted her lips with his tongue and speared her with pleasure that shot like an arrow straight to that hollow ache deep inside her body.

The hand beneath her chin slid around her neck, his spread fingers threaded through her hair to cup the back of her head. His other hand moved downward, slid over her back and hips, grasped her buttocks and pressed her to him rhythmically, matching the undulating movement with the slow, deep thrusts of his tongue.

Tess moaned. She felt on fire, her body clamoring for fulfillment. She wanted to get closer to Ryan, to writhe and clutch and coil herself around him.

Ryan ended the heated kiss with an abruptness that was shocking, but he didn't release her. They stared at one another, breathless, their hearts knocking together, bodies taut.

Without a word, he swept her up into his arms. Plagued by a sudden return of shyness and nerves, Tess buried her face against his shoulder. With long, determined strides he carried her swiftly through the living room and down the short hall to the bedroom.

The lamp on the bedside table lit the room with a soft glow as he set Tess on her feet. The instant he straightened, he bracketed her face with his hands and tipped her head back. In the dim light the eyes that roamed her face glittered like sapphires. "God, you're lovely," he whispered. "Irresistible. I should have known from the moment we met that this was inevitable."

That startled an embarrassed chuckle from her. "How could you? I was pregnant."

"You were beautiful." His thumbs swept the hollows beneath her cheekbones. "I thought then it was just that maternal glow that expectant mothers have, but I was wrong." His gaze dropped to her mouth and his head began a slow descent. "You're still exquisite."

He whispered the words against her lips, his breath striking her skin in warm little puffs. Then his mouth slanted over hers.

Never had Tess had such a soul-stirring experience. The kiss was as different from the previous one as night to day. With impeccable care, his lips rocked over hers. It was the merest contact of flesh to flesh, but oh, so warm and tender. His tongue slicked over her quivering lips, probed the corners of her mouth, then swirled enticingly around its inner edge, without ever quite entering that yearning sweetness.

Tess trembled beneath the sensuous assault. The excruciating gentleness aroused her almost beyond bearing.

One of Ryan's hands slid down and lightly cupped the side of her neck, his fingertips playing softly over the velvety rim of her ear and the sensitive skin behind it. His other arm looped around her back to hold her close.

At last he ended the tormenting caress. Raising his head slowly, he eased back a step. He smiled at her with that rare flash of warmth and tenderness that never failed to steal her breath away. Slowly, he slid his hand down her neck, turning it so that the backs of his knuckles skimmed over her collarbone and chest to the button at the top of the wide V-neck of her suit jacket. His fingers deftly released the top covered button and sought the next one, his knuckles grazing the rounded tops of her breasts on the downward glide.

"You're trembling." Ryan's eyes flared as he felt her helpless response. He released another button...and another. Slowly, his knuckles skimmed down over her bra, the silky skin of her midriff. Encountering the waistband of her skirt, he stopped, watching her. "Do I frighten you, Tess?"

"No. It's...not that," she said in a tremulous voice. "It's just..." Cool air feathered over Tess's skin, sending another delicious shiver rippling through her as Ryan released the last button and eased the champagne-colored silk jacket off her shoulders. He tossed the expensive garment into a chair.

"What then? Tell me what's wrong."

"Nothing's wrong." Tess looked at him uncertainly and bit her bottom lip. "It's just that it's been so long for me, and...and there's never been anyone else but Tom. It's...it's almost like the first time all over again," she said in a rush.

Ryan's hand stilled on the front clasp of her bra. "Oh, Lord, sweetheart," he groaned in a voice that went low and rough with emotion. "Do you have any idea what it does to me to hear you say that?"

He took her mouth in a hungry, hot kiss that left them both shaken. With considerably more haste, he released the clasp on her bra, and it joined the silk jacket on the chair. Tess sucked in her breath and gripped his upper arms as he cupped her breasts and swept his thumbs back and forth across her nipples. He bent and suckled a hardened peak, drawing it deep into his mouth. Each rhythmic tug seemed to pull at her feminine core, making it throb and yearn.

"Oh, Ryan!" Gasping, Tess arched her neck and clutched his head with both hands, burying her fingers in his hair, holding him to her as he lavished the same fierce attention on the other breast. Her heart beat against her ribs like a wild thing, while the rest of her body seemed to grow weak and liquid.

Hazily, Tess felt the easing of pressure at her waist as the button was released, heard the soft rasp of the zipper being lowered. The champagne silk skirt slithered to the floor and pooled around her ankles. Hooking his thumbs under the tops of her beige half slip and panty hose, Ryan went down on one knee and lowered them to her ankles. Tess held on to his shoulders for balance as he removed first one, then the other high heel pump then eased the stockings over her feet and tossed them and the other garments aside. The tiny triangle of toffee-colored silk and lace quickly followed.

Ryan wrapped his arms around her hips and pressed his face against her stomach. "I've lain in my bed on the other side of that wall night after night, tormenting myself imagining this. Going crazy with wanting you," he said in a raspy whisper as he strung hot kisses over her silky skin.

Tess trembled and held him close, her fingers buried in his hair. Her emotions overwhelmed her, and she closed her eyes against the sweet rush of feelings that surged inside her.

Against her belly, she felt the slight rasp of his beard stubble, the hot wetness of his mouth, the warm, silky feel of his hair. The pleasure became so intense it was almost painful, and finally, trembling, Tess gripped his shoulders and urged him upward. "Please, Ryan. Please."

He stood at once. Pausing to look at her, he took in every line, every dip and curve of her naked body, his burning gaze promising untold delight. "Yes. Oh, Lord, yes," he said with throaty urgency.

Quickly, he tossed back the bedspread and covers and eased her down onto the bed. Trembling, Tess watched as he snatched off his own clothes. He pulled impatiently at the buttons on his shirt, and when the last one wouldn't cooperate, he tore it off. Bare-chested, he hopped on one foot, then the other as he yanked off his shoes and socks. He bent and shucked out of the suit pants, and when he straightened, Tess caught her breath at the sight of him in only the brief, dark maroon underwear. Then it, too, was gone.

The lamplight painted that magnificent body with light and shadow. Naked, his shoulders seemed broader, his chest more massive. Muscles rippled in his legs and arms as he lowered himself beside her. His arousal was awesome, and Tess knew a moment's fear.

Then his arms came around her. "Tess. My sweet Tess." The gentleness and longing in his deep voice banished the budding panic, and when he pulled her to him, their soft moans of pleasure blended at the first thrilling touch of warm flesh to warm flesh.

His kiss was deep and penetrating, exploring her mouth with the same urgency that his hands explored her body. He traced the long, lush line of hip and thigh, the inward curve of her waist, the exquisite flare of her rib cage. Tenderly, he cupped his hand around her breast and flexed his fingers against the soft flesh.

In restless passion, Tess's hands ran over his shoulders and neck and back, her fingertips tracing the tiny knobs in his spine, then slipping around to explore his chest and twine in the coarse hair that covered it, tugging gently.

Every touch, every tiny incoherent sound of pleasure pulled their emotions tighter. Their breathing grew rapid, deep, labored.

Tess trembled, her body awash with sensations and driving need. She had not known such voluptuous pleasure existed. It was sweet agony, and she gloried in it, greedily savoring each wondrous rush of emotion. The taut, throbbing ache that consumed her was nearly driving her mad.

A whimper escaped her as Ryan's hand slipped between her legs and cupped her womanhood.

The soft cry seemed to steal the last of his control. He raised his head and looked down at her, his face flushed and taut. "Oh, Lord, sweetheart. I can't wait any longer."

"I don't want you to." Slipping her arms around his well-muscled torso, she urged him down to her. "Love me, Ryan," she whispered. "Love me, now."

It was a cry from the heart, but Ryan was too caught in the throes of passion to notice. He levered up and positioned himself between her soft thighs. Holding her gaze, he entered her in one smooth stroke, smiling tightly as he watched her eyes glaze, her face soften in ecstasy.

He pressed deep, and when he was fully sheathed in her silken warmth, he stilled. "Are you all right?" he asked, his voice gritty from the control he was exerting over himself.

Tess smiled and stroked her hands over his back. There had been a moment of pinching tightness but it had passed quickly. His concern for her touched her deeply and her heart overflowed with love for him. "I'm wonderful," she whispered in his ear.

It was all the encouragement he needed. He pressed deeper and began to rock her with him in an ageless rhythm.

His thrusts were sure and strong and Tess met each one eagerly. Passion built and spiraled. Their movements became rapid, urgent, drawing the knotting tension tighter, ever tighter. At last, the explosion came and together they were hurled off the edge of the earth. They cried out and clung to each other as the world seemed to disintegrate in a starburst of ecstasy.

## Chapter Eleven

Molly knew nothing about newlyweds or sleepless wedding nights—nor did she care.

As always, at precisely six-thirty the next morning she awoke and let out her first tentative grunt and squeak of displeasure. When that did not instantly bring the desired result her complaints worked up into a string of fussy squawks. Then she really turned up the volume.

Across the hall, her mother groaned but Tess wearily raised her head from the pillow and started to climb from the bed.

"Stay there. I'll get her."

Tess jumped, barely stifling a scream at the sound of that voice coming out of the darkness beside her. Then she remembered. Ryan.

She sagged back against the pillow and put her hand over her caroming heart.

The mattress shifted, and she could make out Ryan's naked silhouette as he climbed from the bed and stepped into his pants. Memories of the previous night and the feel of that magnificent body against hers sent a tingling sensation sweeping over her.

Tess had lost count of the times they had made love. Quick and hot, long and languorous, playful and rowdy, desperate and frantic—they had experienced it all. They had been insatiable, greedily indulging themselves to the fullest, she recalled with a blush. She had not known herself. Even now, the memory of their passion brought a surprising return of desire.

When Ryan headed for the door, she tamped down on the feeling and raised up on her elbows. "Ryan...uh, maybe I should get her. Molly is always a soppy mess in the mornings."

"No problem. I've changed her before, remember," he said, giving her a wry look.

"Yes, I know. But she'll be hungry and impatient for her bottle and—"

"Hey, I can handle it. But if it makes you feel better, you can get her bottle and cereal ready and we'll meet you in the kitchen."

"All right."

Ryan flipped the switch beside the door, and the bedside lamp came on. Tess sat up, carefully holding the covers to her, tucking them under her arms, not quite meeting his eyes. His gaze flickered over her bare shoulders and down her body. She felt the touch of that stare like a trail of fire over her skin.

When she made no move to leave the bed, Ryan raised one eyebrow. "Well?"

Tess's hold on the blankets tightened. She hadn't a stitch on. Regardless of the night of passion they had just shared she simply could not bring herself to parade around naked in front of Ryan. "I, uh...I..."

A look of mild surprise came over his face. "Don't tell me you're still shy?" Her blush answered for her and he gave a low, sexy chuckle. "Well, I'll be damned."

Ignoring Molly's indignant wails, he recrossed the room in a slow, hip-rolling saunter, his bare feet soundless on the carpet. When he reached the bed, he grasped her chin in the wide V between his thumb and fingers and tipped her face up.

"Honey, last night I saw every sweet inch of your delectable little body. Hell, I kissed every inch of it," he said in a dark, rasping rumble that brought scalding heat to Tess's face and sent excitement skittering through her. "I plan on doing it again. Often."

He bent and took her mouth. The slow, heated kiss was so erotic, it turned her body to hot wax. Her heart pounded and her pulse thrummed and the delicious quaking she had experienced the night before began again. When he raised his head, he studied her dazed expression, his eyes hot and slumberous beneath heavy lids. He smiled and dropped another quick kiss on her wet lips. "Get used to it," he murmured.

Tess still did not move until he disappeared through the doorway, not out of shyness but simply because it took that long to regain her equilibrium.

Finally she rose from the bed and pulled on a long velour robe, belting the sash tight at her waist. In the bathroom she splashed her face with cold water. Touching one flushed cheek with her fingertips, she stared at her reflection in the mirror. Her mouth was puffy and slightly red, and the skin around it bore traces of whisker burn. Her eyes glowed.

And to think . . . at one time she had thought Ryan was cold.

Over the past few months she had learned, of course, that his abruptness was a shield. Nevertheless, his passion had taken her by surprise. On the outside he was reserved and conservative, even distant, but inside . . . inside he sizzled.

Ryan made love with an uninhibited, smoldering sensuality that had shocked and thrilled her. In bed all the barriers were down, feelings and physical pleasures were explored with unrestrained enthusiasm and joy.

Tess looked at her glowing face in the mirror, a bit dazed. Her wedding night with Tom had been sweet and awkward, a period of fumbling self-consciousness and anxiety. With Ryan those hours in the darkness had been lusty and hot and intense, a voluptuous sating of the senses that had been beyond her wildest fantasies and had filled her heart with hope.

Ryan might not love her yet, but he desired her. Surely a hunger that great would eventually lead to deeper feelings.

Tess had just finished heating Molly's bottle and cereal when Ryan entered the kitchen with the infant cradled in the crook of his arm. He was still barefoot but he had slipped on his wrinkled dress shirt, leaving it unbuttoned, the long tail flapping around his hips.

Earlier, when he had entered the nursery, the baby's furious cries had ceased. However, now that she was dry, powdered and dressed, she was tuning up again.

"I hope you've got her breakfast ready. This child wants something to eat and she wants it *now*."

Tess laughed and snapped a bib around her daughter's neck as Ryan lowered her into the carrying seat that Tess had placed on the small kitchen table. "I know. She's turning into a little glutton. A demanding little glutton."

She picked up the baby's spoon but Ryan took it from her. "Here, I'll do this while you rustle us up something to eat."

Tess looked doubtful, but Ryan scooped up a mound of the mush, stuffed it into Molly's open mouth, and expertly swirled the tiny spoon around her lips, catching the overflow.

While she prepared bacon and eggs, Tess watched them with a twinge of envy. Ryan made faces and kept up a string of nonsensical talk while he shoveled in bites of cereal and gave Molly short drinks from the bottle of formula. In turn, Molly kicked and cooed and flailed her arms, obviously enjoying both the food and the attention.

It was so easy for them. The love between her daughter and this big brooding man was as natural and effortless as breathing. If only it could be that way for her and Ryan, Tess thought wistfully.

Ryan finished feeding Molly at the same time that Tess set their breakfast on the table. After wiping her face and burping her one more time, he transferred the baby to a springy canvas seat and set it on the floor between their chairs. Molly kicked and bounced and banged her rattle happily while they tucked into their meal.

"Did you talk with the apartment manager about us taking a three-bedroom place?" Ryan asked, buttering his toast.

"No. I tried several times last week but she was always out. Things were so hectic and I was so busy getting ready for the wedding, I simply didn't get a chance to check back."

"That's all right. I'll go down later today and make arrangements. With help from Reilly and a few of the guys on the construction crew, we should be moved before I go pick up Mike next weekend."

A forkful of eggs halted halfway to Tess's mouth. "You're not going to work today?"

Giving her a sardonic look, he swallowed the bite of food in his mouth and took a sip of coffee. "I hadn't planned on it, no. Why? Are you trying to get rid of me, Tess?"

"No! Of course not. It's just...that is...you said you were so busy at work, I thought..."

"We are busy, but I think I can afford to take one day off to be with my bride," he murmured. His gaze slid down to the V-neck of her robe where the overlapping lapels were gaping open, exposing a generous amount of cleavage.

Turning pink, Tess tugged the edges together and tightened the belt at her waist.

Something flared in Ryan's eyes. He reached across the table and touched her cheek with his fingertips. "Last night was wonderful," he said in a husky whisper that made her heart jump. "But it wasn't enough. Not nearly enough."

"Oh, Ryan." Tess gazed into those vivid eyes, helplessly enthralled. His words, his hot look, sent a shower of sparks cascading through her body.

The hand at her cheek slid downward and slipped beneath her hair, cupping her nape. Tugging her to him, his smoldering gaze on her parted lips, Ryan leaned across the table toward her. Slowly, they drew closer. Heads angled to the side. Breaths mingled. Eyelids drifted downward.

Molly chose that moment to conk herself on the head with her rattle. The baby let out a piercing shriek and Tess jumped, but Ryan merely looked down at the infant and grimaced wryly. "Molly, girl, I love you but, sweetheart, your timing stinks."

Tess scooped up the baby and cuddled her, kissing the red spot on her forehead and soothing away her tears. When she was calm once again, Ryan reached for her.

"Why don't I take Molly with me while I go next door and shave and get dressed? That'll give you a breather to do whatever you have to."

"Well . . . I do need to sterilize bottles and prepare formula. And wash some of Molly's things."

"Fine." Hoisting the baby up against his shoulder, he headed for the door. "We'll be back in a little while."

The apartment seemed eerily quiet without them. It was the first time she had been there without her daughter since Molly had been born, Tess realized.

Taking full advantage of the peace, Tess rushed around to get done all the daily chores that came with having a baby. She didn't know how Ryan wanted to spend the day, but she wanted to be ready for anything.

She started a load of Molly's things washing, prepared formula, filled the bottles and put them into the sterilizer and changed the crib sheet. When done, she changed the sheets on the bed that she and Ryan had shared, as well.

They smelled like him, she realized as she stripped the wrinkled linens off the mattress. Unable to help herself, Tess buried her face in the rumpled folds of cloth, inhaling deeply Ryan's dark, masculine scent and shivering at the delicious memories it evoked.

She finished making the bed and straightening the apartment and headed for the shower. Steam clouded the glass outer walls of the stall. Tess stood with her face up to the invigorating spray, luxuriating in the feel of the hot water streaming over her body. When the door suddenly yanked open, she let out a yelp and spun around.

"Ryan!" she squeaked when he stepped inside. Reflexively, she crossed her arms over her chest to shield her breasts. "What are you doing?"

"Joining you. I told you last night we would shower together." His gaze traveled leisurely over her, taking in every inch from her wide eyes to her coral-painted toenails.

"Molly—"

"Is taking her morning nap. If we're lucky it'll be a long one."

"But—"

"Shh. Just relax."

Relax? How could she relax with him standing there naked, just inches from her? His nearness intimidated her, with his big body towering over her making her feel weak and defenseless and painfully self-conscious. She had never felt so vulnerable . . . or so excited.

Watching her, Ryan picked up the soap and rubbed it between his palms, working up mounds of thick lather. When his hands were full, he replaced the cake of soap and looked at her.

"Lower your hands, Tess."

"Ryan—"

"Do it, honey."

The sensuality in that coaxing voice sent a shiver rippling through her and she obeyed helplessly. Ryan smiled and slowly, almost reverently, cupped his lather-filled hands around her breasts.

Tess caught her breath. His long callused fingers flexed in a slow rhythm around the soft flesh, and a shiver rippled through her as his callused palms rubbed against her hardened nipples.

The hot shower spray needled against her back and water cascaded down over her buttocks and legs. In front, Ryan's hard hands and the creamy lather caressed her while steam rose all around. With a low moan, Tess closed her eyes, absorbing the voluptuous sensations, her back arching with the pleasure of it.

"Now it's your turn," Ryan murmured.

Her eyes flew open, a look of confusion in the whiskey-colored depths.

"Touch me, sweetheart. The way I'm touching you."

Tess was quaking inside—from nerves, shyness, excitement—she didn't know which. As though in a trance, with a shaky hand she picked up the bar of soap and rubbed it between her palms, her lambent gaze locked with Ryan's.

When her hands were full of rich lather, she hesitantly placed them on his chest and began to move them in slow circles, running her fingers through the silky hair, grazing his collarbone with her fingertips, rotating her palms against his nipples. Tess's gaze followed the motion, fascinated by the white lather and her small hands moving over the dark skin of that massive chest.

"Mmm, that's nice," Ryan almost purred. He looked at her through slitted lids, a naughty smile curving his mouth. "Actually, though, I had a lower place in mind."

Tess's eyes widened, and she jerked her hands back. Chuckling, Ryan took hold of her wrists and returned them to his chest. "Don't worry about it. There's no hurry. I'm sure you'll get there."

And she did.

Ryan's hands slipped around her waist, bringing her against him and up on tiptoe for his kiss. Of their own accord, Tess's hands slid around him and moved over his broad back as Ryan took her mouth in a long, slow, melting kiss that made conscious thought impossible. His tongue swirled, while his big hands caressed and fondled and his body moved against her with an evocative rhythm.

Tess lay against him weakly. Her hands restlessly massaged and explored the long flat muscles in his back, then glided downward, spreading lather over his waist, his firm buttocks, the backs of his thighs, their movements growing more restless and bold as the tormenting kiss went on and on. Her soapy fingers explored his armpits, glided over his ribs, massaged the points of his hipbones. One hand slipped between their bodies and found his navel, her fingers playing over his corrugated abdomen. Then—slowly, deliberately—her explorations began a downward path, and Ryan's low groan rumbled into her mouth as her small hand intimately cupped him.

Every cell in Ryan's body tightened. His heart thudded so hard, it felt like it would club its way right out of his chest. The feel of that small soft hand touching him brought such exquisite pleasure he wasn't sure he would survive it.

Ending the kiss, he slowly lifted his head and stared down at her. Tess didn't move. She stood with her neck still arched to accommodate his kiss, watching him languorously, her eyes glittering beneath heavy lids, her wet lips parted. Her cupping hand flexed around him like a heartbeat.

"Put your hands on my shoulders, Tess," he commanded in a raspy voice. "Hold on to me."

She obeyed, and he bent his knees. His hands smoothed down over her slick buttocks and thighs. Cupping the backs of her knees, he straightened and lifted her, bringing her legs around his waist. His big hands clasped her hips. Their feverish gazes locked. He watched her eyes glaze over and her lovely face soften as he slowly settled her onto him.

"Oh, Ryan. Ryan," she almost sobbed against his shoulder.

With a low growl, he turned and braced her back against the tiled inner wall of the shower. He buried his face in the wet strands of hair at the side of her neck. "I'll never get enough of you," he declared in a guttural voice. "Never."

He surged into her with urgent, powerful strokes. The shower spray continued to pound down on them. The radio on the counter played a soft tune. In the other room the telephone shrilled twice before the answering machine clicked on and a disembodied voice chattered away. Neither noticed. On fire, they clung to one another, unaware of anything beyond the burning desire that drove them.

With each breath, Ryan's movements grew stronger, faster. Clutching his wet head with both hands, Tess whimpered and tightened her legs around him, her body undulating to meet each thrust.

The frenzied loving quickly drove them to the edge. The taut pleasure coiled tighter. Tighter. Then it broke free.

"Ryan! Oh, my darling!"

Ryan gritted his teeth against the exquisite pleasure as he felt her tense, felt her body contract around him as the first pulsing spasms overtook her. "Oh! Oh! *Ry-an!*"

"Yes. Yes!"

The explosion rocked them, and they clung to each other, their hoarse cries blending together as the world shattered in a burst of white hot pleasure.

Ryan sagged against Tess. Leaning his forehead against the cool tile, he gasped for breath and fought to regain his senses and deny what his heart was telling him, but it was too late.

He loved her. Dammit, he loved her!

It was a hell of a time and place to face the truth, but he had no choice. He had tried for months to pretend otherwise. He had tried last night, taking her over and over, sure that once his desire for her was slaked the feeling would be gone. The trouble was—if he lived to be a hundred, his desire for her would never be satisfied. He knew that now.

Ryan rolled his forehead against the tile and squeezed his eyes shut. Damn. Damn. Damn. What was he going to do? He didn't want to love her. He had sworn he would never again give any woman the power to hurt him. Oh, Lord. What would he do if she left him?

The thought was so painful, Ryan's hands tightened reflexively at Tess's waist, digging into her soft flesh. She moaned and stirred.

She was draped around him, boneless and limp as a wet dishrag, her head on his shoulders, arms hanging loose, her looped legs sliding slowly down his thighs.

She was utterly spent, the picture of a well-loved woman. Ryan thought about the passionate way she responded to him, and a warm feeling expanded in his chest. Shifting again, she released a shuddering breath. He smiled wryly when he felt the slight puff of air eddy against his neck.

After reaching back and shutting off the water, he adjusted his hold on her and stepped from the shower. He placed her on the bath mat and she swayed on her feet, clutching his forearms for support. Forcing her heavy eyelids open partway, she looked at him pleadingly. "Ry-an. Please. I want to go to sleep," she moaned.

"In a second." He ran the towel over her, giving her a cursory drying, then did the same for himself. When done, he swung her up in his arms.

Within seconds they were snuggled together in the bed. Tess lay with her head on Ryan's shoulder, her hand curled on his chest, sound asleep. Holding her close, his jaw resting against the top of her head, Ryan stared at the ceiling.

* * *

"If I had known that Ryan was going back to work so soon I would have been over days ago. And I still say a one-day honeymoon stinks."

"Oh, I don't know." Tess handed Amanda a cup of tea and gave her a sly look. "It depends on how you spend it."

"Ooh! Now that sounds interesting. Tell me all about it."

"I'll do no such thing."

Joining her friend on the sofa, Tess curled into the corner with one foot tucked beneath her, cradling her mug of tea in both hands. Over the rim, she gave her friend a censuring look.

Amanda ignored it. Turning sideways as well, she pursed her lips and studied Tess with a speculative gleam in her eyes.

"The man must be a real tiger in bed. He just looks so...so virile and masculine. And so damned sexy. Not to mention the fact that you've got a glow I haven't seen on you in over a year." She leaned forward and her voice dropped. "Tell me. Is he a lusty lover? Or is he one of those take-his-time-and-make-it-last types? Mmm, I get the shivers just thinking about it."

"Amanda! Behave yourself."

"All right. All right, spoilsport," she grumbled, but her voice was tinged with laughter.

Amanda was a terrible tease. Tess knew she didn't expect her to answer the outrageous questions and comments. Even if she had, her one-day honeymoon with Ryan had been too special and private to share with anyone else. A dreamy smile tilted the corners of Tess's mouth at the memory of it. Their lovemaking had been spectacular, breathtaking. And the quiet time they had spent with Molly had, in its own way, been just as wonderful. Both had sent her hopes for their future soaring.

Amanda groaned. "Oh pul-leeze. If you're not going to tell all the juicy stuff, at least have the decency to wipe that lovesick look off your face. It's nauseating. You look positively besotted.''

Tess stuck out her tongue and grinned. ''You brought it up.''

''Yeah, yeah. Well let's talk about something else. Like my godchild.''

''Molly's fine. She's growing like a weed and in perfect health. You'll see for yourself as soon as she wakes up from her nap.''

''How about Mike? When is he coming home?''

''Ryan is going to Crockett tomorrow to get him.''

Amanda looked around. ''You've done wonders with this place, honey, but isn't it a little small for the four of you?''

''I know. We're looking for a three-bedroom apartment. We thought we could get one in this complex but they're all rented. For the past four days since Ryan went back to work I've been looking at other units, but no luck yet. We want to stay in this area because of Mike's school. Plus, Wildwood is only a few miles from here. Until we find a place, we'll keep both apartments. It's not ideal but it's the best we can do for the moment. And there's no sense in moving twice.''

A sound drew their attention. Amanda and Tess looked at each other and grinned, and as one they rose and headed for the nursery.

An hour later, when Ryan and Reilly walked in, Molly was lying on the sofa between the two women, squealing and cooing at Amanda, who was playing peekaboo with her.

''Well, well. Look who's here,'' Reilly said, grinning.

Amanda spared him only the briefest glance, then pointedly ignored him.

Ryan paused just long enough to say hi to Amanda before going to Tess. She looked up to greet him, and he bent from the waist and cupped her chin. Searching her face, he murmured a husky, ''Hi.''

"Hi," she whispered back, smiling shyly. Before she could say more, he kissed her. He made a thorough job of it, taking his time, savoring her soft lips and the delicate shudder that she could not suppress.

"Uh...hey, Hoss. Come up for air, willya. Newlyweds," Reilly added with a derisive snort. "Disgusting, isn't it?"

"Personally, *I* think it's sweet," Amanda said in her haughtiest tone.

Breaking off the kiss, Ryan straightened and sent his brother a challenging look. "Can't a man kiss his wife in his own home without being heckled?"

"Sure. I just didn't want you to get carried away and forget you had an audience." He flashed a wicked grin. "I embarrass easy."

"Oh, brother." Amanda rolled her eyes.

Ryan snorted.

Tess turned the color of a ripe tomato.

"I'll get those plans you wanted," Ryan said, and headed for the bedroom. He returned in less than a minute with a long cardboard tube.

"Thanks, Hoss." Tapping the cylinder against the side of his work boot, Reilly looked at Amanda. "So...how's it going in the news business?"

"Fine." Amanda handed Molly to Tess and stood up. "I'd better be going. Thanks for the tea. Nice seeing you again, Ryan." Bending, she placed a light kiss on the baby's head then headed for the door at a brisk pace. "I'll call you tomorrow, Tess," she called over her shoulder.

"Uh...I've got to go, too. See ya," Reilly said in a rush and hurried after her. "Hey. Wait up, Amanda. I'll walk with you to your car."

"No, thank you. I am perfectly capable of getting to my car on my own."

"Yeah, but I'd feel better if—"

The door closed behind them, and Ryan and Tess exchanged an amused look.

"What a pair. The woman practically bares her teeth every time she sees him and he still won't give up. Not that he's stupid, mind you. It's just that Amanda intrigues him. Reilly's never before run across a woman who didn't like him."

"Oh, I think she likes him, all right. That's what's bothering her."

"What? You're kidding?" Ryan looked at Tess's smug smile and narrowed his eyes. "Wait a second. You're not thinking of doing any matchmaking, are you?"

"No, of course not. I'm just going to let them work things out for themselves."

Ryan lifted Molly from her arms and kissed the baby's chubby cheek. "Hello, sweetheart. How ya doing today, hmm?" He glanced back at Tess, his face serious. "For Amanda's sake, you'd better hope you're wrong. Reilly is not known for his constancy. And he's definitely *not* the marrying kind."

Her face pensive, Tess watched him stroll away into the kitchen, tickling Molly's belly and murmuring nonsense to the gurgling baby. Neither were you, she thought.

"Sure you won't come with me?" Ryan nibbled Tess's neck and lightly nipped her earlobe while his hand made a slow foray across her tummy. She smiled. They lay together, spoon fashion, and she could feel his heat all along her back.

"We can't. Molly won't wake up from her nap for a couple of hours yet. Besides, I think the trip up there and back in one day would be too hard on her." And after the vigorous bout of lovemaking she and Ryan had just shared, Tess wasn't sure she had the energy for the trip herself.

"I guess you're right." Ryan gave her neck one last nibble and climbed out of bed. "I'd better get a move on, though. Mom will have my hide if I don't get there in time for lunch.''

He disappeared into the bathroom, and after a quick shower he emerged and dressed in jeans and a sweater. When he was ready to go, Tess pulled on her robe and walked with him to the door.

''Tell everyone I said hi, and that I'll see them at Easter.''

''I will.''

''And be careful on the highway.''

''Don't fret. Mike and I will be back before you know it.'' He tucked a loose strand of hair back into her sleek pageboy. ''What're you going to do while I'm gone?''

''I guess I'll call around some more about an apartment, although I think I've checked out every one in this area.''

''I've been giving that some thought. Probably the best solution would be for me to build us a house.''

''A house?'' Tess's eyes lit up. ''Oh, Ryan, do you mean it? That would be wonderful! I love that idea!''

Ryan's eyes grew cold and his mouth twisted in a hard sneer. ''Yeah. I sorta thought you would.''

The hateful tone took her by surprise. ''Ryan? What's wrong? Look, if you don't want to build us a house—''

''Don't worry. I said I'd build you a house and I will. I know how much store you women put in those kinds of things.''

You women? What did that mean? Then Tess recalled what Ryan had told her about Julia's reaction when he had been forced to sell the home he had built for her and his comment that every woman had her price.

Pain stabbed at Tess. He was lumping her into the same category as his first wife.

He opened the door, but Tess put her hand on his arm. ''Ryan, please listen to me. A house would be nice, it's true. But it certainly isn't necessary. Really. I'm sure I'll find us a nice apartment eventually.''

"Yeah, sure." He crammed his Stetson on his head and walked out.

"Ryan!" Tess cried. She stepped out onto the landing but he was already loping down the stairs. She watched him go, her shoulders sagging. "Oh, Ryan. When are you going to realize that I'm not Julia?"

## Chapter Twelve

When Ryan and Mike returned from east Texas that afternoon Ryan's bitter mood had passed. He greeted Tess with a warm kiss and cuddled Molly, all trace of anger gone from his expression and manner. If anything, he was in an exceptionally lighthearted mood and bantered good-naturedly with his son for most of the evening.

Mike was his usual exuberant self. He was happy to see Molly and Tess again and excited about the four of them being a family now, and he thought it was "cool" that he would be sleeping next door alone for the time being. All evening he cracked jokes and chattered happily about his visit with his grandparents.

Not wanting to spoil his homecoming, Tess did not bring up the subject of the house until later, when the children were asleep and she and Ryan were alone in their bedroom. However, no matter how much she protested that a house was not essential to her, Ryan would not budge on the issue.

"We need the space, and this is the logical answer."

"But—"

"Give it up, Tess," he said, pulling her into his arms. He had already stripped down to his navy blue briefs, and her hands came up automatically to rest against his hair-covered chest. He held her loosely against him, his fingers laced at the small of her back, and smiled down into her worried face. "C'mon, honey. Admit it. Given a choice, you know you'd prefer to have a house. Now wouldn't you?"

"Well . . . yes. Almost any woman would, but—"

"And I want you to have one. I want to build one for you."

Tess searched his face. She wanted desperately to believe that he had put aside the old hurt and anger. "Do you? Do you really?"

Ryan's expression altered subtly. His eyes took on a smoldering gleam and his smile changed from coaxing to sensual. He freed one hand and traced the low neckline of her nightgown. "Hmm. There are a lot of things I'd like to do for you," he murmured. Bending, he buried his face against the side of her neck, nuzzling his nose into the silken fall of hair. He nipped at her earlobe then licked the tender skin behind it. "And *to* you."

Tess shivered and clutched his upper arms. "Oh, Ryan." Her head went back and she closed her eyes as his marauding mouth moved over her neck and shoulder, the tender skin beneath her jaw. A heavy hotness began to seep through her body. "Ry . . . Ryan, we . . . we have to talk."

"To hell with that." Bending, he swept her up in his arms and crossed the room in three long strides.

His knee dented the mattress. Tess felt the cool sheet against her back, and a second later Ryan's warm body blanketed hers. She struggled to hang on to her purpose and ignore the exquisite sensations buffeting her.

"But Ryan . . . about . . . about the house. . . ."

"Later," he ground out. He cupped her breast and captured her mouth in a long, sizzling, wet kiss. In only seconds Tess's resistance crumbled and her arms tightened around him as her ardor rose to match his.

"Later" never came. Tess tried several times to talk to Ryan but he always brushed aside her protests. He was immovable on the subject of the house, and finally she gave in. One Sunday afternoon a few weeks later, they left a napping Molly in Mike's care and Ryan took her to Wildwood to pick out a lot.

"Oh, Ryan, it's beautiful," she exclaimed as they climbed from the truck. It was a sunny day, but cold and blustery. Tess shivered and pulled her heavy sweater-coat tighter around her, but not even the frigid wind could dim her appreciation of her surroundings. The huge oaks were bare in mid-January, but that did not detract from the beauty of the area.

The development was laid out around a spring-fed lake, whose overflow formed the small creek that meandered through the property. Newly poured, winding streets followed the natural curve of the land. Ryan and Reilly had taken pains to preserve as many trees as possible on the twelve hundred acre plot, leaving each lot dotted with stately oaks and towering pines. A fifty-foot wide strip of natural forest separated each half-acre homesite on three sides, providing a maximum of privacy and a preserve for the forest creatures.

"There will be nature paths through the woods and biking and jogging paths along the roads. The clubhouse and golf course will be over there," Ryan said, pointing to the structure going up on the far side of the lake. "That side is less wooded so we won't lose as many trees to the fairways and greens. Around the remaining two-thirds of the lake are homesites. They're the premium locations. I thought we would take one of them."

"But you'll lose profits if we take one of the most desirable lots. Really, Ryan, I'd be just as happy with one of the less expensive ones."

"Don't worry about that."

"But—"

"Tess, liking the spot we choose is more important than its market value." Slipping his arms around her from behind, Ryan propped his chin on top of her head. Blissfully content, Tess leaned back against him and rested her arms on top of his. "I plan on this being our home for a lot of years," he continued. "I want Molly and Mike and whatever children we may have in the future to grow up here."

Tess's heart skipped a beat. She and Ryan had never discussed the possibility of more children, but he had obviously given the matter some thought. The idea thrilled her, but more than that, it boded well for their future. With his history, Ryan would not consider bringing children into a marriage that he was not committed to.

"I wouldn't even mind living here when we retire. Right on this spot, looking out over the lake and the trees. How does that sound to you?"

Tess's eyes grew misty and her chin wobbled. Her heart was so full she could barely speak. "It . . . it sounds wonderful," she managed to choke out. "Simply wonderful."

Ryan wasn't just building a house; he was building dreams.

The next few weeks were a whirlwind of activity for Tess. At Ryan's insistence, she met numerous times with Bob Carlson, the architect that R & R Construction used. Together, after many changes and alterations, they came up with a basic floor plan that suited both her and Ryan. Then she began the task of making selections of carpeting, hardware, stain, paint, light fixtures and a thousand and one other things.

Ryan came home early one afternoon in late February and found her poring over books of wallpaper samples.

She sat on the living room floor, so immersed in the chore she had not heard him come in. Molly lay on a blanket beside her, industriously chewing on a rubber toy. He stopped in the entrance and watched Tess, his face grim.

His gut was in a knot. How would she take the news he was about to give her? On the way home he'd told himself over and over that she would understand. Tess was resilient and scrappy. She would accept it. But would she? Julia hadn't.

His expression hardened. He walked into the living room and tossed his sheepskin-lined coat over the back of a chair. Spotting him first, Molly squealed and kicked eagerly, grinning from ear to ear, her two tiny teeth sparkling.

Tess looked up, surprised. "Ryan! What are you doing home so early?"

"I want to talk to you about the house."

"Oh, good. I need to talk to you, too." She sprang to her feet with one of the big sample books in her arms. "I want your opinion on this wallpaper I've picked for the entryway. Oh, and Bob Carlson called this morning and suggested that we consider adding a small sunroom off the master bedroom and put a hot tub in it. What do you think?"

"It doesn't matter. There's not going to be a house." Inwardly, he flinched at his harsh tone. He knew he was being unnecessarily blunt, but he couldn't seem to help himself. Aggression was the only defense he had against the terror that was eating at his insides.

Tess blinked three times, her face blank. "Wh-what?"

"I said, there's not going to be a house. We've got troubles. This morning we had a fire at the storage barn."

"Oh, dear. How bad was it?"

"Bad. Most of the heavy equipment is a total loss. We have no choice but to replace it. So far, we've only laid out phase one at Wildwood. We can't continue without that machinery."

"Won't the insurance cover at least part of it?"

"We dropped the insurance a few years back when the building industry here went bust. All our machinery was old. We figured we'd take the risk and cut expenses." He shrugged. "It was a roll of the dice, and we lost."

"Oh dear. I'm so sorry."

"Yeah, well, so am I. Reilly and I are already stretched thin financially with the loan we took out to get the project started. Now we'll have to borrow more money to buy new equipment. For the time being, we'll have to tighten our belts. Which means no new house."

"I see." Tess glanced around at the wallpaper books and tile and carpet and paint samples that had almost taken over her living room for the past few weeks. Her shoulders slumped. She looked down at the book in her hands, only then noticing that she still held it. She bent and placed it on the stack with the others. Glancing at Ryan, she spread her hands in a gesture of defeat. "Well . . . I guess that's that."

His hard stare bore into her. "For a woman who claimed a house wasn't important to her, you sure look down."

"Well, of course I'm disappointed. Who wouldn't be? But I'll get over it."

"And if you don't?"

"Ryan! I'm not a child. This is a letdown, of course, after all the planning and work and anticipation. But I've told you over and over that the house isn't something I can't live without. It can wait until the firm recovers."

Making little grunting noises, Molly was trying to scoot across the blanket to Ryan, but he barely noticed.

He searched Tess's face. The first stirring of hope began to tighten his chest. "You would be willing to do that?"

"Of course. What else can—" An arrested look came over her face. "Wait a minute! There is another solution." She looked at Ryan and bit her bottom lip. "I, uh...I don't know how you feel about this, but...well...I do have the money from Tom's insurance and the sale of my house. You're welcome to it."

The offer hit him like a slap in the face. "No. Absolutely not. I won't take your money." Rage sizzled through him.

"But—"

"Dammit, I said no. That money belongs to you and Molly. Put it in a trust for her if you want, but don't ever offer it to me again. I won't use a dead man's insurance to salvage my business *or* my marriage." Shooting her a furious glare, he snatched up his coat and stormed out.

Molly's little face crumpled and she began to wail.

Salvage their marriage? Tess stared after him, her jaw dropping. Why...he thought she was going to cut and run...the way Julia had done.

Her legs grew wobbly and refused to support her another second. Tess sank down onto the arm of the Queen Anne chair, only remotely aware of her daughter's outraged cries. It hurt. It hurt terribly. Things had been going so well lately. Ryan had seemed content, even happy. She had thought— at least hoped—that the love she showed him in almost everything she did and her commitment to him and their marriage, the joy and pleasure they had found with each other, would heal those old wounds.

Tess gave a mirthless little laugh. Apparently, she was wrong. She supposed she should have known better. Trust, after all, was an essential part of love; without it Ryan would never return her feelings for him. Worse, without his trust, how long would it be before her love for him began to shrivel and die?

Moving like an automaton, she picked up Molly and soothed her feelings with soft words. When the baby was quiet and playing happily once again, Tess went to the telephone and called the architect. He was perplexed when she told him to stop working on their blueprints, but she did not elaborate. After the call she gathered up all the samples, bundled up Molly and returned everything to the suppliers. The rest of the afternoon she spent calling about apartments in the area.

A little after six that evening Ryan called to say he would be working late and would grab a burger. Mike answered the telephone, and when he relayed the message to Tess, he was unconcerned, but she knew that their clash, not pressing work, was behind Ryan's absence.

She and Mike ate the pot roast dinner she had cooked, and afterward they watched a John Wayne movie on television together. Mike had already gone next door to shower and go to bed when Ryan finally came home. Tess jumped when she heard the door open. Her nerves began to hum like a high voltage wire, but she remained at her dressing table and continued to smooth moisturizer over her face and neck.

He stopped just inside the bedroom, and she looked up, meeting his brooding stare in the mirror. A fine tremor quaked through her. Without a word, Ryan crossed the room and pulled her up into his arms.

"Oh, Ryan," Tess cried. She went into his embrace eagerly and wrapped her arms around him, pressing her anguished face against his chest. The top three buttons on his flannel work shirt were open, and she burrowed her nose in the silky chest hair visible through the gap. The smell of sawdust and the crisp cold of outdoors clung to his skin, mingling with his intoxicating scent. He clasped her to him so tightly she could barely breathe, but she didn't care. He was home. And he was holding her.

"I'm sorry, Tess," he whispered urgently.

She squeezed her eyes shut and clutched him tighter. "Ryan, I would never leave you just because we're going through a rough period financially."

"I know. I know."

"The house isn't important. Neither is the money. You've got to believe—"

"Shh. It doesn't matter." He raised her head, and her heart did a wild little dance in her chest. Passion, and something she couldn't name, darkened his face and blurred his features. Homing in on her mouth, his fiery gaze grew slumberous, and his head began a slow descent. "Nothing matters but this," he said in a raspy whisper against her lips, and his mouth closed over hers.

"It's a pleasure doing business with you." Reilly flashed the couple his most charming smile and offered his hand as he escorted them to the door. "As soon as we have your blueprints we'll start breaking ground. Barring torrential spring rains, we should have you in your house by late summer."

"We're looking forward to it. We'll get our architect to start working on the plans right away."

The instant the door closed behind the couple, Reilly whirled around and let out a whoop.

"*Whoo-iiee!* Let the good times *roll!*" Pumping his arms, he did a hip-swiveling dance across the office, waving the Henderson's down payment check.

Ryan smiled at his brother's antics. "Don't get too carried away. It's early days yet."

"Are you kidding? At this rate, we'll be in the chips by summer."

Ryan didn't know if he would go that far, but he had to admit, things had been rocking along surprisingly well lately. In the month since the fire they had gotten the loan with no hassle, taken delivery on the new equipment, and contracted to build eight custom homes—three this week alone.

The last was particularly encouraging, since they hadn't even opened a sales office. In every case, the buyers had wandered into Wildwood and been impressed with the development's amenities and the quality of the three model houses they currently had under construction.

Reilly rose from putting the Henderson's check in the safe and stretched his big frame. "I don't know about you, Hoss, but I'm knocking off early. It's Friday, the world is good, and I feel like doing a little celebrating. Besides, we've earned a breather." He slipped into his windbreaker, a ruminating smile tugging at his mouth. "Who knows? I may even give Amanda a call."

Ryan heaved to his feet and reached for his Stetson. "What for? She's just going to say no. And probably a few other choice words to boot. Why don't you just admit that you've finally met a woman who's immune to your dubious charm and give it up?"

"Heck, no. I'll wear her down one of these days. You'll see."

"Yeah, right. And donkeys fly." Chuckling, Ryan flipped the dead bolt on the door and followed his brother out.

The site was deserted. On Fridays the crew always lit out at the stroke of five, their weekly paychecks burning holes in their pockets. Ryan waved goodbye to his brother and climbed into the Cherokee. It felt strange to be going home so early, but Reilly was right; they had earned a little time off. Maybe he and Tess would go out to dinner and a movie. Just the two of them.

He slipped a Natalie Cole CD into the player, rolled down his window and inhaled deeply of the mild spring air. Feeling happy and mellow, a slight smile softening his stern features, he headed home, his fingers tapping the steering wheel in time to the music.

Ryan was looking forward to surprising Tess, but when he let himself into the apartment the hollow silence told him no one was home. He checked next door but no one was there, either. Not even Mike. He glanced at his watch and frowned. Where could they be? Disappointed, he went back to the other apartment and headed for the shower.

Walking into the bedroom, he pulled his shirt free of his jeans and began unbuttoning it. Halfway across the room he noticed the double doors on the closet standing ajar and stopped in his tracks. An uneasy feeling whispered through him. Changing direction, he walked slowly to the closet. He pushed the doors open wider and stared. It was empty. All that was left were three forlorn wire hangers and a crumpled plastic dry cleaner's bag on the floor.

She was gone.

The vicious pain that sliced through Ryan was paralyzing. He could not move or make a sound. All he could do was stand there and stare at the empty clothes rod and bare shelves, the silent cry of anguish from deep in his soul trapped inside him.

"Oh!"

At the sound, Ryan's head whipped around in time to see Tess skid to a halt two steps inside the door, her hand over her heart.

"Oh, my," she exclaimed in a breathless voice. "You scared me. I didn't expect you home so early."

"Sorry if I spoiled your plan," he snarled between clenched teeth. "No doubt you expected to be long gone before I got here." Oh, God. She looked so adorable, standing there in her shabby jeans and workshirt, with her hair all mussed and a streak of dirt on one cheek. He wanted to go to her and snatch her into his arms and beg her not to leave him, but the hurt was too deep.

A look of confusion flickered across her face. "No, not really. Mike and Amanda and I can only carry so much. And I—"

"You have my son helping you?"

"Y-yes. He's downstairs with Amanda and Molly. Ryan, why are you acting this way? Is something wro—?"

His bark of bitter laughter cut her off. "I suppose I should be grateful that you had the decency to tell me to my face. That's something, anyway. Not much, but I guess it's better than coming home to find a polite little note and all your belongings gone. Of course, you were handicapped— you can't get much in that little car of yours. What did you plan to do, send a moving van back for the rest?"

She stared at him, her expression slowly changing from perplexed to stunned. "You...you think I'm leaving you."

He jerked his head toward the empty closet. "That makes it fairly obvious, wouldn't you say."

For Tess it was the final straw. Ever since they married— ever since she had known him—she had tried to be understanding. Over and over she had forgiven his bouts of bad temper and bitterness and endured his occasional barbs. But no more.

"Obvious? *Obvious?* The only thing obvious to me is that you are a blind fool," she raged at him.

Clearly, Ryan had not expected anger from her. Had the situation not been so painful and serious, the stunned look on his face would have been comical. Tess was too incensed and hurt to notice.

She brushed past him and flung the closet doors so wide they banged back against the wall on either side. "Look at that! Take a good look," she commanded.

"So? It's empty."

"Right. Completely empty. *Your* clothes are gone, too."

Ryan's gaze shot back to the vacant closet, and Tess felt a surge of satisfaction at the startled uncertainty that flashed across his face. Most of Ryan's clothes were still next door, but for convenience he had moved a few things—mostly everyday work clothes—into her closet. Apparently, in his rush to think the worst, he had forgotten that.

"What—?"

"This morning, unexpectedly, a three-bedroom apartment became available in building B—one of the ones you rebuilt after the storm," she informed him in a stilted monotone. "The tenants were behind on their rent and they moved out in the middle of the night. When the manager called and offered us the apartment, I snapped it up. Amanda and I spent the morning cleaning it, and when Mike got home from school, we started moving what we could."

"Why didn't you call me?"

"I did. I called you several times, but neither you nor Reilly were in the office. I even left a message on the answering machine."

Ryan winced. "Damn. I didn't think to check it. We had some home buyers with us when we came back to the office and we were so busy with them I didn't notice. I'm sorry, Tess."

"Sorry just isn't good enough anymore, Ryan. Don't you see? Just because you came home and found an empty closet is no reason to jump to conclusions. If you had any faith in me you wouldn't have."

"Tess . . ." Ryan started toward her, but she held up her hand and took a quick step back.

"No. I'm not through. I am tired of being judged on someone else's behavior. I—am—not—Julia! Do you hear me?" Her voice shook with cold fury and she felt as though she were about to fly apart, but she was determined to get it all out, all the hurt and frustration and disappointment she had endured for the past three months. "For weeks I have done everything in my power to prove to you that I am nothing like that woman, but you're either too thick or too blind to see. Well, I'll be damned if I'll let you keep punishing me for what she did to you."

"You don't understand. I—"

"Oh, I understand all right. I understand that you're a fool. A pig-headed, embittered fool who would rather wallow in the pain of the past than be happy with what you've got.

"I didn't marry you for your money, you idiot. Or for security. Or to have a father for Molly. Or to get a house. Not even to have a bedmate. I married you for one reason and one reason only. I married you because I love you."

The statement had a stunning impact on Ryan. His stony face went slack, and for a moment all he could do was gape at her. Then his expression lit up with pure elation. "Tess. Oh, Lord, honey, you have no idea how happy I am to hear you say that." He started for her again with his hands outstretched, but once more she backed away. He halted, his smile collapsing.

"Tess, sweetheart, don't you see? I love you, too. I think it happened a long time ago, but I knew for sure the day we married. I love you honey. I love you very much."

She returned his hopeful look with a steady stare. She could see by his baffled expression that her reaction was not at all what he had expected.

"Do you?" she questioned coolly. "I don't think so."

"Tess! Sweetheart, I swear it's true. I think, deep down, I've known it all along, but I just couldn't..." He grimaced and made a frustrated gesture. "You've got to understand... this isn't easy for me. But I do love you, Tess. You have to believe that."

"I'm sorry. I would like to. You have no idea how much I would like to believe you. But I can't. Love means trusting someone, Ryan. Completely. Without reservations or doubts. Believing in them, no matter how things appear or what happened in the past with someone else. I have to know that you have faith in me, and in my love for you. Without it..." She stopped and swallowed hard, then lifted her chin. "Without it, we have nothing."

"Tess ... what ... what are you saying?"

"I'm saying that I love you, Ryan. With all my heart. But I don't know how long I can live with your doubts."

She turned to leave and panic stabbed at him.

"Where are you going?"

She looked back at him with sad eyes. "Downstairs. It's time to feed Molly."

After she had gone, Ryan stared at the empty doorway. When he heard the front door close, he sank down on the edge of the bed. Leaning forward, he propped his elbows on his spread knees and held his head in his hands. Dear Lord, what had he done? Had he driven her away? Was she downstairs even now packing to leave him? He groaned at the thought and ground the heels of his hands against his closed eyes. He wouldn't blame her if she was.

She was right; he had to let go of the past. Deep down, he knew that Tess wasn't Julia. She wasn't anything like Julia. She was sweet and giving, the most unselfish person he knew. Intellectually, he knew he could trust Tess. But emotionally he was always braced for the worst.

It had to stop. He had to put what happened in his first marriage behind him and get on with his life. With their life together.

The door slammed. "Dad? Dad, are you here?"

Before Ryan could answer, Mike burst into the room. He came to a halt in the middle of the floor, breathing heavily.

"What did you do to Tess?" His voice broke in the middle of the accusing demand but for once he was too worked up to be chagrined. He bristled with anger, his young face flushed and fierce. "What did you say to her?"

"Why? What's wrong?"

"She's downstairs in our new apartment. She won't tell Amanda or me what upset her but you can tell she's been crying. All she would say was for us to stop unpacking things because she wasn't sure whether we were going to move after all. What's going on? I thought you wanted to find a bigger apartment."

"I did. We do." Ryan felt a tremendous sense of relief to know that Tess was still there. That was something, at least. He couldn't bear the thought of losing her, especially now that he knew she loved him.

Her uncertainty about their future filled him with guilt. It wouldn't be easy, but somehow he had to convince her that he really did love her. He thought about the problem, and after a moment his jaw hardened. He could start by letting her know that he wasn't giving up.

"Well?" Mike insisted pugnaciously. "If it's not the apartment, then what *did* you do to upset Tess? And what are you going to do about it?"

"The problem is between Tess and me. But you're right— I have to do something about it. And I'm going to start right now."

With a purposeful stride, Ryan brushed past his son and went into the living room, where he snatched up the telephone and punched out a number. The instant Reilly picked up his phone, Ryan started talking.

"Good. I'm glad I caught you. I want you to pick up a couple of dollies at the warehouse and get over here, pronto."

"Jeez, Hoss. Whatever happened to saying hello? And what the heck do you want with dollies?"

"Tess found us a new apartment. We're moving tonight. And you're helping."

Reilly groaned. "Ah, man. Gimme a break. I mean, I love you guys, but no way am I spending tonight moving furniture. Sorry, but I got other plans."

"Did I mention that Amanda is here helping?"

A pregnant two-second pause followed.

"I'll be there in twenty minutes."

## Chapter Thirteen

For the next two weeks Tess worked like a demon straightening their new apartment and turning it into a cozy home. She unpacked all the boxes and put everything away, hung pictures, made curtains for Mike's bedroom and, with his help, rearranged the furniture at least a half dozen times.

Even when the place was in apple-pie order she kept up the same pace, inventing projects and doing unnecessary chores just to keep busy. Anything to keep her mind off of the state of her marriage.

The normal routine of their lives had resumed, and on the surface they gave the appearance of a normal, happy couple, but both she and Ryan knew it wasn't so. The basic problem remained unresolved.

Clearing the air had not helped one iota. If anything, they seemed to be growing further and further apart, Tess admitted in desolate moments of painful honesty. They were friendly and polite to each other—excruciatingly so—but the tension was always there, crackling beneath the pleasant facade. Only in the privacy of their bedroom did their true feelings surface.

It was strange, Tess mused one afternoon as she needlessly polished her mother's silverware; the instant the lights went out the terrible constraint between them crumbled. In the darkness they clung to each other, their lovemaking wild and frantic, filled with a silent desperation that stripped away the pretense of the day and revealed their fears.

Adding to the strain, Ryan was seldom home anymore. Night after night he worked late in the Wildwood office, often not getting home until after she had gone to bed. She supposed that immersing himself in work was, for him, as it was for her, a way of escaping the awful strain between them.

They couldn't go on this way. It was unbearable. But she hadn't the slightest idea what to do about it.

The telephone rang and Tess jumped, dropping the fork she was polishing. As she reached for the receiver she wondered if it was Ryan, calling to tell her he would be working late again that night.

"Hello."

"Hello, Tess. It's Charles."

"Charles!" Her eyes opened wide and her hand fluttered to her chest. Oh, dear. She had forgotten all about the Bensons. "Well . . . this is a surprise. How are you?"

"Why are you surprised? I told you I would be back, and here I am, just like the proverbial bad penny."

Tess closed her eyes. He had no idea just how accurate that statement was.

"Actually, I had planned to return much sooner but I got tied up in an international banking deal. I've been in Moscow for the last couple of months. I hope you didn't think that I'd forgotten you?"

"No, no. I didn't think that." She hadn't thought of him at all.

"Good." Charles's voice dropped, taking on an intimate huskiness. "Would it be possible for you to get a sitter for Molly tonight? We have a lot to discuss. Besides... I'm anxious to see you again."

"Charles, I'm sorry. I can't."

"Why not? Look, if you can't get a sitter, I suppose I can come over there. We need to talk, Tess."

She sighed and raked her fingers through her hair. "There isn't any point in it, Charles. I can't move to Boston."

"Look, Tess. I realize you're probably still upset about what my parents did. But, sweetheart, I'm sure if you'll just give them a chance to make it up to you we can all put that bit of unpleasantness behind us."

"It isn't that. Look I'm sorry. I should have written to let you know."

"Know what?"

Tess winced.."That I've remarried."

*"What!* To whom?" he demanded. "When did this happen?"

"I married Ryan on Christmas Day."

"Ryan? Ryan McCall? That...that roughneck construction worker who lived next door to you? I don't believe it!"

"It's true. And Ryan and his brother own their own company. He's hardly a 'roughneck construction worker.' Not that it would matter to me if he were."

"Oh, Tess, Tess," Charles lamented, ignoring her defense of her husband. "How could you?"

She didn't like his tone. Any guilt she felt for being remiss in notifying him and his parents of her marriage dissolved. "How could I what?" she responded coolly.

"I realize that you've been lonely this past year, but to marry a man like that, when we could have given you so much more. What were you thinking?"

"Marriage isn't about things, Charles. Don't any of you men understand that?"

"But, Tess—"

"No. I don't want to hear any more. I'm sorry if you don't approve but the fact is, I'm married to Ryan now," she said emphatically. The words had no sooner left her mouth, however, when a niggling voice in her head taunted, *"But for how long?"*

Charles was too much the shrewd negotiator not to know when a method of persuasion had become counterproductive. In the short silence she could almost hear him clamping down on his annoyance and pulling back to regroup. Even so, when he spoke she could hear the stiff disapproval in his voice. "I see. Well, then. I suppose there is nothing left for me to say except to wish you well."

Relenting somewhat, Tess responded in a gentler voice, "Charles, I'm still willing to let you and your parents get to know Molly and be a part of her life. You are still her family, after all. That hasn't changed just because I married Ryan."

"How kind of you. I'll be sure to tell them. Now, if you'll excuse me, I have a meeting to attend. Goodbye, Tess."

"Goodbye, Charles."

Tess hung up the receiver and sighed. Charles was miffed because he hadn't gotten his way, but she knew he wasn't really hurt. Even so, she didn't like upsetting him. The unpleasant conversation might have been avoided if she had only thought to inform the Bensons of her marriage, but she'd had so few dealings with them in the past that she rarely gave them a thought. That didn't excuse the omission, though.

She would write to them now, she decided, heading for the desk. Better late than never.

Leaning back in his desk chair, Ryan absently twisted and untwisted a paper clip.

"Haven't you got anything better to do than mangle that piece of wire?" Reilly asked with a rare touch of impatience. "Like go home to your pretty little wife, maybe?"

Tossing the mutilated paper clip aside, Ryan shot him an annoyed look. "I have to go over those invoices tonight. I think the brickyard may be shorting us."

"The invoices can wait until tomorrow. One day's not going to hurt. Hell, I'll check them myself if it'll get you to knock off on time."

Ryan snorted. "Who're you kidding? I know you and paperwork." He gave his brother a wry look and reached for the stack of bills.

"For Pete's sake, Hoss, how long are you going to keep this up?"

"I don't know what you're talking about."

"Look, I don't know what's going on between you and Tess, but I've got enough smarts to know it won't get straightened out with you holed up here every night."

"Don't you think I know that?" Ryan snapped. The trouble was, he hadn't a clue how to make things right. He'd been tiptoeing around Tess for two weeks, terrified of saying or doing the wrong thing. So he stayed away as much as he could. It wasn't the answer, but he didn't know what else to do.

He wondered how long Tess's patience would last. Already her usual optimism had all but disappeared and there was a terrible sadness in her eyes that he didn't know how to make go away.

"You wanna tell me about it?" Reilly prodded gently.

Frowning, Ryan picked up the paper clip again and started twisting it. "Tess doesn't believe that I love her," he muttered.

"Well, hallelujah. At least you finally came to your senses and admitted that you do. So, have you tried telling her?"

"Hell yes, I told her. But she says I don't trust her, therefore I can't really love her."

"Mmm. Sounds reasonable to me. So do you? Trust her, that is?"

"With my life," Ryan vowed without a second's hesitation.

"Well then, I guess you'll just have to prove it to her."

"Yeah, right. And just how am I supposed to do tha—"

The sound of a car door slamming cut him off. The brothers exchanged a surprised glance and Reilly got up and went to the window.

"Who is it?" Ryan asked.

"Some slick-looking dude in a Beamer. I sure hope he's not a creditor cause he looks madder than a wet hen."

That was borne out an instant later when Charles Benson burst through the door like an avenging angel.

"McCall, I've got a few things to say to you," he snarled at Ryan the instant he spotted him. Behind Charles, Reilly quietly returned to his desk and settled back to watch the confrontation.

Not by so much as the flicker of an eyelash did Ryan move. Still leaning back, he remained comfortably slouched in his chair, the picture of unconcern. Only the hard glitter in his eyes betrayed his sudden tenseness. "Oh? About what?"

"About Tess and you and this ridiculous marriage. You're despicable, McCall."

"Hey!" Reilly barked, half rising out of his chair.

"Stay out of this," Ryan ordered quietly, never taking his eyes off their visitor. "I can handle Mr. Benson."

"Benson? You mean this is—"

"Charles Benson. Tess's brother-in-law."

Charles did a double take when he noticed Reilly, but he quickly refocused on Ryan. "That's right. And as a member of her family I protest the sneaky, underhanded way you engineered this marriage. You took advantage of a lonely, vulnerable widow, McCall. If you have an ounce of decency in you, you'll release her from this disaster."

Ryan's eyes narrowed dangerously. "Not a chance."

"Damn you. Tess and Molly are Bensons. They belong with my family in Boston, not tied to some Texas ruffian. Molly, after all, is my brother's only child and my parents' only grandchild. And I assure you we can give them much more than you can ever hope to," he added with a sneering look around at the trailer that served as their office.

Ryan's jaw bulged. He managed to keep his voice level but it had a steely edge. "Maybe so. But I'm not giving her up. Not to you or anybody."

The telephone rang before Charles could reply, and Ryan snatched it up. "R & R Construction," he barked into the mouthpiece.

"Ryan?"

The hesitancy in Tess's voice pricked him. With an effort, he struggled for a milder tone but he could not quite erase the grittiness. "Yeah, honey, it's me. Sorry. I didn't mean to bite your head off. Did you need something?"

"I, uh . . . I was just wondering if you were going to be home for dinner tonight? That's all."

Ryan glanced at Charles. "Yeah. I'll be there by six."

When he hung up, he got to his feet and stared at Charles over the top of the desk. "You've had your say, Benson. Now I think you'd better leave."

Charles hesitated. His jaw clenched, and he glared at Ryan. "All right. I'll go. But I'm warning you, McCall, you haven't heard the end of this."

* * *

Tess hung up the telephone slowly. What in the world was wrong with Ryan? Oh, Lord. She hoped there hadn't been another catastrophe. No. No, it couldn't be that. If so, he wouldn't be coming home on time.

Which reminded her; she had better get busy and start dinner.

On the way to the kitchen, Tess paused to toss back into the playpen the toys that Molly had thrown out. Balanced precariously on fat little feet, her chubby fingers clutching the mesh siding of the pen, Molly bounced and crowed with delight.

"I am not doing this for your entertainment you know, Miss Molly," Tess scolded with mock severity.

Gurgling happily, Molly bent her knees, snagged a terry cloth-covered foam rubber block and flung it over the side.

"Why, you little devil." Tess bent down and tickled the baby's tummy. "What do you think I am? Huh? Your personal servant?" Molly squealed as Tess buried her face in the side of her neck and blew hard.

Laughing, Tess straightened and tweaked her daughter's little pug nose. "Now you behave yourself. Daddy's coming home and Mommy's got work to do."

Molly bounced excitedly at the word "Daddy" and started blowing bubbles. Tess's smile turned sad. "I know. You'll be glad to see him. So will I, pumpkin. So will I."

Leaving Molly playing, Tess went into the kitchen. If only they could get beyond this impasse. Ryan claimed that he loved her, and Tess wanted to believe him. She wanted with all her heart to believe him. But she lived in dread of the next incident or crisis, of what his reaction would be.

Tess started washing vegetables for a salad. Barely halfway through the chore the doorbell rang. She dried her hands quickly and went to answer it.

"Hello, Tess."

"Charles! What're you doing here?"

"I've come to apologize for the way I acted earlier. And, if you don't mind, I would like to see Molly."

"Oh. Well..." The request took her by surprise. Charles had not shown any personal interest in his niece during his previous visit. "I suppose it would be all right." She stepped aside to let him in.

"You didn't mention that you had moved. The tenant in your old apartment told me where to find you. I hope you don't mind."

"No. No, of course not." Actually his being there made her uneasy. Ryan was not going to be pleased.

Molly, bless her, was sprawled in the playpen taking a little catnap. Tess knew she wouldn't sleep long but she wasn't going to tell Charles that. She wanted him out of there before Ryan got home. "Oh, dear. I'm sorry, Charles. She's asleep. I would wake her, but when you do that she's so cranky."

"No, no," he said quickly. "Don't do that. I can wait until she wakes up."

"Oh. Well... it may be a while..." she began, but the words trailed away when Charles took her hand between both of his.

He looked into her eyes, his gaze filled with warmth and fondness. "Tess, I might as well admit it—I really came to talk to you."

"About what?" she asked cautiously. She tried to ease her hand free, but he held fast.

"Surely you know. I want you to leave this man you married and come away with me."

"Charles! Stop it!"

"Can't you see that you've made a mistake?" he insisted. "You don't belong with McCall. You belong back East with us. You and Molly."

"I want you to leave, Charles. Now." She snatched her hand away but he took her by surprise and pulled her into his arms. "Charles! Have you lost your mind? Let—me—go!" Tess struggled wildly, pushing against his chest and twisting and turning, but she could not break free.

"You know that you're attracted to me, Tess. If you had just given yourself a little more time to get to know me you would never have made this mistake. But it can be rectified. Come back East with me, honey. Let me take care of you." His gaze dropped to her mouth, and his voice grew husky. "Let me love you, sweet Tess."

"No! Charles, no! You can't—"

His mouth clamped over hers, muffling her fierce protest. Shock and anger poured through Tess. She struggled with all her might, pummeling his shoulders and twisting and kicking. She even tried to bite him, but he would not stop. Charles kissed her with a passionate determination that bordered on violence and frightened her. In desperation, she drew back her knee, but she never got the chance to deliver the painful blow.

"Get your hands off my wife, Benson, before I tear you apart," Ryan growled.

Charles released Tess so quickly she staggered back. Horrified, she looked across the room at Ryan, and felt sick. "Ry-Ryan please...it's not...I wasn't..."

"Don't upset yourself, my dear," Charles said in his maddeningly imperious manner. "I'll handle this." He faced Ryan with calculated arrogance. "You might as well know, McCall, that I'm taking Tess and Molly back to Boston with me."

"Charles, what are you saying? You know that's n—"

"I said stay out of this, Tess." His mouth curled in a sneering little smile that dared Ryan to object. "We're leaving tonight, and there's nothing you can do about it."

With a little moan, Tess put both hands over her mouth and watched her husband, bracing for his attack. To her surprise, it never came.

Crossing his arms over his massive chest, he pinned Charles with a hard look and asked calmly, "Oh really? Just out of curiosity, how do you plan to accomplish that? Kidnapping is illegal."

Charles's face fell. Baffled by the unruffled response, he sputtered and blinked for a couple of seconds, but he tried to brazen it out. "I won't have to resort to kidnapping," he blustered. "Tess wants to go with me. She cares for me. You saw us kissing just now."

"What I saw was you mauling my wife against her will. Tess loves me, Benson. And I love her. And all your scheming and manipulating isn't going to change that," Ryan said in a dangerously quiet voice.

Shock rippled through Tess. By the time Ryan had finished speaking, her eyes were awash with happy tears and an incandescent smile lit her face. She couldn't believe it. Joy swelled her heart and overflowed, gushing through her like a bubbling spring.

"I don't accept that," Charles declared arrogantly. "In her present condition Tess couldn't possibly know what's best for her or what she feels."

It took a second for the arrogant statement to pierce her elation. When it did, indignation nearly choked her. "Now wait just a darn minute. Who do you think you are?" she demanded. "I am a mature adult. I certainly don't need you or anyone else to tell me what to do or how I feel."

Charles met her irate glare with a look of pitying condescension that made her want to scream. "Tess, my dear, you must admit this past year has been rough on you—losing Tom so suddenly, then learning you were pregnant, having Molly all alone."

"She wasn't alone. I was with her."

Ignoring the remark and the challenging look in Ryan's eyes, Charles went on as though he hadn't spoken. "Dearest, whether you know it or not, those things put you under a severe strain. It's not surprising that you've made some mistakes in judgment."

Tess gritted her teeth. He was talking to her as though she were a weak-witted child. "There is *nothing* wrong with my judgment," she said through her teeth.

"Now, now. Don't get upset. I don't blame you, Tess. You were lonely and vulnerable. Naturally you were susceptible and easily swayed." He paused to shoot Ryan a nasty look. "This . . . *person* offered you security and a little affection and you mistook it for love, but he's totally unsuitable. I know you've realized that this marriage is a disaster." He smiled slyly. "The kiss we shared proved that."

Tess gasped. "That's not true!" She cast a desperate look at Ryan, her fear returning. "Don't listen to—"

"Tess. Tess," Charles chided. "My dear, I know you feel obligated to stand by the commitment you've made, no matter how disastrous, and I admire your integrity. Really, I do. But I simply cannot allow you to let a rash decision ruin the rest of your life. Don't worry. This is a mistake that can be corrected easily enough. You just leave everything to me."

His gall left Tess speechless. She stared at him with her mouth agape. Before she could find her tongue, he grasped her elbow.

"Come, pick up the baby and let's go. You'll be able to think much more clearly once we're out of here, I promise you."

Tess tried to pull away. "Charles, let go of me. Ow! You're hurting me!" she cried when his grip tightened cruelly.

Ryan made a subtle move—the merest squaring of his shoulders, his big body tensing for combat—but it was enough to stop Charles in his tracks.

"Get your hands off of her, Benson. Now," he snarled in a low rumble. "Or so help me, I'll beat the living hell out of you."

"If you think you can scare me with your threats—"

"It's not a threat. Believe me, nothing would give me more pleasure than to put my fist through your face. The only reason I haven't so far is because I didn't want to upset Tess. But I'm fresh out of patience."

Charles glared defiantly, but uncertainty flickered in his eyes, and after a moment he dropped his hand from her arm. Tess quickly stepped away, rubbing her elbow, her apprehensive gaze sliding back and forth between the two men.

"Now then," Ryan commanded in the same deadly tone. "You have five seconds to get the hell out of our home."

Charles glared at him, then at Tess, his face a livid mask. "All right. I'll go. But this isn't the end of it, McCall," he blustered. "That child is a Benson, and she belongs in Boston with her family."

"I'll see you in hell first. Now get out," Ryan repeated icily.

Charles's gaze sought Tess. "This is your last chance. Are you coming with me or not?"

She lifted her chin and looked him straight in the eye. "Goodbye, Charles."

His aristocratic face hardened and the look in his eyes turned to icy hatred. "Very well, so be it. You'll be hearing from our attorney." Cursing under his breath, he brushed past Ryan and stormed out.

Ryan watched him go. When the door slammed shut, he turned slowly, and for the first time since arriving, he looked directly at Tess.

Across the space of the room their gazes met and held—hers soft and adoring, his a vivid glitter in his solemn face. Waiting. Expectant.

The air between them quivered with emotion. Finally, breaking the charged silence, Ryan whispered, "Come here, sweetheart."

With a glad cry, Tess flew across the room into his outstretched arms. "Oh, my darling. My love," she sobbed.

"Shh. It's okay," he whispered an instant before his mouth closed tenderly over hers. For several minutes no words were necessary. They kissed passionately, deeply, clutching each other with all their might, their hearts free at last.

When their yearning became more than they could bear, Ryan broke off the kiss and swept Tess up in his arms. His face was stiff and flushed with passion as he strode through the apartment to their bedroom. Beside their bed, he stopped and looked at her intently.

"I love you, Tess." His deep voice vibrated with emotion, and the look in his eyes made her insides melt.

Cupping his face with her hand, Tess gave him a quavering smile as tears spilled over onto her cheeks. "I know, my love," she whispered. "I know."

\*    \*    \*    \*    \*

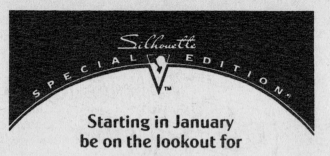

## HE'S MORE THAN A MAN, HE'S ONE OF OUR

## EMMETT
### Diana Palmer

What a way to start the new year! Not only is Diana Palmer's EMMETT the first of our new series, FABULOUS FATHERS, but it's her 10th LONG, TALL TEXANS and her 50th book for Silhouette!

Emmett Deverell was at the end of his lasso. His three children had become uncontrollable! The long, tall Texan knew they needed a mother's influence, and the only female offering was Melody Cartman. Emmett would rather be tied to a cactus than deal with that prickly woman. But Melody proved to be softer than he'd ever imagined....

Don't miss Diana Palmer's EMMETT, available in January.

Fall in love with our FABULOUS FATHERS—and join the Silhouette Romance family!

*Silhouette*
## R O M A N C E™

**Silhouette** SPECIAL EDITION

## It takes a very special man to win

*That SPECIAL Woman!*

She's friend, wife, mother—she's you! And beside each Special Woman stands a wonderfully *special* man. It's a celebration of our heroines—and the men who become part of their lives.

Look for these exciting titles from Silhouette Special Edition:

January **BUILDING DREAMS** by Ginna Gray

February **HASTY WEDDING** by Debbie Macomber

March **THE AWAKENING** by Patricia Coughlin

April **FALLING FOR RACHEL** by Nora Roberts

Dont miss THAT SPECIAL WOMAN! each month—from your special authors.

### AND

For the most special woman of all—you, our loyal reader—we have a wonderful gift: a beautiful journal to record all of your special moments. See this month's THAT SPECIAL WOMAN! title for details.

TSW1

**Silhouette Books
is proud to present
our best authors,
their best books...
and the best in
your reading pleasure!**

Throughout 1993, look for exciting books
by these top names in contemporary
romance:

**CATHERINE COULTER—**
*Aftershocks* in February

**FERN MICHAELS—**
*Whisper My Name* in March

**DIANA PALMER—**
*Heather's Song* in March

**ELIZABETH LOWELL—**
*Love Song for a Raven* in April

**SANDRA BROWN**
(previously published under
the pseudonym Erin St. Claire)—
*Led Astray* in April

**LINDA HOWARD—**
*All That Glitters* in May

When it comes to passion,
we wrote the book.

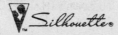

BOBT1R

For all those readers who've been looking for something a little bit different, a little bit spooky, let Silhouette Books take you on a journey to the dark side of love with

# SILHOUETTE Shadows™

If you like your romance mixed with a hint of danger, a taste of something eerie and wild, you'll love Shadows. This new line will send a shiver down your spine and make your heart beat faster. It's full of romance and more—and some of your favorite authors will be featured right from the start. Look for our four launch titles wherever books are sold, because you won't want to miss a single one.

**THE LAST CAVALIER**—Heather Graham Pozzessere
**WHO IS DEBORAH?**—Elise Title
**STRANGER IN THE MIST**—Lee Karr
**SWAMP SECRETS**—Carla Cassidy

After that, look for two books every month, and prepare to tremble with fear—and passion.

**SILHOUETTE SHADOWS,** coming your way in March.

 Silhouette®

SHAD1